POWERFUL ENEMIES

A JAMIE AUSTEN THRILLER

TERRY TOLER

Powerful Enemies

Published by: BeHoldings, LLC

Book Cover: BeHoldings Publishing
Contributing Editor: Donna Kos

For information email: terry@terrytoler.com.

Our books can be purchased in bulk for promotional, educational, and business use. Please contact your bookseller or the BeHoldings Publishing Sales department at: *sales@terrytoler.com*

For booking information email: booking@terrytoler.com.
First U.S. Edition: February, 2022
Printed in the United States of America

ISBN 978-1-954710-09-2

OTHER BOOKS BY TERRY TOLER

Fiction

The Longest Day
The Reformation of Mars
The Late, Great Planet Jupiter
The Great Wall of Ven-Us
Saturn: The Eden Experiment
The Mercury Protocols
Save The Girls
The Ingenue
Saving Sara
Save The Queen
No Girl Left Behind
The Launch
Body Count
Save Me Twice
Powerful Enemies
Deadly Games
Don't Be Careful
Wintervention
Cliff Hangers: Anna
Cliff Hangers: Mr. & Mrs. Platt
Cliff Hangers: The Quarterback
Cliff Hangers: Macy
Cliff Hangers: Not, Not Guilty
Cliff Hangers: The Book Club
The Blue Rose
Triggers
The Book Club
The Book Club Murder

Non-Fiction

How to Make More Than a Million Dollars
The Heart Attacked
Seven Years of Promise
Mission Possible
Marriage Made in Heaven
21 Days to Physical Healing
21 Days to Spiritual Fitness
21 Days to Divine Health
21 Days to a Great Marriage
21 Days to Financial Freedom
21 Days to Sharing Your Faith
21 Days to Mission Possible
7 Days to Emotional Freedom
Uncommon Finances
Uncommon Health
Uncommon Marriage
The Jesus Diet
Suddenly Free
Feeling Free

For more information on these books and other resources visit
terrytoler.com.

Thank you for purchasing this novel from best-selling author Terry Toler. As an additional thank you, Terry wants to give you a free gift.

Sign up for:

Updates
New Releases
Announcements

At terrytoler.com

We'll send you an eBook, *The Book Club*, a Cliff Hangers novella, free of charge.

Prologue

Northern Syria

Arriving early to set off a bomb can be as problematic as arriving late.

Special forces team leader, Kyle Kelly, didn't know firsthand about the second part of that statement. He'd never been late. In his mind, if he wasn't early, then he was late.

Early had its problems, though. Keeping out of sight, being one of them. Fortunately, this mission was at nighttime. The moon was behind the clouds. The desolate area in northern Syria was mainly without power. Everything was pitch black. So much so that he and his team of six men had to wear night-vision goggles to see their own hands in front of their faces.

Intelligence said they were likely to meet resistance. So far, he hadn't seen any, which was puzzling. The targets were supposed to be military outposts. A term he used loosely to describe them. In this part of the world, an army outpost consisted of a dozen or more men with machine guns at one place at the same time.

All Kyle saw in his goggles was a village with a dozen crude structures. If people were inside the buildings, they were asleep. Apparently, confident enough in their safety that there were no armed lookouts.

Kyle decided to make his move. He was the one who set the time of the attack, so he could change it. An uneasy feeling had come over him. Things were too quiet. Going too well. The enemy seemed too absent.

One command in the com and his men sprang into action. They fanned out in six directions to predetermined points in the village. Each carried two explosive devices, which were to be secured outside the front door of twelve structures.

They moved stealthily and with precision. Carefully, even though the bombs weren't armed and couldn't detonate. No matter how well trained a man was, getting used to carrying a powerful bomb without any anxiety took considerable mental fortitude, especially when someone could be in the shadows about to unload his weapon on you.

Kyle wasn't even sure what kind of improvised explosive devices they were. That's how in the dark he was. All he knew was that they were sophisticated mines with motion detectors. Once they were armed, they exploded as soon as they detected movement.

Most mines required direct contact. Someone had to step on one to detonate it. In this instance, as soon as a person opened the door of the house or even approached it, the bomb would explode. Killing anyone in a radius of five hundred feet. The bomb would level the building.

Presumably, when the terrorists in the other buildings heard the first explosion, they'd rush out the doors to see about the commotion and set off the bombs in front of their own structures. If all went well, everyone in the village would be dead by sunrise.

Kyle wasn't sure how many people there were in the village. Something that caused him a great deal of angst in the planning. The last thing he wanted was to engage in a firefight with an unknown number of armed terrorists.

For whatever reason, he wasn't allowed to do his usual reconnaissance. The higher-ups fed him the intelligence. He liked to gather it himself. But this mission was top secret. Came from somewhere near the top of the food chain.

Kyle didn't even know the why's of it. So, he resisted the urge to think about it.

He maintained his vantage point to monitor his men's progress and watch for any hostiles. The radio in his earpiece was totally silent. That meant things were going well. Of course, he could see that from his vantage point. His body was tense anyway, and he was ready to act at the first hint of trouble.

His men neared the critical part of the effort.

The point where they'd all know if they were going to get out of there without being seen or heard or if they'd have to fight their way out.

Kyle scanned the horizon again, searching for any threats. Seeing none, he allowed himself to exhale the breath he was holding and take in a deep one to replace it.

His mind began to wander again. This was an essential mission to powerful people. According to his direct supervisor in D.C., only two people knew about the mission, which added to Kyle's pressure.

All he could surmise was that the secrecy was due to the nature of the mission. Not typical warfare. Technically, the mines were banned by international humanitarian laws—a gray area. In principle, the laws stipulated that care had to be taken to minimize the possibility of civilian contact with the devices.

The rules of engagement were clear. They were allowed to place a mine to kill the enemy. But if there was a one percent chance an innocent civilian could happen upon the mine, then the mines were illegal even if it did give them an advantage in the war.

According to intelligence, terrorists had taken over the town, and its civilians had long since fled to Turkey. Again, something Kyle hadn't been able to verify. He simply had to take his superior's word for it.

Still, the questions remained. Kyle didn't know why the powers that be didn't simply drop the bombs from the air and annihilate the village eliminating any risk to his men. That'd be too simple. Like the running joke about military intelligence being an oxymoron. Suits in an airconditioned room decided what his men armed with guns and bombs had to do in the middle of a raging hot civil war.

Kyle often wondered how they ever got it right.

Sometimes he felt like a pawn on a chessboard. He moved around the theatre at the whim of men who were supposedly smarter than him. Didn't matter. Kyle had learned years ago that his job was not to question orders but to follow them.

Even though the nighttime Mediterranean air was a cool sixty degrees, Kyle wiped the sweat off his brow. He told himself to focus. He wouldn't relax until his six men were back next to him safely. The suits might not care about the risks, but he did. The estimated number of casualties in their calculations didn't have names to go along with the numbers. He was responsible for these men and was determined not to lose any of them.

Kyle fixated on them. He watched them expertly place the bombs. One by one, each man fulfilled his duty, then sprinted back to Kyle's position.

Things were going surprisingly well. Murphy's Law hadn't raised its ugly head and enforced the laws on the situation.

When the last bomb was in place, and the last man was back to the safety of their cover, Kyle armed the bombs remotely with a code only he was given. The bombs were on a relatively short time delay. It would give the squadron time to get to safe ground,

They wouldn't hang around to watch their handiwork.

Another order from someone above his pay grade.

At Kyle's command, the men hiked the three miles back to their camouflaged transportation. Immediately they all jumped on board and made the nerve-racking drive to Turkey across the border. They arrived at their rendezvous point ahead of schedule without firing a single shot from their weapons.

A chopper picked them up and deposited them at a U.S. air base. Within thirty minutes, they were on a military flight to Germany.

They were the only passengers, which seemed strange.

They were only on the ground in Germany for eight hours. Long enough for a hot meal, a shave and shower, and a few hours of shut eye, while completely isolated from the main population.

The men were loaded on another military flight and sent to Afghanistan. Once in Afghanistan, they went their separate ways.

Clearly, someone somewhere wanted Kyle and his men out of sight and out of mind. And busy so they couldn't talk to each other.

As far away from Northern Syria as possible.

For whatever reason.

1

CIA Headquarters
Langley, Virginia

Brad was summoned to Neal Fuller's office. He'd been racking his brain trying to figure out why.

He'd been in Fuller's office only one time, which was one too many in his mind. Fuller was the Director of the Central Intelligence Agency and had been for nearly six months. The newly elected POTUS appointed the Director with the advice, consent, and confirmation of the US Senate.

By one vote.

A sad day for intelligence.

Fuller had risen through the ranks as a diplomat. A butt-kisser who kissed the right ones along the way. Typically, Brad stayed out of politics and kept his nose to the grindstone. His plate was full, trying to keep a handle on Alex Halee and Jamie Austen. A nearly impossible task. He'd managed them for more than eight years and still didn't know who was managing who.

Their photos should be in the encyclopedia next to the phrase 'tail wagging the dog.' In reality, Alex and Jamie were the whole dog, dragging him along by the leash he tried to control them with.

Frustrating. And extremely rewarding.

Two of three people in the world he would take a grenade for. Now only two, since the other one, Curly, died of a heart attack a few months back.

The hostility for Director Fuller was personal. When Alex came to Brad with the allegation that Neal Fuller had put a ten million dollar hit out on Jamie, Brad didn't believe it.

Now he'd seen the proof. Without a doubt, Fuller orchestrated the hit to score political favor and secure his position as Director of the CIA.

Since the revelation, Brad had made it his personal mission to bring the evidence to light and end Fuller's reign as CIA Director. He hadn't been able to do it yet because of the questions that would arise.

How did Brad come upon that classified information above his clearance level?

Could he make the charges against the Director stick?

Would Alex be implicated in the gathering of the intelligence?

While he didn't know for sure that Alex had broken the law to get the information, he couldn't take that risk.

So, Brad made the decision to do nothing. For now. Let Fuller make another mistake. Something he was more likely to do as Director wielding more power. Although, with that power came the ability to cover up almost any wrongdoing. While Congress and the President spouted off ad nauseam about investigating their political enemies, Brad couldn't remember the last time any investigation led to anything.

Never.

As much as he'd like to nail Fuller, it couldn't come with his fingerprints on it. Alex insisted that he'd take Fuller down on his own terms. At a time and place of his choosing. A phrase Alex stole from politicians who tried to sound harsh but rarely followed through with the rhetoric.

Not something Brad was concerned about when it came to Alex. He didn't doubt that Alex would do precisely what he said he'd do. Alex had few enemies who were still alive.

None, actually.

Except for Pok.

That thought brought a smile to Brad's face. He learned a couple of months before that Pok was alive and working for Alex on an island in the Caribbean. Somehow, Brad had earned Alex's trust. To the point that Alex shared with him the inner workings of his organization that he'd built outside the purview of the CIA.

Alex had wanted Brad to come work for him.

"Maybe, someday," Brad told him.

Right now, he could do Alex more good from the inside. He'd have his back. Help keep the powers that be from knowing Pok was still alive and that Alex was working his own agenda.

Brad still couldn't get used to the fact that Pok was alive and working for Alex. At one time, Pok was Alex's mortal enemy. Now they were the best of friends. Pok had turned to the good side. The two best computer hackers in the world, Alex and Pok, were systematically dismantling criminal organizations around the world by stealing their money and crippling their cyberinfrastructure.

Brad was getting a lot of the credit for their efforts.

Of course, no one within the CIA knew Pok was still alive or the extent of Alex's activities. He didn't even fully understand for obvious reasons. Plausible deniability.

He knew just enough to be dangerous.

Dangerous to men like Fuller. Brad considered himself the man's mortal enemy. Fuller was nothing more than a corrupt bureaucrat who put his self-interest over the interests of the operatives in the field who were risking their lives for God, family, and the American flag.

Treasonous as far as Brad was concerned.

But moving on him had to wait. And they had time. Fuller wasn't going anywhere. He was somewhat hamstrung as well because Alex and Jamie were legends in CIA circles. Jamie, especially, had a lot of political capital, as they called it. It was as difficult for Fuller to bring them down as it was for Alex and Jamie to bring Fuller down.

So, a cold war had broken out, so to speak. Between Alex and Fuller.

Inside the CIA. Hidden for months.

Brad was now in the middle of that war. Was he about to be thrust front and center on the front lines?

The meeting with the Director was giving him pause.

Did Fuller know about his involvement in Alex's clandestine activities?

The man was the head of the largest intelligence operation in the world. It was certainly possible.

Brad wasn't worried about himself. All of his activities were above board. Alex ran the CIA operations out of the cyber lab in Virginia. Within the purview of the CIA and with Brad's oversight under a corporation called AJAX which served as their cover.

Brad stuck with what he was authorized to do. Oversee AJAX and feed Alex and Jamie missions as they came up. He hadn't broken any laws.

Unless you considered the untruthful answers he had given on his monthly lie detector test. Or... his looking the other way when Alex and Jamie formed their own missions and were raking in billions of dollars into AJAX.

Brad suddenly felt extremely vulnerable.

AJAX had been his idea. It was an art distribution company that was a cover for their CIA operations. Between the art and the theft of money from bad actors, AJAX was worth more than two billion dollars as far as Fuller knew. It had a seventy-five million dollar jet and a yacht worth three times that.

Stolen from terrorists.

Given to AJAX with the full knowledge and approval of the CIA.

What Fuller didn't know was that AJAX was probably worth twice that. Four or five billion.

Alex bought an island in the Caribbean where Pok ran Alex's cyber warfare operations cleverly hidden from the world. Alex had built a team of more than a dozen hackers. They stole money from terrorists and deposited it into various shell corporations that couldn't be traced back to Alex.

Not for their personal gain.

The money was used to finance Jamie's sex trafficking rescue operations and other worthwhile causes.

Fuller wouldn't approve. He thought all power should flow through him. He was already jealous of Alex and Jamie and how beloved they were.

What Brad wanted to do was not show up for the meeting. Not an option. Technically, Fuller was his boss, although he primarily answered to a deputy director in clandestine services, several rungs down the ladder.

So, Brad stood to his feet and straightened his tie. He took a deep breath and left his office for the meeting. He didn't have far to go. The Director's office was a couple of hallways from his.

He decided to hope for the best. That's what he told his operatives in the field to do. Worry about the things you can control. The meeting with the Director was whatever it was. Nothing he could do about it. He needed to take his own advice.

Easier said than done.

Brad walked through the hallowed, cold, and sterile halls of CIA headquarters to the office of the Director, feeling like a prisoner on death row being led to execution.

Had the Director discovered something?

Did he know Alex was after him?

Fuller had to know that much, at least. Even though Fuller was the Director of the CIA, he had to be concerned about being in the crosshairs of the two most lethal assassins on the planet. Alex and Jamie who'd not forgotten the Director's total lack of concern for their lives.

Brad would soon know.

He walked into Fuller's office and was greeted warmly by the Director. Also present in the room was Brad's direct boss, J.T. Ward.

Fuller offered Brad something to drink, and he passed.

So Fuller got right to the point. "I've been watching you," he said.

Brad's heart started racing faster. It was already doing laps around his chest. He expected his operatives to have the best poker faces in the world. He had to muster one at that very second.

Fuller continued. "I must say I'm impressed. You do good work."

"My operatives in the field do good work, sir. I just ride their coattails."

"You're too modest. Behind every good man is a better woman, as they say."

In the case of Fuller, several women. A trophy wife, a mistress, and a couple of professional hookers on the side. Information uncovered by Alex and his team.

Brad made a concerted effort to keep from grinning.

"Behind every good field operative is a good puppeteer behind the scenes," Fuller continued. "Pulling the strings. I must say I'm impressed by your skills."

"Thank you, sir."

Brad sensed a but was coming.

"But," Fuller said.

Here we go.

"But your skills are wasted managing operatives. I have bigger plans for you."

"I'm very happy with what I'm doing."

Brad meant that. He thrived on the thrill of operations. The adrenaline rush. The planning and execution. The endless phone calls in the middle of the night from an operative in trouble. The split-second life and death decisions that had to be made periodically. Knowing he was making a difference in the world. Helping good overcome evil. Those were the most important things.

"I'm promoting you, Brad. You're taking J.T.'s spot."

Brad forcibly had to keep his mouth from gaping open.

J.T. was Deputy Director Counter-Terrorism. Brad would be jumping several spots ahead in the proverbial rat race.

"I'm flattered," Brad said. "But I feel like my skills are better served managing operatives in the field. Not in administration."

The Deputy position, while it yielded a lot of power and might be a good career move, was several steps removed from the field. Brad would be a paper pusher. He'd become everything he always despised. A suit, as Curly called them back in the day when he was still alive.

Maybe that was the source of his hesitation.

More times than he could count, he'd joined in with Curly, Alex, and Jamie, making fun of people in those positions.

The meeting wasn't going how he had expected it to. Fuller was offering him a promotion. More money. More prestige. A fast track to more promotions in the future. Who wouldn't want that?

"Can I give you a decision tomorrow?" Brad asked.

"No, sorry. Right now. It's on the table for the next two minutes. I don't want a man in this position who's indecisive."

"Okay. I'll take it."

The Director stood to his feet, extended his hand, and Brad shook it.

When Brad got back to his office, he took a burner phone out of his briefcase and exited the building. He called a number he knew by heart.

Alex answered on the first ring.

"You've gotta get out of the country," Brad said to him. "Fuller's coming after you."

2

When Brad called Alex on the unsecured line, and his first words were 'get out of the country,' Alex thought Brad was probably overreacting. When he followed it up with the words 'Cardinal Red,' Alex immediately hung up the phone.

Cardinal Red was the equivalent of the 'nuclear option' and meant the precautions they had in place in the event of a worst-case scenario were to be implemented. The term, Cardinal Red, came from Alex's days in college. He was the starting quarterback for the Stanford Cardinal football team. Their colors were red and white. The Cardinals lost to Alabama in the national championship game by a last-second touchdown given up by the defense. Alex played well and would've been named MVP had the Cardinals won.

One of the few losses he'd experienced in his life.

He wondered if he was about to experience another one.

Cardinal red was like code red. Code red meant life as he knew it was over. The only thing he didn't know was why.

It probably had something to do with Fuller.

Alex hung up the phone and went to work. He packed a few things and left the house as soon as possible. That'd be the first place Fuller would look for him. Alex left his CIA-issued phone at his home so they'd think he was still there. Anything he could do to throw them off his track would be done.

He wasn't going to let Fuller find him if he could do anything about it.

Not that he was sure they were even looking for him or what he'd do exactly if they did find him. Alex would never fire on another CIA or FBI agent. Unless they fired on him first, which he couldn't imagine happening.

They'd have orders to take him alive which wasn't the worst thing in the world either. This wasn't a hill to die on. He had a lot of cards left to play, including turning himself in. Which he considered. But if he did so, he wanted it to be on his own terms. So for now, he intended to run. Go dark.

Curly had taught Alex how to disappear off the face of the earth for as long as he wanted. Fuller would know that and try to spring a surprise on Alex before he had time to react. Having Brad in the office instead of coming to work for him was apparently paying off.

As soon as Alex was off the cell phone tower near his house, he called the airport where his jet was in a hangar. The call couldn't be tracked because he used a burner phone. His instructions were for them to get his plane ready for wheels up in a little over an hour. He also told them to file a flight plan for South Africa.

When he hung up, he was as deep in thought as a mile-long mine shaft. One of Alex's strengths. The ability to focus on the task at hand without emotion. Mistakes were made when one panicked. He'd been in too many dangerous life and death situations for this one to rattle him.

Alex stayed off the main roads and took evasive action to make sure he wasn't being followed. After twenty minutes, he was satisfied that he didn't have anyone tailing him. So, he drove straight to a storage unit that only he and his wife Jamie knew about.

Inside were several fake passports for him and for Jamie. Along with a dozen burner phones, a laptop, and a million dollars in cash which were already in two backpacks for a quick getaway.

He was in and out of the storage unit in less than two minutes and on the road again.

Jamie and Alex both knew this day might eventually happen. Ironically, Alex always thought they'd be running from a terrorist who was out to kill them. Not his own government who he'd risked his life for more times than he could remember.

Wrapping his mind around the sudden turn of events had his head spinning. He could hardly believe it. Though apparently, it was true. His own government. A powerful enemy in a powerful position.

Fuller had almost unlimited resources at his disposal. That's why Alex had to be faster. Smarter. A step ahead.

He'd already be in the air and out of the country except he had to talk to Brad. He couldn't leave the country without knowing what this was all about. It might not even be Fuller, although he couldn't imagine it being anything else.

After more evasive moves meant to lose a tail, Alex drove to a predetermined meeting point. Hopefully, Brad was there. Since Alex didn't know why Brad had instituted Cardinal Red, he also had no idea if he'd be able to break away to meet him.

According to the plan, Alex would wait at the rendezvous point for fifteen minutes. If Brad didn't show up, then he'd leave. The meet was to take place in *Lady Bird Johnson Park*, along the Potomac, just west and south of D.C. Alex had already scouted out the area a number of times.

He knew where to park his car so he wouldn't be seen. In a cluster of trees just off the main road. From his vantage point, he could see the bench where Brad would be if he were coming. He could also view the traffic coming in and out of the park.

Brad wasn't there.

Alex wouldn't have approached him right away even if he was. The extra precautions were to ensure that Brad wasn't followed. In fact, no one was in the park at that time.

The brief respite allowed Alex to catch his breath. His mind wanted to speculate about what had happened, but what was the point? He'd know soon enough. At least, he hoped he would.

As the minutes clicked by, Alex became convinced Brad wasn't coming. He prepared himself for the inevitable. He'd have to drive to the airport, get on his plane, and go dark. Meaning he'd go off the grid until he could sort things out. He wasn't going to South Africa but to his island in the Caribbean.

There he'd be safe. Fuller would have his plane tracked, but Alex had ways to hack in the system and make it look like the plane went to South Africa. When Fuller sent someone there to find him, they'd end up on a wild goose chase. He would disappear into thin air like a puff in the wind.

Fuller would never find him. Not unless Alex wanted to be found.

The real trick would be to get Jamie to the island. She was on a mission in Asia. He'd have to cross that bridge once he had more information.

Out of the corner of his eye, he saw a car approaching. He didn't recognize it. The windows were tinted. The car pulled slowly into the parking lot and stopped next to the bench.

That complicated things. Brad wouldn't approach the bench with that vehicle in front of their predetermined meeting spot. The car sat there for at least five minutes. Alex surveyed the park and determined that the car wasn't being followed and that Brad wasn't hiding in the trees somewhere waiting for the car to leave.

Suddenly, the car door opened.

To Alex's surprise, Brad exited the vehicle, looked around, then sat down on the bench. Alex scanned the area once again, looking for any signs of trouble.

He didn't see anything.

But he still hesitated.

Could it be a trap?

What gave him pause was that he couldn't see inside the car. Could Fuller's goons be hiding there?

Brad would never betray him unless he was coerced. Something Alex had to consider. When the proper pressure was applied to a person's most vulnerable point, self-interest trumped loyalty. Brad wouldn't be tortured, but Fuller had a number of incentives to cooperate at his disposal.

The threat of jail time was one. Brad losing his high-powered job. An enormous cash payoff. Threats against loved ones. Alex wouldn't put any of those things past Fuller. His opinion of Fuller was right up there with cockroaches.

The unknown caused Alex to hesitate again. Finally, he decided it didn't matter. Knowing what was going on was worth the risk. Whatever it was.

And... all things considered, he liked his chances. If it was a trap, Alex had options. Fuller's men would have orders to take him alive. There couldn't be more than five or six guys in the car. There weren't a dozen men alive who could take Alex if they couldn't use their weapons to kill him.

So, he decided to risk it and approach the bench. He called out to Brad, who was staring straight ahead. He'd be able to tell by the look on Brad's face if anything was awry.

If he saw anything, he'd react. And he'd have the element of surprise. If there were men in the car, it'd take them several seconds to exit it. By the time they did, Alex would race back to his car, which was unlocked and running. He'd be down the road before they could get to him.

Brad looked his way and smiled nervously.

Nothing on his face or demeanor told Alex that Brad was not alone. No slight nod of the head. No wink. No tilt of the head toward the car. No hand gestures. Absolutely nothing to deter Alex from approaching the park bench.

Emboldened, Alex let out a sigh and picked up his pace. Brad stood to his feet. Alex grabbed him and pulled him close into a bear hug. Then patted down Brad's back with his hands. In an exaggerated manner.

Half kidding. Half serious. He had to. To be sure. It was necessary even with a dear friend in this type of situation.

"I'm not wearing a wire," Brad said with a grin. "If that's what you're wondering."

The pat down had already confirmed that in Alex's mind. That didn't mean Brad didn't have a listening device on him. CIA spy tools had become highly sophisticated and incredibly small. A microphone could be in his ear and transmitted wirelessly. It could be in a ballpoint pen in his suit pocket. Or in his shoe, on the tip of his toe. In his pants pocket the size of a quarter. Theoretically, it could be anywhere on his person.

Alex wasn't going to search him.

By the way Brad was acting, Alex was no longer worried about a listening device. He was trained to detect deception. Brad was trained to avoid detection.

Alex was better.

His abundance of caution had been unnecessary. But he hadn't survived in this business by being reckless. The inattentive didn't survive in this line of work. They either quit or were killed before they changed professions.

"What's got your hair on fire?" Alex asked him.

"Fuller promoted me to Deputy Director," Brad said, cutting to the chase.

Alex let that sink in.

"Shoot!" he said. "We're screwed."

The situation was more serious than he had imagined it to be.

"I know! How soon can you get out of Dodge?" Brad asked. "Fuller just sprung this on me. I asked to think about it overnight, and he shot me down. Said it was now or never. That means he's coming after you today."

"Thirty minutes from now or less, I'll be on a plane to a faraway destination. We've always been prepared for this, but that doesn't make me like it any more than getting a root canal."

"Where's Jamie?" Brad asked.

"She's on a mission," Alex said with a sigh.

"Rescuing girls?"

"No. She's rescuing paintings."

3

Khorog, Tajikistan

Jamie and her team were in one of the most dangerous parts of the world.

While the small landlocked country of Tajikistan in central Asia was open to American tourism, they weren't open to a heavily armed team of highly skilled operatives sneaking into the country across the Uzbekistan border without a visa. Or them entering the restricted GBAO, the Gorno-Budakshan Autonomous Region, to kidnap one of its most prominent citizens.

The CIA didn't sanction the mission, nor did Jamie care. The operation was sanctioned by AJAX, consisting of Alex and Jamie sitting around the dining room table brainstorming, then deciding to do it.

That was the way most of their missions developed. To an outsider, it may seem like they were going off half-cocked, but it had been their method of operation for many years. It worked for them, and they accomplished more than the suits who sat in their offices, who spent ridiculous amounts of time and money formulating plans that seldom worked in the field.

If you hadn't been shot at several times or killed someone, you couldn't possibly understand how many things could go wrong on a mission or what will and won't work when bullets start flying.

The Colonel developed the plan for obvious reasons. A trusty operative who'd been with them for several years now. He really was a Colonel in his life before AJAX. Tajikistan bordered China on the east and Afghanistan to the north. The Colonel ran more missions in Afghanistan during the war than almost any human alive. He knew the language, the customs, the terrain, and how to navigate governmental control.

Or lack thereof which was often the case in these tribal areas where Russian influence dominated. Independent tribal leaders rebelled against all authorities who tried to impose their will upon them. They had their own way of doing things, and the Colonel knew the ins and outs. His expertise was invaluable when it came to planning the details of a mission. Even more so in this part of the world.

Two other members of the AJAX's A-team supported the mission. Bond and A-Rad. The best of the best, which meant they had a high probability of success. Although on paper, missions always looked easier than once you were in the field. Nothing ever went precisely according to the plan.

The four of them finished the surveillance necessary and were ready to execute. They'd followed the target for three days and were satisfied that they were prepared. Things seemed to be straightforward.

A-Rad was loitering outside an irshod, the equivalent of a convenience store in the United States. Bond was outside a bank just off Lenin Street positioned with a direct view of *Khorog Jamat Khana Park*, which ran along the Gunt River. The Colonel was positioned by the *Summer Theatre*. He was closest to Jamie. Just in case she ran into trouble and with a clear line of sight to the *Shirinsho Shotemur Statue* where Jamie was standing waiting on the mark to arrive.

The radio suddenly burst into activity all at once.

"Smolt is not alone!" more than one of them said, clearly sounding the alarm. The mark was expected to arrive alone. So was she. That was part of the deal.

Smolt was the codename for the target. Clement Salomon was French, living in Tajikistan so he'd be outside the reach of most governments who would like to get their hands on him. The code name, Smolt, was chosen because it meant young trout. Salomon was in his twenties, which was young for one of the foremost art thieves in the world.

The din in the radio hadn't let up. A-Rad said in a much too loud voice, "Private. They should be coming into your sight about. . . now!"

Private was the Colonel's mission name they used over the radio.

Nicknames were meant to be funny. Jamie was Dolly. As in Dolly Parton. Because she was tall and thin. Athletic. Her breasts were barely an A-Cup. Pretty much the opposite of the iconic, glamorous Dolly Parton.

Today she wore a padded bra and dress for Clement's benefit. He was well known as a playboy who couldn't keep his hands off attractive women. He had a weakness for beautiful women and Jamie fit the bill, although she felt naked without her wedding ring on her finger. Curly, may he rest in peace, had warned her before he died, that she had the look of a married woman and needed to wipe it off her face if she intended to enter the field as a single woman. That look could get her killed.

How did she get rid of it, when she didn't even know what look he was talking about, and he wasn't around to coach her on it?

"He's got two goons with him," Colonel said to Jamie interrupting her thoughts. "We should abort."

"Let's let it play out," Jamie said.

"He doesn't know you from Adam. Walk away and he'll think he was stood up. He won't be any the wiser."

Out of the corner of her eye, Jamie saw the three men turn onto the sidewalk and begin walking her way. She turned away from them and looked at the statue so they couldn't see her talking to herself.

Jamie understood the concern. In their surveillance, they'd never seen Clement with bodyguards. He'd brought them along today, probably because of the nature of their transaction. Nineteen million dollars was a lot of money. Clement was being cautious. Perhaps he suspected a trap. Whatever the reason, this could be a game-changer.

Maybe she should abort.

"Everybody stand-by," Jamie whispered after dismissing her own concern. "If things go south, you know what to do."

The more missions they did, the more cautious her team was becoming. Probably a good thing, but it was annoying. Jamie knew the risks going in and didn't get nervous when the risks played out. The guys were just overprotective of her. If Alex had been standing there instead of her, they would not have suggested they abort the mission so soon.

It's not that they didn't think she was capable. She was, as much as Alex or any of them. It's just that they'd become too attached to her. Relied on her too much. Felt like they had a personal responsibility to protect her. Which they did from a professional standpoint. Not emotionally. Not personally. She understood because she had to tamp down those same feelings when she was on a mission with Alex.

The two of them had somehow managed to figure it out. At some point, she'd have to have a frank discussion with the team about it. Now wasn't the time.

The men were near. It was game time.

Jamie turned away from the statue and faced them. The two bulky men were Russian. They were wearing high-priced jet-black suits, she assumed with weapons under the jackets. They each looked to outweigh Jamie by more than a hundred pounds. She noted four points on each of their bodies that could have them writhing on the ground in agony or dead if that was the route she chose.

"I assume you're Clement," Jamie said, extending her hand.

He didn't take the handshake. Instead, he said, "You're American."

"Is that a problem?"

"Maybe. I was expecting Slava Smirnova. You told me you were Russian."

"Davayte poznakomimsya!" Jamie said to him in Russian. Meaning, let's get acquainted.

"Kakova vasheh nastoyashcheve imya?" he responded by asking, "What's your real name?"

"Occupe-toi de tes oignons!" Jamie said in French, causing Clement to burst out laughing.

She told him to 'Take care of your onions.' A French way of saying 'mind your own business.'

"You speak French, Russian, and English, as do I. I'm impressed. You're a woman of many talents. I like that."

His expression had turned from skeptical to interested. Jamie's beauty and charm usually worked on disarming a man's defenses. It hadn't taken long with the Frenchman.

"Seriously," Jamie said, changing her tone of voice to reflect the business she was interested in transacting. "I'm here to buy a stolen painting. I'm sure Clement is not your real name either."

It wasn't. His name was actually Charles Bonfils. He graduated from the Beaux-Arts de Paris, a world-famous art school in France. His parents were Francois and Brigitte Bonfils, from Nantes, France. He came from humble beginnings. His father was a starving artist whose charcoal drawings never took off.

Charles had more promise but was lazy and always getting into trouble. He'd been arrested as a child for any number of petty crimes. While quite bright, he got bored easily. Excitement was what engaged him. The thrill of the chase. The possibility of getting caught. He found running from the law far more interesting than his father's ideas regarding his future.

His first foray into stealing paintings was on his graduation day. He stole a famous painting hanging in the halls of the Beaux-Arts de Paris. The authorities caught him. He said it was a graduation prank, and he had intended to return it. The judge didn't find it amusing and sentenced him to ninety days in jail.

For most people, that would have made a lasting impression, perhaps even turning them away from the dark side. But the opposite happened. Clement was hooked. The isolation in jail gave him time to plan his next caper. He took full advantage of that void and came out of jail with numerous heists to orchestrate.

Over the following four years, his thefts became more brazen. The value of the paintings stolen, more mind boggling. Bonfils was quoted as saying it was as easy to steal a fifteen-million-dollar painting as it was a ten-thousand-dollar one.

So he focused on bigger prizes. Interpol had him on their most wanted list. No one was sure exactly how many millions of dollars of paintings he had stolen, but they were adding up. His reputation as an art thief was growing every year.

"I like to know who I'm dealing with," Clement said.

"You're dealing with someone who is about to give you nineteen million dollars," Jamie replied. "My name is unimportant."

Clement landed on Jamie's radar when she was searching the dark web for stolen paintings for sale. One, in particular, caught her attention. A Van Gogh self-portrait was reportedly given to Van Gogh's mother as a gift. It had been on display in a French gallery when it went missing. The crime was never solved, although there was much speculation that Clement was behind it.

When Alex tracked the website back to Clement, she had her confirmation. That's when they formed the plan to come after him. While she mostly invested her time rescuing girls, she had a softness in her heart for art. She minored in art in college. When Brad approached them about starting a corporation to act as a cover for their covert operations, a company who bought and sold fine art seemed like a natural fit.

In the short period of time they'd been running AJAX, they now owned more than three hundred million dollars in paintings. When she got back to D.C., Jamie intended to sign a lease and open a new art gallery near the White House and Union Station. She hoped Clement might lead her to some paintings to go in her gallery.

With some prompting from the Sig semi-automatic handgun hidden on her.

Clement reached into his pocket and handed Jamie a business card. On the backside were some numbers. Jamie assumed they were the routing and account information for the bank. Wiring instructions.

"I need to see the painting first," Jamie said.

"Once the money's in my account," Clement said, "I'll take you to the painting."

"That's not the deal," Jamie said sternly. "We met here in a public place so I could see the painting. I need to verify it's real."

"You don't trust me?"

"I don't trust my own mother when it comes to nineteen million dollars," Jamie retorted.

Clement smiled.

Jamie winced on the inside. Her mother died of breast cancer when she was seventeen. She only invoked the name of her mother for effect. She regretted not saying husband or best friend, but there was no time to overthink the comment.

"I will take you to it after I get my money," Clement said.

"You don't trust me?"

"The middle of Khorog is not the place to examine a Van Gogh."

"Don't do it," Jamie heard Colonel say in her ear. "Abort."

"You chose the place. It was your idea to meet here."

Clement let out a noticeable sigh.

"I will take you so you can see the painting."

"I take it, the painting is not here," Jamie said.

"No. But it's not far. My car is this way," Clement said, gesturing with his hand.

"After you," Jamie said, using the same gesture. She didn't like men with guns at her back.

She followed behind the three of them.

The pleads in her ear were coming fast and furious from everyone at once. If she had a way to turn off the radio, she would, but that wasn't an option. The radio would stay on while she was in range until the mission was complete. Everyone listening would know what was going down. Jamie hoped they would pipe down. Having three people chattering in your ear was annoying.

Jamie tried her best to ignore them.

On the street was a black SUV with the engine running. A man was inside behind the wheel.

The din in her ear became more frantic as the Colonel started shouting instructions to the team.

One of the bodyguards opened the back door for Clement. He got in first, and Jamie slid in beside him.

The last thing she heard in the com before they drove off was the Colonel yelling at her that she had screwed up his plan.

4

The park was calm and peaceful. Alex's insides were anything but. The gentle breeze did little to calm his emotions. They were stirring around like a boiling volcano about to erupt, destroying everything in its path.

While Alex was anxious to get to the airport and out of the country, he still had more questions than answers. The longer he and Brad talked, the angrier he got. What he'd really like to do was march down to Fuller's office and drag him out by his hair, tie a weight around his legs, and dump him in the river, so he'd never have to see that smug look on his face for the rest of his life.

Of course, only after he'd given Fuller a chance to unburden himself with a confession of all his misdeeds that had gotten him to the position of CIA Director in the first place. Alex knew Fuller was behind the hit on Jamie, he'd just like to hear the scumbag admit it.

Alex and Brad both knew that wasn't going to happen. Fuller would never spill the beans on all of his gross misdeeds voluntarily. Fuller probably saw nothing wrong with his actions since they led him to the coveted position of CIA Director. People like him considered it collateral damage if the end justifies the means. He didn't care who he destroyed along the way. The man had no conscience.

But bringing Fuller down required finesse, not strength. A problem Fuller had as well. He couldn't just take a scorched earth approach with Alex. He'd have to take an indirect approach. A blitz, so to speak, going back to Alex's football days. Bring an attack from every angle until Alex was overwhelmed.

Alex wondered where he'd attack first. Brad knew Fuller better than most.

"How do you think Fuller will play it?" Alex asked him.

"I don't think he'll arrest you right away. He doesn't have anything that'll stick. But he'll be looking."

"That means he has to find something," considered Alex.

"If he doesn't find anything, I wouldn't put it past him to make something up. Create an appearance of wrongdoing."

Alex stood up from the park bench, put his foot on it, and stood over Brad. He was too worried to sit. He knew this would be a three-ring circus with someone getting eaten by the Bengal tiger at the end of the show. Hopefully, he'd be the one controlling the tiger.

Brad continued. "I suspect Fuller is at your house right now. When he finds you aren't there, he'll start seizing everything. Computers. Laptops. Phones. Documents. He'll take anything and everything if he thinks it will help take you down."

"He won't find anything. There are no documents. We don't leave a paper trail. Everything's electronic. The only thing he'll find is what I want him to find."

"Good. He already knows that stuff anyway."

"Exactly. Everything else is behind a firewall. Which is behind ten more firewalls. He'll never crack it."

"He'll have his best people on it. You know that. He won't stop."

"I'm his best person. We're the ones the CIA comes to when they want to breach a firewall. Fuller has to know that."

"He does. But he can make things unpleasant. Get you angry enough to make a mistake. It's going to be difficult at best, but you're going to have to keep your cool."

Alex didn't respond. He did a quick glance around the park to see if there were any threats. He saw a few joggers on the path and some Canadian geese wandering around.

Brad was making sense. Alex needed to control his emotions. Now more than ever. For his and Jamie's sake, as well as the essential clandestine work they were involved in.

"Fuller will start seizing assets," Brad said. "He'll freeze all your bank accounts. He'll do everything in his power to break you and take you down."

The anger inside of him was nearing a boiling point. Fuller's tactics were becoming clearer to him. He'd hit Alex where it hurt. All the hard work he and Jamie had done over the past few years was going to be dismantled. For the purpose of humiliating him. A wounded animal will make mistakes. Lash out in anger. That's what Fuller was counting on.

That didn't mean Alex could easily control his emotions. This was an attack on him personally.

"All those assets are in AJAX's name!" Alex expressed what he was feeling. "What right does he have to seize them? They're not hidden. I give you a report every quarter, and we account for every dollar we take in and spend. It's all on the up and up."

"Doesn't matter. Those funds were secured while working on CIA missions. Fuller will say that you're entitled to a salary like everybody else. But he'll argue that you don't have any right to become a billionaire at the CIA's expense. There's nothing you could say to have Fuller understand the situation. If he isn't benefiting, nobody is going to reap any rewards if he has anything to say about it."

"It's not the CIA's money!"

Alex bit his lip to keep from exploding further. He had to be careful not to raise his voice too loud. There were people around. So he lowered it a few decibels. "We steal the money from terrorists. We take it from oligarchs. Bad actors. We're doing the world a favor by taking that money out of their hands. The world is a safer place because of us."

"I know that, and you know that. So does Fuller. But he'll make his case. Some of the higher-ups will be sympathetic to it. There's a new regime in town. Fuller has filled the higher ranks of the CIA with his own men. Many share his sentiment that you've become too powerful. Too wealthy. Jealousy drives them as much as anything else. They can't stand to see you accomplish so much, especially since your work is charitable. They probably don't even understand the concept."

"Still, it's not illegal. Everything is above board. The previous CIA director authorized the setup."

Brad furrowed his brow and twisted his lips into a frown. Alex knew what he was thinking. That statement wasn't true. Fuller knew about the two billion in assets. He didn't know about the rest. The offshore accounts. The operations on their island. Cryptocurrency. The cyber lab run by Pok had secured another three billion hidden worldwide.

As altruistic as those endeavors were, and as much good as they undoubtedly did, the money was unreported. Alex considered the money an extension of AJAX. Unauthorized, but necessary to rid the world of the scum of the earth who trafficked in arms, drugs, and even humans.

Alex considered himself the Robin Hood of the cyber world. The money was put to good use. Fuller would say it was laundered.

If he ever found out about it.

Alex could hear Fuller's argument. Alex was an American citizen. Fuller would say that the money should be reported to the IRS even though it was earned outside the U.S.

A gray area.

Fuller could never know about it.

Brad and Alex would be wise to drop the subject. Leaving the details unspoken between them was in their best interest. That afforded Brad plausible deniability if he was ever questioned. He couldn't share information he didn't know. It was safer for both of them that way.

Probably knowing this, Brad changed the subject. Unfortunately, to something equally as unpleasant.

"You'll lose the yacht," Brad hypothesized.

"They wouldn't even have that yacht if not for Jamie! She risked her life to get it. That's ludicrous."

A Sheikh in Abu Dhabi held women on that yacht as sex slaves. Jamie rescued the women and seized the yacht. The Sheikh was out of the picture. Dead or in prison somewhere. At the time, Jamie was a hero for rescuing the girls and putting out of commission a ruthless tyrant who the American government couldn't touch on their own.

Alex could barely contain his anger, but he kept his voice down anyway. "AJAX owns that yacht! Everybody knows that. We don't use it personally. Jamie uses it to rescue girls. The yacht is needed to get the girls out alive."

The yacht had been redesigned to have a hidden holding room. Jamie rescued girls in foreign countries, hid them in the yacht, and transported them to safety.

Jamie would hit the ceiling if she learned that Fuller was taking the yacht from them.

"Be that as it may, they'll seize your plane as well."

"Jamie has the plane. She's in Tajikistan on an AJAX mission."

Brad only nodded. He appeared to be deep in thought as his brow was furrowed. Alex was pacing now. Back and forth in front of the bench, like a cat on a hot tin roof.

"I need to figure out how to warn Jamie and get her to the island before she comes back to the states."

Brad shook his head from side to side in an exaggerated way.

"No! That's not a good idea. Jamie needs to come back to Washington D.C. If you both run, it'll look like you have something to hide. She needs to say that you're on a mission. Out of pocket for a few weeks. Make it look like you aren't running. That'll buy you some time and make Fuller waste valuable resources looking for you."

"I don't want to put her at risk. What if Fuller arrests her?"

"Not going to happen. Jamie is untouchable. She's royalty at the CIA."

"And I'm not?"

Brad rolled his eyes at his friend.

"Not like Jamie. They think she walks on water."

"I think I did see her do that once," Alex commented, trying to lighten the mood if only for himself.

Brad smiled slightly, but then continued in his serious tone. "If Fuller came after Jamie, he'd have a mutiny on his hands. Half his employees would walk out in protest. Jamie will be fine."

"I suppose you're right."

"I am right! Jamie needs to come back here and fight for you. Confront Fuller. Make it hard on him. Rally support. She'll be your eyes and ears. I'll do what I can, but Fuller promoted me to get me out of the way. So that I'm no longer close to you. I don't think I'll be of much help. I really didn't want the promotion, but there was no way around it."

"You've already been a huge help. I appreciate you meeting me here to give me the skinny on what's going down."

Brad stood to his feet and leaned in so he was speaking in Alex's ear.

"You need to find out what Fuller's up to," Brad said. "There's some reason he's moving on you now. I don't know what it is. He's done something that he needs to cover up, and he's afraid you're going to find out what it is. That's why he has to discredit you. So, if you do find it, no one will believe you over him. Your job is to find out what that something is."

"Any ideas?"

"Not a clue. But if you start digging, you'll hit something. No one is better at a deep dive for information than you. I have great faith in you. You have to get inside Fuller's head."

"That's a scary thought. Who'd want to be inside that depraved mind? It sounds like hell on earth, in my opinion, but I'll do it. I have to figure it out for everyone's sake. He has to be stopped before he does any more damage. A man like that with unfettered power is dangerous to our democracy."

"Figure out what he has to gain. Fuller is motivated by power and prestige. His position in life is what drives that guy. He wants to be President someday, and he doesn't care whose toes he steps on along the way. He's ruthless and has no conscience. It's a dangerous combination."

"When I get through with him, he won't be fit to run for the local dog catcher. Not to mention what'll happen when Jamie finds out what he's done. She's going to get all up in his face. He has no idea what he's gotten himself into. I wouldn't want to be Fuller when she gets her hands on him."

"That's the spirit. Let's bring him down."

Alex and Brad did a sort of man hug and Alex thanked him again. Then went back to his car and drove to the airport.

Emboldened.

He didn't choose this battle, but he intended to win it.

5

As soon as Brad was out of the office, Director Fuller called Jack August in. He had been out of sight in the conference room so Brad wouldn't see him.

August came into the room and stood at attention, waiting for instructions.

"It's done," Fuller said to August. "Brad's out of the way. He won't be a problem. But, you have to move quickly. Brad and Alex are thick as thieves. I'm sure he's trying to get in contact with Alex as we speak. Are the wheels in motion?"

Fuller stared at August as the man shifted his weight from one foot to the other. The answer had better be yes. Time was of the essence. Fuller expected that the plan was already underway. He'd been working with August for three weeks, planning the first move. Every detail. Numerous times until he was sure August had it embedded in his thick skull.

The man wasn't stupid, or he wouldn't be where he was today, but Fuller didn't like not being in control. No one else was as smart or as efficient as he was when it came to executing plans.

Which was why he was Director and the grunt standing in front of him wasn't.

"Everything's set!" August finally confirmed. "All I need is your order to proceed."

"You already have my orders!" Fuller barked. "Follow the plan. Where is Alex now?"

"According to his cell phone, he's at his house," replied August nervously.

"Have him picked up and brought in for questioning. More importantly, I want all his bank accounts frozen right away. Seize the yacht and his plane and any other assets we can get a hold of."

"The bank accounts will only take a few phone calls. The yacht is in the marina in Miami. I already have agents standing by with the legal paperwork to freeze it. Jamie has the plane. I don't know where she is. She's on a mission to Central Asia. No one knows when she'll be back. Do you want me to seize the paintings as well?"

"What kind of mission?"

"I don't know. It's not authorized by the CIA. It's an AJAX deal. I assume a sex trafficking rescue, but I'm not sure. She's off the radar."

Fuller paused to think for a moment. He hadn't given Alex and Jamie a CIA mission on purpose. Both of them were supposed to be in town when he made his move. This complicated things.

"Find her," Fuller said. "Call Jamie back from her mission. Tell her to get back here as soon as possible. Tell her we would never pull her off a mission as important as rescuing girls from a sex trafficking ring if it wasn't imperative that she come back. I'm sure she'll be hard to convince, but you have to make this happen. When she steps foot on US soil, have her detained and brought in for questioning."

The wheels in Fuller's head were spinning a mile a minute. Then another idea came to light causing him to change his mind.

"August, forget looking for Jamie for now unless I deliver different orders," said Fuller. "Now. . . what were we talking about?"

He'd lost his train of thought.

"The paintings? Do you want me to seize them as well?" August asked. "According to the records, AJAX has more than two hundred million dollars in paintings in a warehouse downtown. Apparently, Jamie plans to open an AJAX art gallery across from the White House."

"That's absurd!" Fuller roared. "The nerve of those two. They are clearly using their positions with the CIA to become filthy rich. It's about time they were brought down to size. I've had enough of them acting as though the rules and regulations they signed up for don't apply to them. The party is over."

"I don't disagree, sir."

Fuller fought back a smirk.

He was rich but not as rich as Alex and Jamie. Since he became Director, his assets had quadrupled. He was now worth more than thirty million dollars. A colossal sum in most people's eyes, but a pittance compared to them.

That alone made him angry. Very angry. It was time to level the playing field.

While he despised the two, he did admire their creativity and ingenuity. The part of his plan that August didn't know about was that Fuller intended to keep AJAX operations intact. He wanted his son, Norm Fuller, to run it. If he could keep his idiot son away from drugs and prostitutes long enough to implement some of his strategies. No easy task based on his son's previous behavior.

Norm was currently in rehab at a facility in upstate New York, checked in under an assumed name. If all went well, he'd be out in two weeks, clean and sober and ready to make the family a small fortune. Hopefully, the promise of big money would get his attention and keep him on the right track. Only time would tell.

For obvious reasons, Fuller couldn't be making financial deals on the side in his position with the CIA. But his son could. That shady practice had been going on in Washington long before Fuller arrived and would continue after he was gone. It was politics as usual. He considered it a perk of helping run the country. He felt like it was a right he had earned, and he intended on taking full advantage of the opportunities that came his way. Making sweetheart deals on the side was as easy for a politician as shooting fish in a barrel.

Hopefully, the kid was up to it. If not, he'd use his brother. Although, he didn't trust him any further than he could throw him. Which wasn't far since his brother weighed nearly three hundred pounds. Forty more than him. He really ought to make time to exercise regularly. Who had the time? That's why he'd never done any field work and was more comfortable behind a desk. Where he could use his brilliant mind.

His mind was wandering again. He realized he still hadn't answered the question about the paintings.

"We know where the paintings are located," August said in a confused voice. "I can have those seized as well."

He needed to quit focusing on the dollar signs spinning around in his head and get back to the conversation.

"Like I said, take everything you can find!" Fuller said with exasperation. "Once we get Alex's computers and laptops, I want our cyber lab to go through them with a fine-toothed comb. Alex is dirty. Now, let's prove it."

Even if they couldn't find any evidence that Alex was dirty, he'd find a way to plant evidence. It shouldn't be hard once he had custody of Alex's personal items.

"I'm on it," August said as he did an abrupt turn and left the room.

Fuller was pleased with his choice of Jack August to replace Brad. What he needed were loyal soldiers. August was the right man for the job. For now, he'd take Brad's place and be in charge of Alex and Jamie. It'd also provide him with some cover. August would say that he initiated the investigation when he took over for Brad and found some irregularities in the books.

He could use the standard 'no comment' line when challenged on it. Afterall, they couldn't comment on an ongoing investigation of one of their own.

If August toed the company line, then eventually, he'd take Brad's place as Assistant Deputy Director and Brad would be fired or jailed. If they did find wrongdoing on Alex's part... actually when they found wrongdoing, then Brad will become collateral damage. At worst, Brad participated in the schemes. At the very least, he was negligent in not discovering them. Either way, it was only a matter of time until Brad was gone as well.

That reminded him.

Jamie.

A problem that needed resolving.

Fuller picked up the phone and called his Station Chief in Ukraine. Another loyal soldier in the vast network he'd built over the last six months. Paul Dietrich answered the secure line on the first ring.

"Director Fuller. It's good to hear from you," Dietrich said. "Your ears must be burning. I was talking to my staff about how good a job you're doing as Director."

Dietrich was also a brown noser. A quality Fuller liked, even demanded from his subordinates. It meant they were ambitious and willing to say or do anything to further their careers.

Dietrich's career was a career-CIA man on a fast track. His career stalled when it was learned that he had an affair with a subordinate in the London office. He'd been ousted and exiled to Ukraine. His wife also left him. Because of his plight, Deittrich was hungry and eager to get back in the good graces of management. Something Fuller would use to his benefit.

Fuller thought the punishment had been harsh. He didn't like laws against fraternizing in the military and wouldn't stand for those policies within the CIA. Women should be allowed to use their feminine wiles to get ahead. If a male superior used his position to take advantage of a subordinate, he didn't see the harm in that either as long as they were two consenting adults. He'd do the same thing if in their positions.

"I need a big ask from you," Fuller said to Dietrich

"Name it."

"Are you familiar with Jamie Austen?"

"Of course. Who isn't?"

"I understand she's running an unauthorized mission in your part of the woods."

"I hadn't heard anything about it."

"My point exactly. We can't have our officers working outside the purview of the agency. Find her and detain her. Hold her for questioning. We need to find out what she's up to."

"May I ask why? Jamie is one of our finest officers. I'm sure she's not doing anything illegal."

Fuller exploded. He hated when people questioned his orders.

"No! You may not ask why! I want her detained, and her plane seized. It's a CIA asset. Do as you're told!"

"Of course. What I mean is... Should I expect trouble from Austen? What if she doesn't want to come in? How do I make her?"

Fuller could hear the nervousness in Dietrich's voice. He often wondered why everyone was so afraid of Jamie and Alex. He knew of the pair's reputation, but no one could be as good as everyone claimed those two were. He always thought it was more of an urban legend of sorts.

"Send in enough men to make sure there's no trouble," Fuller said sternly. "Take her to a safe house. I want her under a twenty-four-hour guard. Once you have her secured, wait for my instructions. Don't let me down. Failure is not an option."

Fuller heard a noticeable sigh, on the other end of the line. He was about to yell at Dietrich again. Before he could, Dietrich said, "I'll get on it right away. First, I have to find Ms. Austen."

"Now! Find her now," Fuller bellowed. "I want her in custody by nightfall."

He slammed down the phone. Letting fly a volley of expletives meant for Jamie Austen. Why did she screw up his plan by being out of town?

They needed to find Jamie before Alex had a chance to warn her. In fact, they probably couldn't. Nightfall was unrealistic. Jamie would probably go into hiding and not be found. Couldn't be helped. At least he could get Alex detained for the time being.

The main thing was to take control of the assets. That would cut both of them off at the knees. They'd lose their wealth. Then their reputation. Hopefully, their freedom. If not, they'd disappear.

Something he could make happen.

Alex and Jamie wouldn't be the first operatives in the history of the CIA to meet an untimely death.

He put out a hit on Jamie once, he could do it again.

6

Khorog, Tajikistan

When Jamie got into the vehicle with Clement, the art thief, she was doing what she did best. Improvising. Doing whatever it took to get the job done. Things didn't usually go precisely as planned. It was the nature of the spy business.

No regrets. At least not yet.

Curly used to say that a person without regrets was a fool and destined to repeat his mistakes over and over again. Her wise CIA trainer also said, on more than one occasion, that the biggest regrets would be from the things she didn't do, not the things she did do.

In this instance, she did what she deemed necessary. Which was the right decision even if it went south.

That's why she deviated from the plan and got in Clement's car despite her team screaming in her ear over the wire to abort the mission. After considering it briefly, she knew she must follow through on the mission. The ultimate goal was to purchase the Van Gogh painting for nineteen million dollars. The transaction would hopefully lead her to more stolen items.

While she wasn't sure which high-profile thefts of art Clement committed, he was behind many of them. Jamie ultimately wanted to determine which were his and, hopefully, what happened to the paintings. With that information, they might be able to recover some of them. Jamie knew by his reputation alone that he must have a sizable collection worth many millions of dollars.

Maybe where he was taking her.

A smile formed on Jamie's face when she thought about her team.

She pictured Colonel and the guys scrambling to find her. By the time they got to their vehicle, Jamie would be out of radio range. The only thing they could do was drive around until they picked up her signal again. While Khorog only had a population of approximately 28,000 people, the guys wouldn't find her unless they got lucky and happened upon them.

They'd first go to Clement's house. The one they'd been surveilling for the last three days. But from the route the driver was taking, it didn't appear that's where they were going. She didn't recognize any of the landmarks.

That would make things more difficult for the Colonel. The guys would begin a search no more straightforward than finding a needle in a haystack. She had her cellphone on her, but they couldn't track it. Tajikistan didn't have GPS locating services for international travelers.

While it almost made her laugh, she did feel bad for them. They were only doing their job which was to protect her.

Now, she couldn't count on them. Jamie was on her own. It wasn't the first time, and provided she got out of this alive, she suspected it wouldn't be the last either.

The guys were probably cursing her about now while scrambling to find her.

It caused her to smile again.

Clement noticed.

"Is something funny?" he asked.

More improvisation was needed.

"I was thinking about how I'm getting a seventy-two-million-dollar painting for nineteen million dollars. That makes me happy."

That caused him to frown. "Perhaps I'm selling it too cheap."

"You and I both know I can't get that for it," Jamie retorted. "The market for stolen paintings is limited. Besides... I don't intend to sell it. I have a place in my master bedroom reserved for this exact painting. Right above my bed."

"Perhaps I can come to your house and see it sometime. I'd like to see the inside of your bedroom." Clement had a lustful grin on his face when he made his forward and lude remark.

That was precisely the reaction Jamie had hoped for. A man with his mind on sex didn't think as clearly.

Jamie envisioned what Clement's face would look like if she backhanded him with enough force to break his jaw. Or what Alex could do to the man's head with his massive football hands.

She tamped down those thoughts.

"Perhaps you'll get that chance," Jamie said, flashing her own seductive smile.

Improvising again.

She could play any role necessary for the sake of the mission. Even pretend to be interested in him. A clever move. Unlikely that Clement would let his goons put her in danger if he thought she might be interested in him, and he could get more than money out of her.

That wasn't going to happen. But he had no way of knowing that fact, and Jamie had no qualms about leading him on.

The vehicle suddenly came to an abrupt stop and pulled into a warehouse drive. Jamie took a quick glance around at her surroundings. They were in an industrial area. With few buildings. No residential housing nearby. The metal building in front of her had no identifying signs. It would be hard to help her team find it, even if she was in communication with them.

The only consolation was that the warehouse was on the same side of the Gunt River as the park where she first met Clement. That'd make it easier. Slightly. It put the odds of them finding her from ten thousand to one to a thousand to one.

Couldn't be helped. In retrospect, they should've had one of her team in a vehicle. When arrangements were made with Clement, he said he'd bring the painting to the park. Jamie would inspect it there. If satisfied, she would wire the money on her phone. Then leave with the painting.

So much for best laid plans. Clement had changed the arrangements. The question was why? It had to give her pause. Was she walking into a trap? Did he intend to take her money but keep the painting? Was there something else he wanted from her and would take if she didn't offer it?

Even though the car was stopped, no one was moving to exit the vehicle. Jamie didn't feel like she should be alarmed, so she didn't say anything.

A few seconds later, Clement pulled out his phone and entered some numbers. The massive door to the warehouse began to open. Once it was high enough, the driver pulled the vehicle inside. The entrance was big enough to drive a small semi through.

The lights suddenly came on.

When the vehicle came to a stop, Jamie tried to open the door to get out, but it was locked.

While she didn't like being confined, it still didn't cause her to be alarmed. She was alone in the back seat with Clement armed with a weapon and hands that could kill him in a hundred different ways.

One of the Russians opened the front door and got out. He then opened her door, and she exited. Clement followed her.

Jamie glanced around, gathering more intelligence, stowing it in her rock-solid memory. This wasn't a typical warehouse. It was well fortified and had security cameras throughout. No windows and no doors led to the outside other than the large bay door which was now closing.

Trapping her in. She fought back the alarm bells ringing in her head.

Jamie could see a highly sophisticated security system complete with motion detectors. The kind of security one would expect to find protecting millions of dollars in artwork.

A wave of excitement pulsed through her like a raging river. This was why she had taken the risk. The possibility of finding a treasure trove of stolen and valuable paintings in the warehouse exhilarated her.

One of the goons approached and reached for her, replacing her excitement with anger. He grabbed her roughly like he was going to pat her down.

She pulled back.

"Touch me again, and I'll break your arm!" Jamie said in no uncertain terms.

The goon didn't say anything. He only looked at Clement. Waiting for instructions. She still hadn't heard either of the Russians speak.

"I can never be too careful," Clement said. "He's checking you for a weapon."

"You can assume that I have a weapon and that I know how to use it!" Jamie said it in a stern voice so he'd know how serious she was.

"Why would you bring a weapon to purchase a piece of art?" he asked calmly.

"Same reason your two men have weapons," Jamie retorted. "I can never be too careful either. I'm a single woman, alone in a warehouse with three armed men. Are you afraid of me? I'm outnumbered three to one."

Before Clement could respond, Jamie added, "My understanding was that this was a friendly transaction."

She was purposefully trying to keep the situation from escalating.

The warehouse where they were standing was completely empty. The paintings weren't stored in that room. She wasn't sure where they were. Better if Clement showed her voluntarily. Without her having to kill somebody.

"I'm not armed," Clement said, correcting her. "I'm a lover, not a fighter. I came here to make a deal. Perhaps make a new friend.

I find guns to be... what do you Americans say, child's play? For the weak."

Jamie couldn't disagree more. Her weapon made her very strong. Was there anything more powerful than having the ability to take another man's life?

His words caused her to relax slightly, though. She was happy to hear that he intended to complete her purchase of the stolen Van Gogh. Jamie kept reminding herself why she was there. She'd learned to control this side of her in the sex trafficking. More times than she could count, she had to cozy up to the bad guy to gain his trust and get into his inner circle. For the purpose of rescuing the girls he controlled.

In this instance, the target was valuable paintings. Not worth the price of a human life, but worth the restraint to gain Clement's trust.

However, if Clement insisted on taking her weapon, that would complicate things. Although he hadn't issued any orders for his goons to do so, if he changed his approach, she'd have to deal with the fallout and act.

Which was fine. A confrontation was coming. Sooner or later. The painting was likely in the warehouse. She wasn't leaving there without it. While she preferred later, she was more than willing to kill the two Russians, take Clement hostage, and force him to talk to accomplish her aim.

A better plan was to let it play out. Even complete the transaction. She would force a confrontation under her terms when she had the element of surprise on her side.

She'd soon find out Clement's intentions.

Jamie eyed the Russians carefully and assessed the threat they posed. They were professionals. One was standing next to her, the other on the other side of Clement. They hadn't stood side by side since the moment she first saw them.

A wise strategy for bodyguards. Many stood right next to the person they were protecting. If they did, it would make it easier for

Jamie to take them out if it became necessary. By distancing themselves, they made it nearly impossible for her to disable both of them with one strike. By the time she took one down, the other would likely have time to draw his weapon.

Jamie had her own weapon, but it was hidden under her dress on her inner thigh. She preferred to be wearing a jacket, but with Clement's reputation as a lady's man, she wanted to play on that weakness. While she had practiced drawing the weapon thousands of times from under her dress, brandishing the gun, aiming, and firing it, always took longer when hidden in a dress than it did hidden in a suit jacket.

The Russians would be slower at the draw than her. An equalizer. Jamie put the odds at fifty-fifty that she could take out both of them before they got a shot off at her. Not the best odds she had dealt with but not the worst either.

Still, not good enough odds to force the issue.

Talking her way out of this rendezvous was the better option. Confidence and bravado seemed like the best strategy. Strength but with vulnerability. Friendliness with sincerity.

She struggled to find the right tone.

"I came here to do a deal as well," Jamie said with an attitude. Deciding on sassy. "But you're not taking my weapon. If you don't want my nineteen million dollars, then take me back to the park. I'll get on my plane and go home. If you want to make a deal, then let's get on with it."

Forcing Clement into a corner seemed like a good strategy.

He hesitated.

Jamie tensed on the inside. She moved her hand down to her side. Shifted her weight, so her legs were further apart. She prepared to draw her weapon.

Depending on his response.

They all waited.

The Russians must've sensed the tension as well because she could see them react. Itching to draw their weapons.

Jamie wondered if she would regret getting in that car after all.

7

Jamie's cell phone vibrated, causing a humming sound that everyone in the warehouse could hear. The phone was hidden in a specially made pocket sewn inside the slit of her dress.

Probably the Colonel calling, because he'd been unable to locate her. That and to complain about her disappearing.

She started to ignore it but then realized that the phone was near the gun and gave her a justifiable reason to reach her hand inside her dress. With that excuse, if she needed to draw her gun, the extra one and a half to two seconds saved shifted the advantage decisively in her favor. It gave her the confidence that she could get to the gun, pull it from the holster, aim it, and fire before the two Russians could get a shot off at her.

Curly always said that Jamie didn't need a significant advantage. If he trained her right, a slight edge would do just fine.

Jamie reached her hand toward the phone. The Russians' demeanor noticeably changed as their eyes widened then their hands reached for their pockets.

"Relax, men," Jamie said, twisting her lips to put an annoyed look on her face. "I'm just getting my cell phone."

She slowed down her motion anyway. The last thing she wanted was two trigger happy men to overreact. With an exaggerated slow motion, Jamie carefully reached inside the slit. Her hand brushed the gun for reassurance, and then she pulled her cell phone out of the inside pocket.

Raising it in the air, she mockingly showed it to Clement and the two bodyguards for effect.

"See—cell phone. Nothing to worry about," she said casually.

She raised her phone to look at the screen while keeping a wary eye on the two Russians. The phone was in her left hand in case she needed to reach for the gun with her right.

It took all of Jamie's self-control to keep from gasping at the two words on the screen.

Cardinal Red.

The words sent her heart spinning in circles like a cheerleader's baton.

The message had to be from Alex. Sent to her from a burner phone.

How was that possible?

It meant the sky was falling. Or the equivalent in their business. Why? Things were going incredibly well with AJAX. What could possibly have happened to cause Alex to execute the equivalent of a Code Red?

It had to be related to Fuller. Ever since the man became CIA Director, Alex had been on edge. Jamie half expected to get a message or a call in the middle of the night saying Fuller was dead from suspicious circumstances. Which meant Alex was probably responsible. Alex was also constantly worried that Fuller would put out another hit on one of them.

Was Cardinal Red evoked because of what Alex did or what Fuller did?

How could she possibly know?

Was it a joke?

No way! That was impossible. Cardinal Red was exclusively meant to activate extreme measures. It was supposed to mean they were in grave danger.

Alex would never kid about a Cardinal Red. He might test her though.

That had to be it.

In the past, Alex always warned her ahead of time when he was going to test out his emergency systems. This time, he must've wanted to test her in real-time to see how well she responded.

She suddenly felt relief and anger at the same time.

"Is everything alright?" Clement said, interrupting her thoughts which had shaken her to the bones like she had just survived the effects of an earthquake.

"Your face is as white as a sheet," he added. "You look like you've seen a ghost."

It did feel like the blood had drained from her face and was pulsing through her body like a fire hose set on full blast.

She quickly composed herself. If the Cardinal Red was a test, it came at the worst possible time. Which was probably what Alex was hoping for. She'd give him a piece of her mind later. He couldn't possibly know the danger she was in at that very moment.

Jamie said the first thing that popped into her mind. "I got bad news from home."

"Boyfriend troubles?"

"That's none of your business! Besides, I don't have a boyfriend."

Which was true. She had a husband. One she wasn't too happy with at the moment. She'd strangle him if the alert weren't as serious as it was intended to be.

She saw relief in Clement's face when she said she didn't have a boyfriend. Although truthfully, she doubted if he cared if she had a boyfriend or not, or even a husband for that matter. Scruples weren't his high suit.

With the phone in her hand, an idea popped into Jamie's head. The distraction gave her the perfect opportunity to call the Colonel and give him her location.

"I thought the call was from my driver," Jamie said to Clement. "It reminded me that I forgot to tell him where I went. He's probably still sitting at the park, twiddling his thumbs."

Jamie looked over at the Russians and they didn't seem as antsy. Their shoulders had dropped back to a normal position and they were standing at attention again with their hands folded together in front of them.

Jamie didn't ask or wait for permission from Clement to call the Colonel. She just dialed the number.

He answered immediately. "We grabbed a bite to eat without you," he said jokingly. "Hope you don't mind." His words came out with a mix of sarcasm, disrespect, and bitterness. He was clearly not happy that she had ditched them.

"I'm sorry. I went with Monsieur Clement to see the painting. We're at a warehouse south of the city. On this side of the river."

She'd like to be more specific but couldn't be. So, Jamie put her hand on the phone and asked Clement, "What's the address to the warehouse?"

Clement scowled. "We'll take you back to the park when we've concluded our business."

It didn't seem like an issue she could press. The location probably didn't even have an address. And if it did, Clement wouldn't be sharing that information.

Jamie pressed the phone back to her ear. "The messieurs will drive me back to the park. Feel free to grab a bite to eat."

"Don't worry. We'll find you," Colonel said emphatically.

"That sounds delightful."

"Did you see the Cardinal Red?" he asked.

The words sent a chill down her spine.

"We can discuss that later."

She hung up the phone with new information. Alex had sent the Cardinal Red to everyone. That meant the problem was more widespread than she had anticipated. Protocol said she was supposed to drop everything and go to a safe place.

How could she?

She was this close to securing the Van Gogh painting and bringing down one of the world's most notorious art thieves. Of course, it might be a moot point. If AJAX was under attack, and personal and professional Armageddon was upon them, then what difference did it make if she recovered the painting?

It wasn't like she was rescuing fifteen-year-old girls from sex slavery.

It was only a painting. Stolen from a rich person who could afford to lose it. Someone who probably already collected the insurance money and was made whole. It hardly seemed worth risking her life over. Especially considering her other potential problems that had suddenly reared their ugly heads.

Jamie pretended to disconnect the phone but left it on so Colonel could hear what was happening. Even though they couldn't do anything about it. They wouldn't have a clue where she was.

She slipped the phone back in the pocket of her dress and resisted the temptation to pull her gun and bring her own Cardinal Red to Clement and his boys.

Jamie's patience was waning. Clement had better stop yanking her chain. She wasn't in the mood. Especially now.

"Are you going to sell me the painting or not?" Jamie asked roughly. "Or shall I call my driver back and tell him to come and get me."

Clement turned his head to the side like he was offended. Jamie didn't care. The Russians suddenly stood up straighter like they were ready to act as the tension in the room suddenly escalated.

She was on high alert as well and anxious for a fight. She'd just as soon shoot the two goons as look at them.

Then find the painting and leave.

Clement let out a sigh of resignation. Perhaps he was ready to move past the potential confrontation as well.

"This way," he said tersely, and began walking toward the back wall. When he got to it, he entered a code on a keypad. A series of six numbers which Jamie memorized. He didn't try to hide them from her, which meant he'd likely change the passcode as soon as she left.

The wall promptly separated with a groan that seemed to echo throughout the warehouse. Behind the wall was an elevator. It opened, and Clement stepped in first, then Jamie, then the two Russians. It only had two unmarked buttons. Clement pushed the lower one, and the elevator door closed, and the elevator creaked its way slowly down to what had to be an underground basement or storage area.

As the elevator doors opened, Clement stepped out into an expansive room. It was pristine, with concrete walls and shiny floors. Several paintings hung on every wall. The humidity in the air was one of the first things Jamie noticed. Fine art needed to be stored at seventy to seventy-two degrees and forty percent humidity and clearly Clement had spared no expense to protect the paintings.

She found the source controlling the climate. A large humidifier sat in the corner, blowing a gentle spray into the air. Under different circumstances, Jamie would've used the opportunity to pick Clement's brain and find out what humidifying system he used. She'd need something similar in her art gallery in D.C., especially in the storage area.

Would she still have an art gallery?

She pressed that thought out of her mind and focused on the paintings and their condition. From her experience, she knew that paintings were resilient although the extra care was helpful.

Numerous masterpieces had survived for centuries in environments that weren't climate-controlled. People kept them in their cellars. They were stored in attics. Often they were found lying on the floor, which was the worst thing for the treasured fine art. No telling how many were destroyed over the years from cracked paint, warping, mold growth, rats, and yellowing of the paper.

The spacious room was like a mini art gallery—albeit filled with ill-gotten gains. Jamie temporarily put Cardinal Red out of her mind.

She was in her element now and was fascinated. Some of the paintings on the walls she recognized. Most of them she didn't, but she could tell they were expensive by the way they were framed and cared for.

She went straight to one of the walls and stood in front of the paintings, admiring them like she was in an art gallery. Clement came and stood next to her, and they both stared without saying a word. He seemed to genuinely enjoy looking at the pieces as well. Jamie wondered if he appreciated the paintings for how extraordinary they were or for just the money they put into his bank account.

Did he spend this much money caring for them because he genuinely wanted to preserve them for posterity or because he wanted to protect his investment? Or both?

An interesting philosophical question for another time. This whole mission was unusual and full of questions. This was the first time paintings had been the focus of the operation and not just a cover for rescuing girls. Sex traffickers cared nothing for the people they tortured and abused. Money was their only motive. Clement seemed to have a fondness for the paintings. An appreciation for fine art.

For ten minutes, they had an engaging conversation about the paintings. He explained what they were and who painted them.

Finally, he asked, "Are you ready to see the Van Gogh?"

"Yes. Very much!" Jamie said, barely able to contain her excitement.

As they walked toward a table on the back wall, Jamie reached inside her dress and disconnected the call with the Colonel. They were in a basement with concrete walls and no windows. The phone wouldn't get reception. The Colonel wouldn't be able to hear the conversation anyway.

That's when the reality hit her. As much as she was enjoying looking at the paintings, she was in a lot more danger now than she was when she was upstairs. For a moment, she had lost track of the Russians. They were in a corner discussing something.

She found that troubling.

Then a more sobering thought struck her.

If the Cardinal Red was real, she might be in more danger when she got outside the warehouse, than she was inside it.

8

Clement walked to the far corner of the downstairs room that held the paintings and entered a number into the keypad. The wall opened up, and a large walk-in safe, more like a converted bank vault, appeared. He emerged seconds later with an art portfolio case. She recognized the case as one commonly used for transporting expensive art. The sturdy case would be both waterproof and fireproof.

He sat the case on a table.

She watched him warily, with her eyes darting back and forth between Clement and the two Russian goons who had moved closer to them.

Clement was practically giddy as he unlocked and opened it. Despite the circumstances, Jamie almost liked the man. Almost. If they'd met under different circumstances, they might've been friends. That was if he wasn't a thief, and she wasn't about to steal all his money, right before either killing him or hauling him away to prison.

He removed the painting carefully then motioned for her to come and stand next to him.

"Van Gogh painted approximately thirty-five self-portraits," Clement began to explain.

Actually, closer to fifty, but Jamie didn't want to correct him. The discrepancy came about because the experts disagreed on the authenticity of some of the paintings. For years, many were thought to be fakes. The style and brush strokes were different. Later, other experts determined that Van Gogh painted them in his latter years while suffering from insanity. Hence the difference in style.

"Look at his eyes. They seem so sad," Clement added.

That's the first thing Jamie noticed. The painting was clearly from Van Gogh's days in the insane asylum. The oppression was easy to see in his face.

"His head is facing to the right," Jamie said. "Probably so he didn't have to paint his left ear. Which he cut off. That must mean he painted this after 1888. The work is magnificent."

"Such a tragedy," Clement said. "The man died before his time. I still think he was murdered."

Van Gogh died from a gunshot wound to the stomach.

"There's debate about that," Jamie said. "The official version is that he committed suicide."

"Either way, he was a brilliant man who never was able to enjoy the fruits of his labor."

Jamie noticed the sincerity in Clement's voice.

He continued. "I wonder what Vincent would think now. I'm selling his work for nineteen million dollars!"

That statement reminded Jamie that Clement, though sincere, was a thief. He was a brilliant man, but he used his skills for evil.

A tragedy in and of itself. Too bad he hadn't used his considerable skills for good.

There were worse things than being a thief, though. The sex traffickers, for instance. They were not only immoral but depraved.

Alex said they were irredeemable. Jamie disagreed. She felt like everyone could be redeemed by God. Even the worst of the worst. Alex was more cynical. He lumped them all in the same category. Low-life scums who needed to die. He'd include Clement in that group if he was around to postulate.

A lot of people thought the same thing about the prostitutes Jamie rescued. Many considered them the lowest of the low. Evil. Women who made their own choices and were wasting their lives.

But Jamie had seen God's redemptive power in many of them. She saw them more as women who were being sinned against than women who were sinning. Especially the younger girls.

Not that she condoned their behavior. But Jamie understood the horrors those women had experienced. She had witnessed firsthand what it took for them to get to that point. Most were physically and sexually abused as kids. Some were sold into sex slavery as children. For many of them, that's the only life they had ever known. Once they were trapped, voluntarily or not, they lived without hope.

Until Jamie came along and rescued them.

While not all could escape and many returned to selling their bodies, Jamie had seen many more redeemed through the *Save The Girls* organization. The Christian group she worked with who helped the girls heal from their past and start a new life. That's why Jamie did what she did. Not to kill the bad guys but to see redemption and freedom for the victims.

If the criminals had to die, then so be it. If the miscreants wanted redemption as well, she'd help them find it. It just had never happened. Maybe someday it would.

It dawned on her that it had actually happened once, with Pok.

Clement began speaking again, which interrupted her thoughts. "Let me go over the provenance."

Provenance meaning the history of the painting from its known origin through the history of ownership. It detailed the chain of custody, so to speak.

Clement said, "The painting was believed to be painted in 1889, as you suggested, while Van Gogh was in the insane asylum. Later it became part of the Heikkinen collection in Helsinki, Finland. It was purchased by a French Museum in 1932. That's when things become sketchy. The painting surfaced again in 1952. It was owned by a German couple, Hans and Marie Weib."

Alarm bells went off inside Jamie's head. Many paintings in France resurfaced in Germany after the war. They were stolen by the Nazis and given to prominent German families. Jamie put those thoughts away for the moment but reminded herself to revisit them later.

"Feel free to examine the painting," Clement invited.

He stepped back away from the table, giving her room to stand closer. While she didn't like him being behind her, she did want to get an up close look at this rare and expensive piece of art. Not so much to examine it. She already knew it was real to the extent she could without taking an X-Ray and conducting a forensic test on the paint and canvas. Her desire was to admire it while she had the chance.

She played up the examination for Clement's benefit though. She wanted to fuss and fawn over the painting before she wired the money and pretend to be looking it over carefully.

"Oil on canvas," Jamie said. "I'd guess 51 x 45 centimeters."

"That's a good guess. Fifty-one and a half by forty-five."

"I don't want to touch the painting without gloves," Jamie said.

"Would you like me to get you a pair?"

"That's not necessary. May I turn it over? I will only touch the frame."

"Of course."

Jamie flipped the painting to the side and looked at the back. She saw what she expected to see—several dealer stamps from sales after the turn of the century.

"Are you familiar with the Dutch master, Geert Jan Jansen?" Jamie asked, still holding the painting on its side.

"I'm not," Clement said.

"He was one of the great art forgers of his time. He specialized in Van Goghs in particular. It's said that Jansen made more than ten million dollars selling forgeries. But he made a critical error. He forgot to put dealer stamps on the backs of the paintings."

Jamie pointed to the stamps on the back of the Van Gogh she was holding.

She continued. "See these stamps. They were from dealers who sold the paintings around the turn of the century and afterward.

The stamps were used to prove the ownership. Not all paintings had them, of course. This one does. I'm satisfied it's an original."

Jamie laid it back on the table. Clement clapped his hands together.

"Shall we finish the transaction and then toast it over dinner with a glass of wine. My treat."

"I will have to take a raincheck for dinner. I'm flying out as soon as we're done here."

The Cardinal Red came flashing into her mind. It had to be dealt with immediately.

Jamie reached into the inside pocket of her dress and pulled out her phone, and the card Clement had given her earlier.

The two Russians flinched, but they maintained their distance.

"Please confirm that I'm to wire the money to the account on the back of this card," Jamie said, holding the card in the air.

"That's correct," he answered. His face flashed her mixed emotions. He was happy about the transaction but disappointed she wouldn't have dinner with him.

An impossibility for more reasons than just the Cardinal Red. As soon as Jamie wired the nineteen million dollars into Clement's checking account, Pok would get an alert back on their island. Within seconds, be it day or night, he'd be on his computer hacking into the banking system. Ten minutes later, all the money in Clement's account would be gone. All but one dollar.

Jamie would have the painting, and AJAX would have all of Clement's money, including the nineteen million dollars.

This was where Alex was a genius. He showed Pok how to go through a criminal's past banking transactions, looking for links to other accounts. Transfers, checks, credit card transactions and corporate ID numbers that could be linked to other accounts. When he found them, he could empty those accounts and disperse the money into AJAX accounts worldwide. The scheme had made billions of dollars for AJAX and taken the money out of the hands of numerous bad actors around the world.

By sundown tonight, Clement would be destitute and livid. All his money would be gone. She couldn't wait to see his face when he found out that information. Hopefully, by that point, they'd also have stolen from him all the paintings in the warehouse.

If Jamie got out of the warehouse without a confrontation, she intended to return with her team immediately to empty the basement and vault of all their contents. Then she planned to go to Clement's house, kidnap him, interrogate him, and search for evidence of more transactions. Hopefully, they would find what paintings he had stolen and who he sold them to.

Armed with that information, they'd travel to those locations, steal the paintings back, and return them to their rightful owners.

Assuming they didn't have to go into hiding from the Cardinal Red.

If Clement forced a confrontation as soon as she wired the money, Jamie would have to figure out how to overcome the two Russians and Clement and either kill them or disable them to the point she could tie them up. Then contact her team, and they'd come to the warehouse and execute the same plan.

Either way, they intended to put Clement out of business for good.

Hopefully, without killing him. She'd like to turn him in to the proper authorities so he could face the music for what he'd done.

She put that out of her mind and concentrated on the task at hand and logged into her account and entered the routing number and account number for Clement's bank. The amount of the wire was already pre-entered into the wire transaction from her bank.

With one stroke of the hand, the wire was sent. It should instantly appear in Clement's account.

"It's done," she said.

Clement pulled out his phone. He typed in some numbers.

His eyes widened.

"The money's there," he said excitedly. "You've got to love technology. It's been a pleasure doing business with you. I wish you'd reconsider dinner."

"Next time. I hope you consider me for future transactions. May I have the travel case," Jamie asked. "I have one, but it's in my vehicle back at the park."

"Of course."

Jamie carefully returned the painting to the container and closed it. She picked it up with her left hand so her right hand would be accessible if she needed to reach for her gun.

She'd soon know if everyone was going to leave the room alive.

9

Jamie was rethinking her options as she walked toward the elevator with Clement in front of her and the two Russians next to him.

Tactically, the situation was as good as it would ever get. She could pull her gun and take control of the problem right then and there without having to fire a shot. If she waited, she'd have her entire team with her, but they'd have a number of obstacles to overcome. They'd have to break into the warehouse, disarm the security system, and get in and out without being seen.

Even if all that went smoothly, they'd still have to find Clement. What if he didn't go back to his house? What if he went straight to the airport and boarded a plane for Monte Carlo for a few days of gambling and sun?

If they did find him at home, which wasn't a guarantee, the two Russians would have to be dwelt with.

She was already in the room with the paintings and Clement was there. She could deal with the two Russians on her own terms. They were in her crosshairs now. The element of surprise was also on her side.

The elevator was less than five steps away. She had to decide quickly.

Her mind processed the plan with the speed of a supercomputer.

Set the Van Gogh on the floor. Pull her gun from inside her dress. Let out a shout to confuse them. Stick the gun in one of the Russians back. Kick the back of his knee, sending him to the floor. Threaten to shoot in a commanding tone. Once he was on the ground, stick the gun in the ribs of the other Russian.

Force him to his knees.

Shoot them if she had to.

Clement was unarmed. She'd deal with him last. Order him to put his hands in the air.

Just as she mentally signed off on the plan, Clement abruptly stopped. He turned and faced her. With a gun in his hand pointed directly at her.

What?

Jamie stopped in her tracks but kept her cool.

"So, you're a liar and a thief," she said calmly. "You did have a gun on you. Why am I not surprised?"

Her heart sped up by a ratio of two.

Both Russians pulled their guns in unison. Looking like a synchronized dance team. Her heart pounded as if it was trying to warn her of the danger. Like it would if she was walking in the woods, saw a bear, and fear erupted.

The warning was unnecessary. She now had three guns pointed at her. She already knew how much danger she was in without her vital signs going crazy.

Three to one. Not the best odds. Jamie was kicking herself for not coming up with her plan sooner and acting when she had the advantage.

"What do you want, Clement?" Jamie said, almost rudely. "The painting? Are you going to take my money and the painting?"

Clement moved his head from side to side like he was trying to release some tension in his shoulders.

"I haven't decided yet. I gave you a chance to go to dinner with me. You should've taken me up on it."

"We can go to dinner. I'll even buy."

Clement smirked.

"I don't want dinner. I want you."

"That you can't have."

"Like I said. I gave you a chance to be with me voluntarily. What girl would turn down that opportunity? I'm a good-looking, rich guy."

"What makes you think I can't find a good-looking, rich guy on my own?" she quipped.

Clement waved the gun in the air dismissively, which caused her to tense up even more. Guns could go off accidentally.

The Russians' eyes were steeled on her. They were prepared to shoot. Their guns concerned her more. They were too far away to make a move against.

"I thought we had a pleasant time together," Jamie said, softening her tone. "Now you're ruining it."

"As I said, I want you, and I intend to have you. You can do it the easy way or the hard way."

"I don't know what you mean."

She knew exactly what he meant but wanted to keep him talking until she thought of something.

Then Jamie realized prolonging the conversation was a bad idea. The clock was ticking on the wire transfer. At any moment, the money would be transferred out of his account and back into hers. If Clement checked it again or received an alert, all hell was going to break loose.

Although, that could be her leverage. She'd promise to return the money if he let her go.

"You aren't walking out of this room with the painting unless you sleep with me."

"Oh! Is that all you wanted? I misunderstood. Are you tired? Do you need a nap? I'm not sleepy, but if you'd like to lay your head on my lap, I'll sing you a lullaby."

Her words dripped with all the sarcasm she could muster.

Agitating a man with a gun might not seem like a good strategy, but it was. The more frustrating she became to him, the more indecision he'd have to deal with. It might make him want her more, knowing she wasn't going to give herself voluntarily. The harder she was to get, the bigger the conquest she became.

Men liked that.

He'd want to keep her alive long enough to prove his superiority.

"You think you're funny, don't you?" Clement said smugly.

Now was the time to test his manhood.

"Quite the opposite. My friends say I'm not funny at all. I don't think this situation is funny either." Her tone changed considerably. "You double-crossed me. I paid you good money for the painting. Now you want to change the terms of the deal. Having sex with me was never part of the deal. That doesn't sit well with me."

"What are you going to do about it?"

"I haven't decided yet," throwing that line back in his face.

"From where I'm standing, you don't have many options."

From Jamie's vantage point, she didn't see many options either.

"I could kill you and your two friends and take all your paintings," Jamie said.

That caused Clement to laugh.

There was a limit to pushing him. She didn't feel like she had reached it. If he wanted to sleep with her, he needed to keep her alive. That meant eventually, he'd have to get close to her. When he did, she had a lot more options.

As expected, Clement took the personal challenge. He took two steps closer to her. The Russians held back. Of course, they would. Four was a crowd when it came to sex. Clement didn't seem like the kind interested in sharing his prey with the hyenas.

Now was the time to act scared.

Jamie retreated.

She wanted to draw Clement away from the Russians. With Jamie and Clement on the other side of the room, the Russians would hesitate to fire their weapons for fear of hitting their boss. A handgun was also much more accurate if you were within ten feet of the target. At twenty to thirty feet, the best shots lost at least fifty percent of their accuracy.

Not Jamie. She could hit a worm out of a bird's mouth, fifty feet away. With each step backward, the situation improved for her considerably. Clement still had his gun, but he wasn't going to use it. Having sex with a bloody bullet-ridden dead person wasn't his goal. Not as much fun.

"Leave me alone," Jamie shouted like she was afraid.

She raised the carrying case holding the Van Gogh out in front of her like she was cowering behind it. It was a shield if a gun was fired. It also created an obstacle for Clement to overcome. He'd want to be protective of the painting even if it was in the case.

"You are playing hard to get," he said lustfully. "I like that. Makes it more fun."

"Why are you doing this?"

Clement ignored her.

Jamie was against the far back wall now. Clement bent over and gently placed his gun on the floor and kicked it backward toward the Russians who were still on their side of the room.

He began unbuckling his belt.

"This ain't no peep show," he said to the Russians roughly, who were still looking their way.

One of the Russians picked up the gun, and then they both turned away.

A stroke of luck for Jamie.

The best possible scenario. The Russians had their backs to them. Clement was unarmed, and she had a weapon under her dress.

The only question was which way did she want to play it.

Curly taught her there was only one way. Overwhelming force.

In the movies, the fight scenes were long and drawn out. Back and forth. The good guy would get in a blow, then take one. He'd eventually win in the end but not before taking a lot of damage. If there was a gunfight, the bad guys got off dozens of shots, always missing the hero.

The movies were unrealistic. One blow can disable you. A dozen shots close range, and one would hit its target.

75

She relied on Curly in these situations. He was always in her head.

Don't hit your attacker to inflict pain. Hit them to inflict damage, she could hear him say.

Preferably one blow—two at the most.

She wanted Clement alive and the two Russians dead. Holding them prisoner until her team came would be a nuisance.

Clement was in her personal space now. He was so close she could feel his hot breath on her face. He wasn't making eye contact. His hand reached for the slit in her dress. Her hand was already in the same area. Prepared to draw her gun.

Jamie grabbed his wrist with her left hand and twisted up and to the right, dislocating his elbow. He let out a howl of pain. She twirled him around, so he was facing the Russians, who reacted quickly.

It hardly mattered.

Jamie already had the gun in her right hand. The Russians didn't even have the opportunity to aim their weapons.

Tap. Tap.

Tap. Tap.

Two shots for each. Forehead. Chest. Forehead. Chest.

Overkill, as they say. The two men were both dead as soon as the first shot hit their foreheads. They fell to the floor with a thud.

Jamie maintained her grip on Clement's wrist and forced him to his knees. His face was taut and twisted in agony.

The best of both worlds. Pain and damage.

Jamie knelt beside him. His head was slumped. He was already defeated. She took his chin in her hand and squeezed it hard, then raised his head so he could look at her. A burning question had been nagging her for several minutes.

"Did the Nazis steal this Van Gogh during World War II?" she asked.

Clement looked up and to the left. That's all she needed to know. It was.

She had a way of verifying it later.

She grabbed his right arm at the elbow, which hung limply at his side. Clement writhed in pain.

"Are there more paintings like this?" Jamie asked roughly.

Clement's expression said it all. He didn't mean to give away his secrets, but they were written all over his face.

"You're going to tell me where they are, or I'll break your other arm. Nod your head if you intend to cooperate."

She twisted his arm harder and could feel and hear the tissues, cartilage, and bones crunching. Ripping. Probably irreparable even by the finest surgeon.

"Yes. I'll tell you whatever you want to know. Please don't kill me."

It didn't take long to break him. He was right. He was a lover, not a fighter. Probably not very good at either.

Jamie stood and pulled out her phone. Still no signal.

She jerked Clement to his feet and made him take her upstairs, where she called Colonel.

"I've got things handled," Jamie said. "Where are you?"

"Right outside the warehouse."

That brought a smile to her face and reminded her to never underestimate her men.

She hung up the phone and forced Clement to open the bay door.

The Colonel and the guys drove into the bay. When they got out of the car, Jamie said, "What took you so long?"

The Colonel glared at her, so she decided to drop the kidding around.

One confrontation was enough for one day.

10

Alex made it to his plane, and it took off without incident. He breathed a noticeable sigh of relief when they cleared US airspace.

He felt slightly better. Until he logged into a secured internet connection and pulled up the security cameras at his house.

FBI agents and CIA personnel were busy ransacking it. The hair on the back of his neck rose from the anger churning inside of him like molten lava.

The men in his house had no regard for his or Jamie's things. They seized all their computers and electronics. He watched them rip out walls and ceilings. Alex wanted to shout through the screen to leave his stuff alone. That they weren't going to find anything and destroying their property was unnecessary.

The men reminded him of a bunch of out-of-control monkeys at feeding time.

Alex could actually talk to them through his security system but resisted the urge. He didn't want to give Fuller the satisfaction. It's a good thing he wasn't there. No telling what he would've done. He probably would have made things worse than they already were.

He racked his brain to make sure he'd covered all his bases, hadn't been careless, or forgotten something. When nothing came to mind, he switched to the security cameras at his office. As expected, the authorities were there as well.

Surprisingly, things were more orderly. Nothing was being seized. No property was damaged.

As he watched the live stream, he could see that his employees weren't at their desks. They were standing off to the side and congregating together. A man was addressing them. Alex turned up the sound so he could hear what was being said.

"My name is Jack August. I am Assistant to the Director of the CIA. I'm in charge now."

Alex knew of him. August was a lower-level field agent. Support staff more than anything else.

How did he get to be Assistant to the Director? Did he take Brad's place? What experience did he have in cyber warfare?

He's the boss?

Alex shook his fist at the computer screen. If he could reach through it, he'd grab August by the neck and throw him out the window.

Then a frightening thought occurred to him. He hoped the man didn't screw up all the systems that he'd worked months to perfect.

"I'm here by the authority of Director Fuller," August continued. "The AJAX corporation is now under the control of the CIA Director. He has assigned me to management duties of the day-to-day operations. Business will continue as usual. From now on, you will report to me."

A chill went down Alex's spine. Fuller didn't intend to dismantle AJAX! He intended to control it. The ramifications of such a move were enormous.

Alex couldn't even wrap his head around all of them.

One of his employees, Ryan Heathcoat raised his hand. "Where's Alex?" he asked.

Ryan was one of Alex's right hand men in the operations. A trustworthy and loyal employee.

"I'm not at liberty to say at this time," August replied coldly.

"We take our directions from Alex," Ryan said defiantly.

That statement caused Alex to smile. It had the opposite effect on August.

"Not anymore, you don't!" he growled. "I'm in charge now. I want a report on my desk from each of you by the end of the day. In that report, you will describe in detail what you are working on. Don't leave anything out. I also want the passcodes to all your computers and cell phones."

"What if I have a problem with that?" Ryan asked.

"Yeah!" Alex was cheering him on.

August walked up to Ryan and got right in his face. "Why would you have a problem with it?" he asked.

"I work for Alex and Jamie. I'm not doing anything until they tell me to."

"You tell him!" Alex shouted.

"Seize this man," August barked. "Take him down to CIA headquarters for questioning."

Alex could hardly believe what he'd just seen and heard. They were arresting Ryan? On what charge?

This was war!

Two FBI agents were at Ryan's side within seconds. They grabbed him by the arms. He tried to pull away, but they shoved him against the wall. A couple of Alex's employees screamed. Several shouted out their disapproval.

Alex jumped to his feet and let out his own shout.

August glared at the other employees and their protests while they dragged Ryan away.

"Anyone else want to join him?" August said.

The employees grew quiet. No one protested. Alex didn't blame them. They must be in shock at the sudden turn of events. If Alex were them, he wouldn't know what to think either.

"Good!" August said. "Anyone who doesn't cooperate will be arrested. I'm in charge of this operation now, and you'd best remember that."

"You sorry S.O.B," Alex shouted at the computer screen.

"Is everything okay, sir?" a voice said through the intercom.

The pilot, Bennett Storvik, was the one speaking and had been one of AJAX pilots for about six months. Bennett was a retired Air Force pilot who'd flown covert missions into South America for years. After retiring from the service, he flew commercial airplanes for twenty years until he retired from that job. When Alex offered him the job, he jumped at the chance to get back in the air.

Bennett was another trusted employee who would never betray Alex. Although, he had no idea at the moment that he was probably breaking the law. Helping a fugitive flee the states.

How did it come to this?

"I'm good, Bennett," Alex said. "What's our ETA?"

"A little less than four hours," Bennett replied.

Alex couldn't wait to get on his island. There wasn't much he could do from the air. All he could do was watch helplessly as the miscreants were threatening his employees and destroying his home. Alex didn't know which was worse—watching them tear his house apart or watching another man running his business. It made his blood boil.

He lowered his tone and spoke to the image on the screen again. His tone might've been softer, but his anger was barely under control.

"You can't do this, Jack August! AJAX is my company! Jamie and I built it with our own sweat and blood! You'll rue the day you ever stepped foot in my building."

The words of bravado sounded good in his head, but really, what could he do? Even from the island, if the Director of the CIA wanted to seize his assets, and take over AJAX, could he really stop him?

Fuller didn't have the authority. Not legally. But that didn't matter. Powerful men didn't need legal authority. They took what they wanted. If the weaker tried to stop them, it would be of no use. As strong as Alex was in ingenuity and resolve, he wasn't as powerful as the Director of the CIA, who had the support of the President of the United States.

Alex sat back down so he could listen more closely to what August was saying to his employees. He at least had that advantage. August didn't know he could spy on him.

"Go back to your desks and get to work on your reports!" August barked to the AJAX employees.

The men and women of his cyber lab scattered like ants in a disturbed anthill.

Alex slumped back in his chair. It wasn't often that he felt powerless. Impotent. Weak. Indecisive. This was one of those times. He needed to get to the island and regroup. Find out what Pok knew about the situation. He'd sent Pok a Cardinal Red alert. Everything on the island was protected and outside Fuller's reach, but additional precautions needed to be taken.

More importantly, he needed Pok's help to bring Fuller down if that were even possible.

Alex logged into his bank accounts. Knowing what he'd find. They were all frozen—even their personal accounts. Beyond frustrated, he slammed his fist down on the table.

More than two billion dollars was now under Fuller's control. Alex didn't even want to think about what Fuller would do with that pile of cash. Undoubtedly, something underhanded, illegal, and of no help to the causes he and Jamie fought so hard for. Ironically, Alex didn't care about the money. He'd give it all back to the US government, if it was the right thing to do. But AJAX was authorized. He and Jamie accumulated that money at considerable risk. They were using it for God.

At least he had the money Fuller didn't know about. Another three billion was outside of the grimy reach of the Director. Alex needed to focus on the positive. He had more than enough resources to continue his operations and bring Fuller down. Pok and the cyber team and lab on the island were arguably more effective than the lab ten times its size back in Virginia.

His thoughts turned to Jamie. She was dangling in the wind. On her own in Tajikistan. The only information she had were the two words he sent her by text. *Cardinal Red.* She probably hit the ceiling when she saw them. He wished he could contact her but didn't dare take the risk.

At least Jamie wasn't entirely alone. She had the Colonel, Bond, and A-Rad with her. And the AJAX corporate jet. Which Fuller would no doubt try to seize. Hopefully, Jamie could put two and two together and do something to protect that asset.

The team was resourceful. They had the ability to go dark if necessary. Jamie would find a way to contact him. She'd know her phones were being monitored by Fuller's team and would work around it.

Alex wasn't as sure as Brad had been that Jamie should go back to Washington, D.C. There was a lot to consider. What was there for her to go back to? The house was in shambles. Their bank accounts were frozen. Fuller seized all their cars. More than likely, he took the yacht which was moored in Miami.

If Fuller would do that, what wouldn't he do? He arrested Ryan. At the drop of a hat. All Ryan did was put up a mild protest.

Why wouldn't Fuller arrest Jamie?

Brad said because the employees of the CIA would protest. That Jamie was beloved.

And while that might be true, so what? Alex wasn't sure that fellow employees in an uproar would be enough to stop a man like Fuller, who was drunk on power.

Fuller could hold their jobs over their heads if they didn't cooperate. They might protest, but were they willing to lose their jobs over it? Be ready to go to jail for Alex and Jamie like Ryan had been?

No way.

When push came to shove, they'd relent to the more powerful. That didn't mean they wouldn't help Alex behind the scenes. He just had to figure out how to communicate with them.

He needed more information, so Alex turned his attention to the events occurring at his office. Curly always said information was like gold. Intelligence was the key and he had the ability to watch August's every move.

He went into Alex's office and closed the door. Alex switched to the camera in his office and the one on his computer. August sat down at Alex's desk and stared at his computer. He reached over and powered it on.

"What is your passcode, Alex Halee?" August said aloud even though no one was in the room to hear it. Of course, August had no way of knowing that Alex was watching him.

Alex scrambled to log into his computer remotely. Undetected. He changed the settings so August could access his computer without a passcode. That way Alex could monitor him.

Let him see only what Alex wanted him to see. The rest was hidden behind a firewall. Alex wanted him to have access so he could track his every move. His communications. Email correspondence. Perhaps he could learn something. If Fuller was going to be the acting boss of AJAX, Alex intended on keeping a close eye on his every move.

"Lookie here," August said. "Alex was being careless and didn't lock his computer. What an imbecile!"

Alex ignored the comment. He had more important things on his mind.

The camera on the computer was set to record audio and video so Alex could monitor all of his conversations. At least one side of them. Search engine history would secretly record the websites he visited. Alex would capture all the passcodes he entered. Hopefully, gaining access to August's home computer and cell phone logs.

He was furiously getting those things set up.

Satisfied, Alex logged off and hacked into the transponder system that tracked his plane. He changed the plane's serial number and FAA registration ID, so it appeared the original plane followed the flight plan to South Africa. By disguising the tail number, the plane he was on couldn't be tracked to his island.

This plane was not owned by AJAX but by a separate shell corporation. Fuller would not be aware of its existence.

Once that task was completed, Alex logged back on to the security camera at his office and monitored August's activities for the duration of the four-hour flight.

August was agitated by a number of phone calls. From what Alex could gather, August's men had no luck finding Alex.

That brought the first smile to his face.

They'd never find him on the island.

Bennett eventually came over the intercom and said, "We'll be landing soon."

Alex shut down his laptop and slumped back in the chair for a few minutes to give himself a chance to relieve some of the tension.

Bennett brought the plane in smoothly as usual. Alex raised the blind on his window.

He let out a gasp. He knew immediately that something was wrong.

11

Sigao Cay

Alex and Jamie named their island Sigao, the Greek word for hidden. Ideally located, the island was north of Aruba and secluded. Just off the coast of Venezuela. It was in international waters but close enough to the socialist dictatorship that American military ships avoided the area. It was the perfect location for covert operations.

And disappearing if necessary as was the case now.

They paid eighty-nine million for the island, which had a fifteen-thousand-square-foot home on it along with many amenities. It had two large guest quarters. One for Pok and the other for the rest of the employees. Alex built a building to house the computer cyber warfare lab and installed state-of-the-art computers in the lab.

The biggest issue to getting the lab operational had been securing the high-speed internet. Alex found a way to work around that problem with a lot of effort. By the time he was finished, the lab was as sophisticated as any in the world and as secure as was humanly possible.

The island was usually bustling with activity. While the team spent hours inside the lab, Alex couldn't remember a time when he landed and hadn't seen people on the tennis courts, in the swimming pool, or laying out on the beach.

Bennett brought the jet to a stop and Alex could feel a sense of gloom come over him.

The island looked abandoned.

No signs of life at all.

The lights were off in the lab and all the houses. No one was milling around. He stared at the deserted tennis courts, swimming pool, and beach. He couldn't believe his eyes. Even the boats in the marina were gone.

Alex assumed the worst.

Did Fuller know about the island? Had everyone been arrested? Was he walking into an ambush?

Bennett had flown Alex in and out of the island more times than he could count and must've noticed the same thing. Before he came to a stop, he went on the intercom and said, "Things don't look right, boss."

"I know. This place should be teeming with people. Someone should be around. This isn't good."

"Do you want me to bring the bird to a stop or go back up and circle around while you take in the scene from the air?"

"Keep the wheels on the ground. Bring her to a stop but keep the engines running. I'm going to deplane and check things out. See what's up."

About that time, a figure slowly emerged from the guest house and was headed toward where the plane usually came to a stop.

"Radar's here," Bennett said.

"I see him. He'll know what's going on."

Alex felt relief that someone was there. Maybe everyone was in a team meeting inside the lab.

Milton Gunter was one of the first people Alex hired for the new cyberlab. They called him Radar because he looked like the corporal on the television series MASH. Short. Geeky. He wore wire-rimmed glasses, like the character on the popular show of the seventies. Typical computer nerd.

He walked with a slight limp. When he first came to Alex, he had limited skills. Alex had taken him under his wing. Radar was sharp as a butcher's knife and a fast learner. His ability to absorb information impressed Alex from the get-go. Not to mention he was incredibly loyal, almost to a fault.

It appeared that Radar was the only person on the island. But, why? There wasn't anything about this that felt right. Not a single thing.

Alex opened the cabin door and exited the plane. Radar's face was as serious as a heart attack.

They didn't exchange any pleasantries.

"What's going on?" Alex asked, getting straight to the point.

"Pok's gone!" he said with as much emotional intensity as Alex had ever seen from Radar's normally stoic personality. "He took everyone with him."

What did that mean?

Alex looked up at Bennett in the cockpit and gave him the sign to cut the engines so they could hear each other talk.

When the powerful engines quit spinning, Alex demanded answers.

"What do you mean Pok's gone?" he asked, even though the question sounded ridiculous in his head and even more so after he said it roughly.

"He left."

Alex's heart was circling his chest like a racehorse coming in for the final lap in the Kentucky Derby.

Rather than ask another stupid question, Alex waited for Radar to explain.

"This morning, Pok came into the lab with his hair on fire. He said everybody's got to get out of here. That the Feds are coming. He told us to scrub our computers of everything."

Alex was pacing now. "And everyone believed him?"

"I didn't. He said the order came from you."

"I never gave that order."

Alex had done some emergency Cardinal Red drills before with Pok and the team. None of them ever included vacating the island. This was the safest place on the planet for Alex and Jamie to flee to. It was becoming abundantly clear. Pok had betrayed him. His worst fear since he started working with the man.

"Pok gave everybody a million dollars," Radar continued. "He said the payment was from you and that their services were no longer needed on the island."

"Why are you still here?"

"I refused to take the money. Everybody else did, though. They got on the boats and left. I stayed behind. I wanted to hear it directly from you. It just didn't feel right in my gut."

Alex put his hand on Radar's shoulder and pulled him into a side man hug. Alex was six foot four and dwarfed the man who was barely five feet five inches tall.

"You did the right thing," Alex said. "Pok was lying."

"I don't understand what's happening."

Alex knew exactly what was going on. Pok had double-crossed him. More than likely, the three billion dollars was gone. Pok was in the wind as well. With a head start. Nothing he could do about it now. He had bigger things to worry about than tracking Pok down.

A monumental task anyway. Even if he had the time, Pok had likely been planning this for months. Waiting for his opportunity. With the computers scrubbed, the trail to the money was destroyed.

Alex had searched for Pok for several years. Jamie was the one who found him in Hong Kong. Actually, Pok found her. Finding him a second time would be even harder. Pok had more skills now, thanks to Alex.

Alex was shaking his head roughly from side to side. He couldn't believe he was in this atrocious situation.

Kicking himself in the backside would have to wait. He had more pressing problems to address.

The lab for instance. Was it functional?

Pok likely took all the backups to his computers. Hopefully, Pok didn't destroy them. All the work the team did over the past months was gone. Vanished into thin cyber air. Alex had taken precautions knowing full well that Pok could betray him. He just never thought he would. Not this soon.

The computer systems had backups to the backups. It had alerts that were supposed to warn Alex if Pok tried anything nefarious.

While he never fully trusted Pok, he felt like they had developed a friendship. Pok also knew Alex's skills. He'd kill him if he ever got his hands on him. Apparently, that was a risk Pok was willing to take. When he sent Pok the Cardinal Red, the North Korean probably thought the ship was sinking, which was his opportunity to get out.

Alex felt a mix of sadness and anger. Almost resignation. This was a blow to the gut he wasn't expecting. It's practically like he was living a nightmare. How could five billion dollars disappear from his grasp in the course of a few hours? Unfortunately, Alex knew the answer to that question. All Pok had to do was strike a few keys on his computer, and poof, the money was gone.

Pok must've figured out how to get around all his safeguards.

"I didn't scrub my computer," Radar said to Alex, shocking him back to reality. "I pretended to."

That caused a sudden burst of energy in Alex. Adrenaline began coursing through his veins again.

He practically ran to the building that housed the computers. Radar tried to keep up. Alex's stride was much longer, and Radar could only limp along. Alex went directly to Radar's cubicle and powered up his computer. It was password protected, so he had to wait for Radar to catch up anyway.

Radar told Alex his password. Alex entered the complicated combination of numbers, letters, and symbols. It didn't take him long to find what he was looking for—access to the main server.

The excitement left him almost as fast as it had come upon him. While Radar's computer wasn't scrubbed, his pathway to the main computer was.

"Gosh darn it," Alex growled. "Pok thought of everything. It's all gone. This computer won't help me."

"I backed it up last night. We can restore it back to last night," Radar offered optimistically.

Alex shook his head no.

"I know how Pok operates. He scrubbed everything, including the backup. He stole all my money. He also probably planted a virus in the system. So if we try to go back and restore it, it'll scrub everything. I want to avoid that. Right now, at least the computers are operational."

"I'll find the virus and get rid of it," Radar said.

"Good idea. And thanks for sticking around. That couldn't have been an easy decision to make, not knowing what the outcome would be."

Alex stood up, making way for Radar to get to work removing the virus they both knew Pok had implemented. The computer whiz sat down in his place and began flailing away on the keys to the computer. Alex looked at him with admiration. Few people would have his sense of loyalty.

How could he repay him?

Radar should've taken the million dollars Pok offered when he had the chance. All Alex had to his name was the million dollars he brought from the storage unit which was still in the plane.

An overwhelming desire to give up hit him like a mack truck.

He heard Curly's voice trying to snap him out of it. *Focus on what you have. Not what you don't have. Things are never as bad as they seem.*

The words didn't make him feel better, but it did get him thinking. He began to assess his situation like a CIA analyst.

He did have resources.

Jamie. The most important one.

Well... God. He had to trust God. All things would work together for his good. He couldn't see the good in things at the moment.

Just give it time.

He had a million dollars. More money than he ever thought he'd possess at any one time.

The island.

The plane. Two planes if Jamie could keep the other one out of Fuller's grasp.

People are more important than things, Curly reminded him.

He had Bennett and Radar. A-Rad, Colonel, and Bond. They were with Jamie. They'd be loyal to them to the bitter end. Alex had no doubt those three would take a bullet for Jamie or him if they had to.

And Brad. He was working behind the scenes.

Things are never as bleak as they seem.

Another Curlyism. He missed his friend. What he wouldn't give to spend ten minutes with him and pick his brain.

Although Alex practically knew what his mentor would say.

Don't do anything rash. Don't make the situation worse by acting foolishly. Gather information. Assess the risks. Employ resources.

Get your revenge.

Alex didn't think of it as revenge as much as setting things right. Three billion dollars in Pok's hands could be a disaster.

While Alex felt no optimism that things were going to turn around anytime soon, he did feel resolve.

He'd find Pok and kill him. He might not ever find the money, but he would find Pok, and he would be a dead man when Alex got ahold of him.

He had another enemy. Fuller. He knew where he was. In Washington D.C. Sitting in his ivory tower. It might be easier to get to Pok than to Fuller.

Fuller or Pok?

That was the question. Who should he go after first?

Definitely Fuller!

12

John F. Kennedy Conference Room
White House

CIA Director, Neal Fuller, was in the situation room of the White House with the National Security Advisor, Henry Feltman, and the Chairman of the Joint Chiefs of Staff, General Jose Gonzalo. They were waiting for the President of the United States to make an appearance so they could discuss a crisis brewing in Syria.

A television was on, and they watched the breaking news. Noted news anchor, Charles Slack Jr., was behind the news desk with a red breaking news alert scrolling across the bottom of the screen. Slack was nearly seventy and one of the most respected newscasters of the past thirty years.

Fuller didn't hold him in as high of a regard. Far too often, Slack didn't report the news in the way it was fed to him by the administration. The CIA Director rarely gave press conferences but did issue press releases periodically. Slack had a tendency to add his own commentary to the party line. Something that was very annoying. In his opinion, the networks should report the news, not commentate on it.

Slack had a furrowed brow and spoke in a serious tone with his deep, resonant voice, "The international chemical weapons watchdog group said last night that Syrian armed forces carried out a chemical attack on the village of Al Khanlib, a small town in Northern Syria held by opposition groups of Syrian President Al Nashad Merali. More than thirty people were killed in the attack, including ten children and seventeen women. Numerous victims of the attack were taken to a local hospital thirty miles away. It's reported the victims suffered from severe burns and acute injuries to the eyes and lungs."

Slack paused to catch his breath and held his hand to his ear. Presumably to get direction from his producer since they were reporting in real-time and things were breaking at a rapid pace.

"The first pictures are coming in," Slack said. "I must warn you they may be difficult to watch. Please take precautions if your young children are in the room."

The newscast cut away from Slack, and images of horrific chaos appeared on the screen. Village huts were leveled from what appeared to be several bomb blasts. Dozens of locals were seen digging through the rubble for survivors. Bodies were lined along the side of the road, covered by stained white sheets. Numerous people sat on the ground in a daze with severe trauma to their faces, hands, and legs. Makeshift bandages loosely covered the wounds but did nothing to hide the agony on their faces.

Fuller saw the NSA director wince and the General clench his jaw and make a fist in anger. This was the exact response he was hoping for from the group. Images like the ones on the screen were precisely what was needed to garner support for a war with Syria which he intended to argue for when the President arrived in the room.

The broadcaster continued with the images rolling across the screen like a movie.

"There can be no question that President Merali of Syria has used chemical weapons as a deliberate campaign of violence against his own people," Slack said. "The evidence is irrefutable. Why would he do so? Namely, to target and silence opposition groups."

An example of Slack interjecting his opinions into the newscast. He wasn't necessarily wrong. Just annoying.

Slack touched his ear again and Fuller sat forward in his chair when he said, "Let's go to the Chief White House Correspondent Ellen Winebrenner for the White House response."

The disturbing images from Syria left the screen, and a pretty blonde appeared. Fuller had always liked Winebrenner. He wished all the big networks hired lookers to report the news. He had difficulty focusing at press conferences when she was in the audience asking questions.

"Thank you, Charles," Winebrenner said. "The White House has not responded to a request for a comment."

"Give us a chance, lady!" Fuller snarled.

She might be pretty, but that didn't mean she couldn't make him mad.

"That's why we're meeting today," Fuller said for the benefit of those in the room, even though they were well aware of that fact. "When the President gets here, we'll craft a response."

Winebrenner continued. She brushed her hair out of her eyes, sending a wave of desire through Fuller. Forbidden lust. He could never have her for obvious reasons. That didn't stop him from thinking about it. Although he generally preferred weaker, more subservient women. Those who could be controlled. One day of being married to Winebrenner, and he'd probably despise her. Sharing a bed might be fun. Anything else, and the woman would get on his nerves the first time she opened her mouth.

The correspondent continued. "In the now-famous news conference, President Rutledge drew a line in the sand meant for the President of Syria. He said that the use of chemical weapons crosses the line, and if Merali ever used them against his own people, the United States would respond with military action and remove him from power. If the report coming out of Syria today is true, then Merali has crossed that line."

"Have you heard anything out of the Pentagon?" Slack asked her.

"My sources at the Pentagon and intelligence officials have told me that they've not been informed of any impending strikes against the Syrian regime."

In due time, lady.

Fuller expected not only a strike but an all-out war to follow. The U.S. Navy already had a strike group off the coast of Syria, and additional forces were on their way. At least, he hoped they were. He'd get a confirmation in the meeting today from the Joint Chiefs of Staff.

Ellen Winebrenner continued with her report from the White House lawn. "A Syrian spokesman has denied that the regime is behind the attacks. He said, and I quote, "We do not possess chemical weapons, and have not, and would not use them if we did."

Fuller knew that statement to be a lie. According to his intelligence, the Syrian government had chemical weapons but hadn't used them in the last ten years. Didn't matter. The report and images were all the President needed to launch his attack.

They heard a commotion, and the President abruptly entered the room with his White House Chief of Staff, Elwood Cunnard.

Everyone knew to keep their seats.

President Rutledge sat down at the head of the large conference table. He leaned back in the black leather chair and put his hand to his chin.

"Okay, fellows," he said. "We need to get ahead of this story. I don't want everybody running around telling everybody what's in their guts. Everyone must keep their heads on straight."

Fuller had to keep from smiling at the inane sentence structure of the Commander in Chief. President Rutledge wasn't the best wordsmith in the room. In fact, Fuller didn't really care for him at all. The only smart thing Rutledge had done was appoint him Director of the CIA. That's why Fuller had to act behind his back to get this war with Syria started. Hopefully, Rutledge had the guts to follow through and do what was right.

"That's why we're here, sir," Fuller said, when no one spoke up.

"What's your intelligence telling you?" Rutledge asked Fuller.

"That the reports are true. Two days ago, President Merali ordered a chemical attack on the village of Al Khanlib. According to our sources on the ground, thirty people were killed. Including ten children and seventeen women."

Fuller didn't actually have any intelligence or any sources on the ground, but based his numbers on the report he'd heard on the news seconds before. He'd written down the numbers on a pad when he heard Slack mention them.

"Why would Merali target a village?" Feltman, the Director of the NSA, asked. "What's the political or military benefit to a chemical weapons attack on innocent civilians?"

Fuller knew Feltman would be the skeptical one.

General Gonzalo spoke up before Fuller had a chance to answer. "To strike fear in the hearts of the people! Merali is a madman. He can't control that region. A few more attacks and the people will be so afraid of him, they'll do whatever he says."

Fuller was glad Gonzalo was there. He had counted on his support. The military brass, when given a choice, usually supported war over detente.

It justified their existence.

"Anyway, Mr. President," Fuller interjected, "I can confirm that, for whatever reason, the Syrian government did indeed use chemical weapons on innocent civilians."

"What are we going to do about it?" the President asked.

"I suggest we raise the alert level from normal to standby," Gonzalo said. "That way, we can move at a higher degree very quickly."

"Done," Rutledge replied.

"I suggest a measured response," Feltman said. "My intelligence hasn't confirmed that the regime was behind the attack. It could've been the opposition forces who launched the attack to bait us into taking action against Merali. They'd like nothing more than to let us do the fighting for them. Even if Merali did do this, which I'm highly skeptical of drawing that conclusion, it's only been this one time."

"How do we know this is an isolated incident and that he won't do it again?" the President asked.

"He will," Fuller said. "You drew a line in the sand. You said if Merali used chemical weapons against his people that you would take out his regime. He used chemical weapons. If you don't act, you'll look weak to our allies and our enemies. Merali will feel emboldened to do it again if there are no consequences to his actions. I don't think you have a choice but to take him out of power."

"Wait a minute!" Feltman said with a raised voice. "Surely, you aren't suggesting declaring war on Syria."

"Only Congress can declare war," Fuller answered. "But we can respond when our national interests are at stake. I think that applies to this situation."

A vigorous debate went on for more than twenty minutes. Fuller and Gonzalo on one side, Feltman on the other. The President remained neutral like Switzerland.

Fuller began to wonder if the President had the guts to pull the trigger, so to speak.

Finally, after the heated debate died down, White House Chief of Staff, Cunnard, spoke up. "Director Fuller is right, Mr. President. A strong response is warranted. Maybe you shouldn't have made the statement about the line in the sand. It painted you into a box. Be that as it may, you did say it. Now you have to back it up, or no one will ever believe anything you say."

He paused to let that sink in.

"In addition," he continued, "the economy is flat. GDP growth is stagnant. A war might be just what this country needs to pull itself out of the doldrums and get you reelected to a second term."

Fuller didn't want Rutledge re-elected. He intended to challenge him in the primary. A long drawn out war in Syria would drag Rutledge down in the polls and give him the opening he needed to unseat an unpopular president.

President Rutledge sat forward in his chair. He had a pen in his hand and was tapping it rapidly on the table. It was getting on Fuller's nerves.

The president took a deep breath then let it out in the form of a dramatic sigh.

"Jose, dust off the war plans for taking out Merali."

"They don't need to be dusted off, sir," the General replied. "The military is prepared to act at a moment's notice."

"Good. I want to reconvene here, this time tomorrow. I want all your military heads at the meeting. Prepared to discuss an invasion of Syria and a regime change. I want to know how long it'll take."

"We're on it," General Gonzalo said.

Feltman grimaced but kept his mouth shut.

So did Fuller. He learned a long time ago not to say anything when he was winning.

The meeting adjourned with Fuller satisfied.

He got his war.

13

Neal Fuller left the White House meeting and got in his awaiting vehicle to take the short five-mile trip back to CIA headquarters in Langley, Virginia. Once back in his office, he made the first of three important phone calls.

The first was to his Station Chief in Ukraine, Paul Dietrich. He needed an update on the whereabouts of Jamie Austen. "Tell me you have Austen in custody," Fuller said without giving Dietrich time even to say hello. He was in no mood for niceties.

"Not yet," Dietrich replied. "We've located her plane in Turkey. I have guards watching it. When she comes back to get it, they have orders to arrest her."

Fuller felt the anger rising inside of him, even though it wasn't all bad news. He was as concerned about securing the plane as he was about getting Jamie Austen into custody. The Gulfstream was worth a lot of money. AJAX owned it, and he wanted it in his possession as soon as possible.

At least Dietrich found the plane and had it in his custody. Soon the plane would be his to do with what he wished.

Not soon enough. Not with Jamie Austen out there running amok.

"Get a pilot to Turkey immediately," Fuller said gruffly. "I want that plane flown back to Washington immediately."

"I suggest we leave it there for a few days," Dietrich said. "Jamie will come looking for it. That's our best way to nab her. Otherwise, she'll go into hiding and we'll never find her."

"Do as I say!" Fuller exploded. "I don't want to give Austen a chance to steal the plane. I want it back here. Now!"

"But"

"Now!"

"If I can't use the plane as bait, how am I supposed to find the girl?" Dietrich asked. "I have no idea where she is."

"You're in the friggin CIA! You're an intelligence officer. Are you telling me you don't know how to find someone?"

"Jamie Austen is highly trained. If she doesn't want to be found, we won't find her."

"Are you saying you aren't highly trained? You must not be. I'm going to have to get someone in your position who knows what they're doing. You have to find her. I strongly suggest you make this your top priority or think about another line of work."

"That won't be necessary. I'll find her," Dietrich said nervously. "Give me a little more time. I'll get the plane sent back to you right away."

Fuller slammed the phone down in frustration. Then he took out his cell phone to make the second call. Hopefully, Jack August would have better news than Dietrich.

August answered on the first ring and managed to get out a greeting before Fuller started his rough questioning.

"Do you have Alex Halee in custody?" Fuller asked roughly.

"No, sir."

"Why not?"

"We don't know where he is. He wasn't at the house when we got there. His phone was there, but he wasn't."

Fuller wanted to slam the phone down again but exercised some restraint since it was his cell phone and would shatter to pieces on his desk. He mimicked smashing the phone in an exaggerated motion hoping it would help him release some of his anger.

It didn't help.

"That means Halee's onto us," Fuller said. "He's gone into hiding. Make sure TSA and all the borders are alerted."

"I've already done so, sir."

"Have we recovered all of AJAX's assets?" Fuller asked.

He needed to change the name of the corporation. It irked him every time it came out of his mouth. AJAX was a combination of Alex's and Jamie's names. That wouldn't do.

No name came to mind so he put it on the backburner. He'd come up with something clever later.

"I think we have everything that's on the balance sheet," August said. "All we know about anyway. I've met with the employees of AJAX and told them I was in charge now. Everyone cooperated and gave me their passwords except one guy. He refused, saying he would only take orders from Alex. He made a stink about it, but I had him taken in for questioning. Other than that, things are going smoothly."

"That's good to hear. Keep looking for Halee, though. It's imperative we find him as quickly as possible. Hold that guy indefinitely as a material witness. We will slow walk his release."

"I will. I do have one lead. Although I haven't been able to verify its authenticity at this time."

"What is it?" Fuller barked. "Get on with it."

"I got an anonymous tip on my computer that Alex has left the country. That he's on a plane to an island somewhere north of Aruba."

"Aruba? That's strange. Did you track the plane? There can't be too many private planes flying out of D.C. to the south Caribbean Sea."

"That's the thing. The tip gave me the tail number of the plane. I tracked it. It left today for South Africa."

"That has to be Halee! That'd be too big a coincidence. That's good news. We should be able to take him into custody in South Africa. Notify the people on the ground there."

"That's what I thought before, but now I'm not so sure."

"Why not?"

"The plane's not in South Africa."

"You're not making sense. You just said it followed a flight plan to South Africa. Make sense boy!"

"The FAA tracker shows the plane followed the flight plan to South Africa. But I called the airport there, and they have no record of that plane ever landing."

Fuller stared at the wall as he realized what had happened.

"Halee must've hacked into the FAA computer tracking system."

"He is a clever one," August said, stating the obvious.

"Not as clever as me," Fuller boasted. He never thought anyone was more intelligent or more clever than himself. In fact, he was sure of it and didn't hesitate to say it out loud.

"Where's this island you're talking about?" Fuller asked. "That's where Halee went."

"The latitude and longitude were included in the same email that had the tail number of the private jet."

"Why didn't you bother to tell me about it before now?" Fuller bellowed through clenched teeth.

"I wanted to verify it first, sir. I thought it was probably a hoax. But after finding out the plane never landed in South Africa, I'm not so sure."

"Pull up satellite photos of the island. Confirm Halee is there. I'll scramble a team together and put them on hold in case they need to go there. They can be on the ground by dawn."

"I'm on it, sir."

Fuller hung up the phone. Then allowed a big smile to form on his face. He was pretty pleased with himself. He could almost taste the sweet satisfaction of getting his hands on Alex Halee and putting him in jail, where he belonged.

Things were going better than could be expected.

While he wouldn't sleep well until he had Alex and Jamie in custody, he was hot on their trail. Fuller knew that the Bonnie and Clyde of the CIA were not to be taken lightly. They were both skilled assassins. He knew they wouldn't take this lying down. There was too much at stake. The duo was as dangerous as a couple of great white sharks swimming around in a backyard pool full of kids.

He'd have to tread carefully. Be smarter than they were. Catch them off guard. Halee obviously thought he was safe on the island. Fuller would have the element of surprise on his side. The bonus was that he would have Halee trapped in a confined space. Fuller would have the island surrounded with no means of escape.

The magician's trick Halee did with the plane was clever. Fuller would give Halee that. But Alex Halee was not as smart as he was.

That was becoming more and more apparent by the hour.

Hopefully, by this time tomorrow, Alex and Jamie will both be behind bars where they belong. He could almost taste victory. Fuller couldn't wait to see the looks on their faces. Like the credit card commercial, priceless.

Fuller picked up the phone and made the third and final call. To Judge Georgia Smithson. The Judge and Fuller went back to their college days. She wouldn't be in her position without Fuller's influence helping her along the way. She'd repaid the favor many times over with her sexual favors.

Regardless, she still owed him. Smithson was ambitious and didn't mind using unethical behavior to get her what she desired. She wanted to be on the fourth circuit court of appeals and Fuller had practically promised it to her. The fourth circuit was a stepping stone to the Supreme Court. Several Chief Justices had come from that court, and it was the most powerful and prestigious in the United States.

Smithson would do whatever it took to move ahead. When Fuller became President, which he knew he would, he'd make it happen, and she knew it.

"Hello Neal," the judge answered in a sultry voice that no longer turned him on. The relationship was now about leveraging power. Fuller had moved on to younger and sexier models to satisfy his need for sex. Now he used Smithson for her power and intellect more than for her body, which was not as sexy as it was when she was younger.

"Hello, sweetheart," Fuller said. "How is my favorite judge today?"

"I hear an ask coming," she said.

"Of course you do."

"Why do you only call me anymore when you need something?" she asked coldly.

"Ouch! That hurt. And it's not true. You're sticking a dagger in my heart with such harsh words. You know I love you."

"The truth does hurt. What can I do for you, Director?" she said in her professional judge's voice.

"I need a hearing. On an emergency motion."

"What's the nature of the motion?"

"The CIA has seized the assets of a couple of its operatives. We've frozen their bank accounts and assets. I want them unfrozen and assigned to a new corporation."

Hopefully she wouldn't ask very many questions.

"How much notice do you need for a hearing?" she asked, to his relief.

"I'd like to do it tomorrow. Or as soon as possible. The CIA has vital national interests in that property becoming functional again."

"Tomorrow is fast. Can you notify the other party by then?"

"They've fled the country and are in hiding."

"You really do want a favor, don't you Director."

"The biggest one yet. I wouldn't ask if it wasn't important. Is there a problem?"

"None at all. I'll see you tomorrow. I hope you appreciate my help, Director, and will remember it in the future."

He knew what she meant.

Fuller hung up. Things were happening so quickly it almost made his head spin. By this time tomorrow, the two billion dollars would be released to his control. The AJAX corporation would be in his name and he could change it. As would the yacht and the plane which he'd have control over.

Even Jamie Austen's rare collection of extremely valuable paintings would be in his possession.

What was he going to do with millions of dollars in paintings?

Hang them up in his house, of course.

14

Tajikistan

Jamie and her team painstakingly and carefully packaged up all the stolen paintings in Clement's warehouse and loaded them into the two vehicles. They put the two dead Russians in the vault and sealed it. At gunpoint, Clement reset the alarm for the warehouse. More than likely, it'd be months, if not years, before anyone discovered the bodies. Whatever family the men had were in Russia, according to Clement.

They drove the two vehicles back to Clement's house in search of more information. Jamie wanted to know which paintings Clement stole and who he sold them to.

He was defiant.

They searched his house and didn't find a paper trail.

Jamie was growing impatient and called for A-Rad.

"Take Clement in the back room and make him talk," Jamie said to him in front of the art thief, whose eyes suddenly widened.

A-Rad was a landmass. A huge man. All muscle. Most of the time, he was as gentle and goodhearted as a lamb. Unless anyone on the team was threatened, especially Jamie, then A-Rad became a fighting machine. With a gun in his hand, he was fearless and ferocious.

His knuckles against a man's jaw could do some severe damage.

"What are the rules?" A-Rad asked.

"There are no rules," Jamie said. "You can do anything you want to him. Just don't kill him. Not yet. Make him talk first."

Jamie gave A-Rad a wink off to the side so Clement couldn't see it. They weren't against torturing someone if a life was in danger, but Jamie wouldn't authorize extreme bodily harm to find some paintings. Clement didn't know that, though.

A-Rad jerked Clement from the chair where he was sitting and dragged him into a room by his hands which were tied behind his back. He cried out in pain as A-Rad strained the man's shoulder muscles, arms, and upper back. A-Rad closed the door behind him and she could hear Clement pleading for him not to hurt him.

Jamie found a chair and sat down. With all the excitement, she hadn't had a chance to contemplate the ramifications of the Cardinal Red. She welcomed the respite. It'd been an eventful few hours.

While her body was resting, her mind was spinning out of control. She still hadn't heard from Alex. Not that she expected to. The protocol in a Cardinal Red situation was to go dark. Standard communication was out of the question. The priority was to get off the grid to a safe place before contact was made. At some point she would hear from him. Hopefully, sooner rather than later.

She really didn't know what to do, where to go, or how to proceed. Did she go back to Washington? To the island? Did they go dark for a few days until she made contact with Alex?

Was Fuller behind the Cardinal Red?

A terrorist?

Was Alex in danger?

Was she?

So many questions. Before she could come up with any answers, A-Rad came out of the room where he had taken Clement.

Jamie sat up in the chair.

"What's wrong?" she asked.

"He's talking," A-Rad said with a satisfied look on his face. This was the closest she'd seen to him acting smug. A-Rad didn't have an egotistical bone in his body.

"That didn't take long," Jamie said, standing to her feet. The adrenaline was suddenly flowing again.

"I didn't even touch him. I raised my fist like I was going to hit him, and he began crying like a baby. Pleading with me not to hurt him. I'm pretty sure he peed his pants. Now he's singing like a canary in a petting zoo."

"What did he say?"

"I cut him off and told him to tell you. You know more about all these paintings than I do. I warned him what would happen if he lied to you, though. I think he's more afraid of you than he is me."

"He saw me kill those two Russians. He probably thinks that's what I'm going to do to him."

"What are you going to do with him once he spills the beans?"

"I'm not sure. This whole Cardinal Red thing has me confused. I don't want to kill him, but I do want him to pay for his crimes. Alex would probably tell me to cut him loose and get out of here. That's probably what we'll do. I want to at least gather the information first."

They walked toward the room and entered it. Jamie felt a tickle in her nose when she got a whiff of urine. She raised her voice so Clement would be sure to hear her.

"If he lies to me, then kill him," she said to A-Rad. "We'll take his body back to the warehouse and put it with the Russians."

Clement squirmed in his seat. He was tied to a chair. Jamie got in his face.

"What did you do with the paintings you sold?" she asked roughly.

"I... I sold them to a Russian in Uzbekistan."

"What's his name?"

"Veniamin Zakarov."

Not the answer she expected to hear.

"The arms dealer?"

The Israelis had been trying to get to Zakarov for years. He financed a number of terrorist attacks in the Golan Heights and also helped prop up the Syrian President by supplying him with arms.

Cutting Clement loose was no longer an option. Not if he was affiliated with a known terrorist.

"I don't know about all that," Clement said. "I just sell him paintings. His money is good, and he pays well."

"Who else do you sell the paintings to?"

"That's it."

"You're lying!"

A-Rad took two steps toward Clement, who cowered back in his chair. To the extent, he could, considering his hands were tied.

"I swear. He's my only customer."

"You're lying. You tried to sell me a painting."

Clement's eyes flitted back and forth like he was trying to think of an explanation for the obvious discrepancy in his story.

"That's the first time I tried to sell a painting on the dark web. I wanted to see if I could get more money for one. A big mistake, as it turns out. I should've stuck with selling to Zakarov."

It seemed like Clement was telling the truth.

"What did you sell to him?" Jamie asked, keeping the pressure on him. "Tell me about all of the paintings that he has now."

"I'm not saying anything else unless you promise not to kill me," he whimpered.

"I promise I *will* kill you if you don't start talking right now."

Clement fidgeted nervously. His eyes were still flitting back and forth in every direction. Obviously, he was considering his options, which weren't many.

"I want some guarantees," he said. Like he was in a position to negotiate with her.

Jamie turned away from him and started for the door.

"See if you can make him talk," she said to A-Rad.

Clement went crazy and started bouncing the chair up and down.

"No! Okay! Okay! I'll tell you what you want to know."

Jamie stopped in her tracks and turned around, and walked back toward him. She leaned against the table with her hands folded in front of her.

"Quit wasting my time," she snarled. "Tell me what I want to know, or I'll turn my bulldog loose on you. This time I won't stop him."

"Do you know about the Queen's Birthday Heist?" Clement asked.

"Of course. Everybody knows about that."

Clement was talking about the most significant art theft in history. It happened on the Queen's birthday in London, which was a national holiday. Businesses were closed, and revelers were on the street. A night watchman at the Royal Art Gallery of London reported that a man entered the building dressed in a police uniform.

"I'm here about a disturbance," the fake cop had said.

The watchman buzzed him in. The thief proceeded to steal fifteen paintings worth more than six hundred million dollars. The perpetrator was never found, even though they had him on security footage. Jamie scrolled through the images in her mind and could see where the man in the video fit Clement's description.

"I stole the paintings," Clement said. "That was me."

"I don't believe you," Jamie said roughly, even though she did.

"I don't care if you believe me or not. I stole them and sold them to Zakarov. He has them at his home in Uzbekistan. Or at least that's where I took them."

"Where in Uzbekistan?"

"I can take you there."

"Give me an address!" Jamie demanded.

"No. I'll have to show you where he lives. That's the deal."

That comment almost made her smile. She didn't because he couldn't know that he did have leverage to make a deal. Zakarov's location was intelligence gold.

She had to admire Clement's survival instincts. He was obviously trying to find a way to stay alive. He probably had deduced that if he gave up all the information at once, she'd just kill him. Something she wouldn't do, but had no qualms about threatening to do so.

Jamie decided to toss him a bone.

"Okay. Take me to Zakarov and I'll let you live."

She motioned for A-Rad to leave the room with her and closed the door. She called her team together in Clement's living room.

"Clement has given us some actionable intelligence. He knows where Zakarov is."

"What about the Cardinal Red?" the Colonel asked impatiently. "Aren't we supposed to drop all missions and wait for instructions?"

"Who is Zakarov?" Bond asked. "The name rings a bell."

"He's a Russian arms dealer. Apparently, he also collects stolen paintings in his spare time. He's in Uzbekistan. We need to go there and recover the paintings and capture or kill him."

"The Cardinal Red, Jamie!" the Colonel repeated, with more urgency in his voice. "We have strict instructions we have to follow. We need to go back to the plane and await to hear from Alex."

"I agree," Bond said. "Until we know what's going on with Alex, we need to lay low."

"Zakarov is a high-value target," Jamie argued more vehemently. "The Israelis would definitely be interested in him."

"Then give them his location and let them handle it," Bond said.

"Zakarov has the Queen's paintings," Jamie added.

"The ones stolen from the Royal Art Museum in London?" Bond asked. His eyes had widened with considerably more interest. Bond was British and a former officer with British intelligence. He was probably on staff at the time of the thefts. Maybe even helped investigate them.

Jamie played that card on purpose. She was playing on his nationalism.

"We never found the thief," Bond said.

"He's in the other room. Clement stole the paintings and sold them to Zakarov."

116

"We need to nail him then!" Bond said with as much vitriol as she'd ever heard come out of his mouth, doing a complete one-eighty.

"We can't!" the Colonel bellowed. "The Cardinal Red. We have to follow protocol and go back to the plane."

"Zakarov's house is on the way back to the plane," Jamie argued. "It's in Uzbekistan. Like I said. We'll go right by it on the way to Turkey."

While Jamie wanted the team's input, she was still in charge and could force them to go along with her plan if push came to shove. She preferred that it was everyone's idea.

"I say we do it," Bond said.

"Me too," A-Rad added.

If A-Rad had a choice between a gunfight and a night at the movies with a pretty girl, he'd choose a gunfight every time. That's how he was wired. He would always choose a dangerous mission over anything else.

She hated to disappoint him but had no other choice.

"A-Rad. You need to drive the paintings back to Turkey. Warm up the plane and wait for us to get there. Then we'll regroup."

His shoulders sagged in disappointment, but he didn't put up any resistance.

"We're going to need a large box truck," Jamie continued. "When we get to Zakarov's house, we'll need a way to transport the paintings back to the plane."

Jamie pulled out her phone and searched for a place to rent a large moving truck. She found one and dialed a number to make a reservation. She'd send Bond and the Colonel to pick it up.

"I'll need a credit card to hold it," the man on the other end of the line said.

Jamie pulled out her wallet and gave him the number of the card.

A few seconds later, he came back on the line.

"I'm sorry, but that card was declined. Do you have another?"

Jamie hung up immediately.

15

Jamie paced around the living room of Clement's house like a tiger in a zoo.

"What's wrong?" the Colonel asked her.

She'd just hung up the phone from the truck rental place, having learned that her credit card was declined. The Colonel was obviously responding to the shocked look that had to be on her face.

What did it mean?

She wasn't really sure.

"My credit card was declined," she said, not even believing the words coming out of her mouth.

"Maybe it was a mistake," Colonel said.

"I don't think so. I think it has to do with the Cardinal Red."

"Can you use a different card?" he asked.

"That's the only card I have in the alias I used for this mission. I made sure it had plenty of credit on it before I left the States."

The card was in a fake name. As was her passport to enter Tajikistan. The card should still be good, though.

Then reality hit her. The name and card were both associated with AJAX. Fuller would have access to it. He had to be the one who froze the card. Probably put a hold on all of their cards and bank accounts.

She didn't panic. At least she had the accounts and cards Fuller didn't know about.

"Let me check something," Jamie said.

She pulled up one of their AJAX bank accounts on her phone. As expected, it showed the balance was on hold. Frozen. She couldn't access it.

She tried several more accounts with the same results. No reason to check all of them, so she checked her personal accounts. They were frozen as well.

She was starting to get a better picture as to why Alex had instituted Cardinal Red.

"This is not good," Jamie said to her team. "All my cards and accounts are frozen. At least all the accounts associated with AJAX."

"Who would do that?" the Colonel asked.

"Fuller," Bond answered on Jamie's behalf. "The man has wanted to get Jamie ever since he put the hit out on her."

Bond was in Hong Kong with Jamie when those events went down and knew firsthand the danger they'd been in because of Fuller.

Colonel went into leadership mode. "A-Rad. Do we have enough fuel to get home?" he asked.

A-Rad nodded his head up and down. Then said, "I refueled as soon as we landed in Turkey. So we're full. The Bombardier has a range of eleven thousand kilometers. That's thirteen hours of flying time. We can pretty much get anywhere in the world. Including back home."

"That's good," Colonel said.

"If your credit cards and bank accounts are frozen," Bond said, "I don't think we should go back to the States. Jamie will be arrested as soon as she steps off the plane. We might be safer staying right here."

"Let's go to the island," A-Rad said. "We can definitely make it back there."

Jamie shook her head no.

"Fuller will be able to track the plane. We can't lead him to the island. Alex is the only one who knows how to mess with the tail number so the plane can't be tracked."

Bond let out a huge groan followed by an "Oh no!"

"What?" Colonel asked. "What's wrong?"

"Fuller will know the plane is in Turkey," Bond said. "He's probably got someone there watching it as we speak. Waiting for us to show up. He'll try to arrest Jamie before she gets on the plane. Even before she gets to the States. So he can detain her indefinitely. That's what we did in the MI6 when we wanted to take down a rogue agent. We froze his accounts and credit cards and put out a travel alert and had him picked up if he tried to cross a border or board a flight."

"Jamie's not a rogue agent!" A-Rad retorted.

Bond raised his hand to stop him. "I'm not saying she is. I'm just saying what Fuller will do to capture her is like what we always did."

Jamie said, "A-Rad, call the airport and see if anyone showed up inquiring about the aircraft."

A-Rad left the room. He returned moments later.

"The plane's gone!" he said excitedly.

"What are you talking about?" Jamie asked.

"The guy I talked to said some men showed up and demanded to take the plane. They had all kinds of credentials and were armed. They boarded the plane, and it took off. The flight plan was for Washington, D.C."

"There goes our ride," Colonel said. "I guess we are stuck here."

"This is worse than I thought," Jamie said soberly.

"What do we do now?" Colonel asked. "I guess we could hide out here. Does Fuller know you're in Tajikistan?"

"I don't think so," Jamie said. She was carrying a phone that Fuller wouldn't know about or be able to track. Then she remembered the credit card she tried to use at the rental truck company. Fuller would be able to track that.

"We can't stay here," Jamie said. She tried to calculate in her mind how long it'd take Fuller to get someone to Tajikistan. Probably four to six hours.

"The problem is that we don't have any money," Bond said.

"Jamie, I've got money. You can use mine," A-Rad said. "I don't even care if you pay me back or not."

She walked over and hugged him.

"You're a good friend. Thanks, A-Rad. But this is my problem. I'll figure it out."

"Just know it's available if you need it."

"I appreciate it."

"Me, too," Bond said. Colonel chimed in and offered his resources as well.

They did all have credit cards and checking accounts that probably weren't frozen, but Fuller might be smart enough to put a trace on them. She couldn't be too careful.

Jamie patted each of them on his chest and let out a sigh. This wasn't the first time she'd been in the field with no money and no means of support. It hadn't happened in a long time, though. Not since they started AJAX and fell into billions of dollars.

Be resourceful, Curly always said. *Think inside the box. Not outside*, he told her on more than one occasion. That was counterintuitive but she kind of knew what he meant in situations like these.

Thinking of Curly brought a smile to her face. His training had mostly been to prepare her for adversity. He said she didn't need as much training for when things were going smoothly.

An idea suddenly came to her, inside the box.

The nineteen million.

She wired it to Clement's account earlier that day. Pok was to pull it out and put it in an AJAX account, but one Fuller wouldn't know about. Jamie felt like she'd had a B-12 shot. She could feel the excitement all the way to the tips of her toes.

Jamie pulled up that bank account, expecting to see millions of dollars in it.

Zero.

Not frozen. Not on hold. There was no money in the account at all. She blinked several times as if what she was seeing would suddenly change.

How was that possible?

Alex must've taken it. That had to be it. Alex transferred it out to protect Fuller from getting it. But why? Fuller wouldn't know about it.

Nothing was making sense.

"What's wrong now?" Colonel asked.

Jamie didn't answer. She walked over to the table and grabbed Clement's phone. She had to know something. She looked through the cell phone for his banking information and found it, but it was password protected.

She stormed into the room where Clement was still being held. A-Rad, Bond, and Colonel were close behind.

Jamie waved Clement's phone in his face.

"What's the password to your bank account?" she demanded. "The one I wired the money into."

He turned his head to the side in defiance. She wanted to rip it off his shoulders.

"Tell me the password!"

"I'm not letting you steal my money and the painting."

"Do I need to remind you that that's exactly what you were going to do to me? Or have you forgotten!"

He just stared at her.

Jamie reached inside the slit in her dress and pulled out her gun. She pressed it against the side of Clement's head.

He started whimpering.

"What's your password?" she shouted. "Tell me now, or I'll blow your brains out!"

"What difference does it make?" Clement said sheepishly but with a hint of resolve. "You're going to kill me anyway. The money will do me no good. At least you won't have it."

A-Rad was by Clement's side in a flash. He grabbed him by the hair and jerked his head backward.

Clement let out a yelp.

"You're right," A-Rad said. "You'll never see that money. And we are going to kill you. But I can make sure your death is slow and painful. A bullet in your head is too good for you."

"We won't kill you if you cooperate," Jamie said.

"Why would I believe you?"

"Because I give you my word."

After more threats and coaxing, Clement relented and gave Jamie the password.

She pulled out his phone and logged into his bank account. To her shock, the nineteen million was still in Clement's account. It hadn't been touched. The balance was more than thirty million dollars.

What was going on? Why didn't Pok take the money? Why were their accounts showing zero, but Clement's accounts were untouched?

Something must've happened to Pok.

Relief washed over her. Surprisingly. At the moment, she was glad Pok didn't take the money. Now, she had access to it.

Jamie pulled out her phone and redialled the number to the truck rental facility. "I want to speak to the owner," she said.

"I'm the owner. How may I help you?"

"I want to buy one of your trucks."

"They aren't for sale. We rent them. I'll be happy to rent you one with a credit card."

"I'll give you a hundred thousand American dollars for one of your trucks."

"I'm sorry, but they aren't for sale."

"Five hundred thousand then."

"Sold," the owner replied joyfully.

Why did she care? The money was coming out of Clement's account. He'd never have the opportunity to use it. While they wouldn't kill him unless they had to, they would see to it that he went to jail for the rest of his life. Either in Israel or in Great Britain. She wouldn't let Fuller take the credit for her bust.

"I'll need cash to finalize the transaction," the owner said.

"Tell me where to wire the money, and it'll be in your account within the hour."

Or at least she hoped it would. She wasn't really sure how fast the banking system worked in Tajikistan. The only thing she knew was that her nineteen million appeared in Clement's account immediately.

"Hold on," the owner said.

He left the line and came back on with the wiring instructions to his bank. Jamie found a pen and paper and wrote them down. She went back to the room where Clement was still tied up and untied his hands.

She handed him the piece of paper and his phone. "Wire five hundred thousand dollars to that account," she said, pointing to the numbers on the paper.

Clement didn't ask why. Clearly, he didn't want a gun in his face again. When it was done, she tied him up again. He protested mildly.

"I'll let you loose soon," Jamie said.

She left the room and motioned for her team to follow. Once they were outside his earshot, Jamie gave them instructions.

"I purchased a truck. Bond and Colonel, go to the trucking company and pick it up and bring it back here."

She looked on her phone for the address and showed it to them.

"Do you still intend to go to Uzbekistan?" Colonel asked.

"Why not? I don't know where else to go. We might as well be doing something productive."

"Good. I want to find the Queen's paintings," Bond said.

Colonel didn't protest further.

He and Bond left the house, and Jamie sat back down in the chair, trying to wrap her mind around the events of the day. Things were starting to come together. A sobering reality was hitting her all at once. Fuller put a hold on their bank accounts. He probably seized all of AJAX's assets, including the plane.

The yacht!

Jamie was suddenly steaming. She used that yacht to rescue girls. Fuller had no right to seize it. She'd risked life and limp to get it.

Jamie was standing again. Filled with resolve. Fuller would rue the day he started messing with her.

Feelings of revenge were a waste of emotional and mental energy, according to Curly, if you couldn't act on them right away. At the moment, she couldn't. Her mind needed to focus on the more pressing issues.

My house!

The realization of what was happening was hitting her like Chinese water torture. Like a slow drip. The bank accounts. Her credit cards. The plane. The yacht. She remembered back to when times were simpler and they didn't have so much to lose.

She really shouldn't think about the house either. But couldn't help herself. Jamie pulled up her phone and logged into the security system at their home in Virginia.

What she saw floored her. The house was in shambles. Ransacked. Walls were torn out. Papers were strewn on the floor. Dishes were out of the cabinets and broken on the floor. The cushions in the couches and chairs were cut up.

My closet!

Many of her clothes were ripped and thrown on the floor.

Everything was destroyed.

A tear formed in her eye.

Mixed emotions flooded her soul. A mix of anger and sadness.

It felt like she was losing everything.

Then she remembered Alex. She still had him, which was the most important thing.

Or did she? She really had no idea where he was or if he was even safe.

If he was alive, he'd certainly know all the things she knew.

What would he do?

Now she had a new worry.

I pray to God Alex doesn't do something stupid!

16

The next morning

Fuller was in the office early. He was still reeling with frustration because he hadn't gotten a call in the middle of the night telling him that Jamie Austen and Alex Halee were in custody. Something he couldn't control.

He had a bounce to his step, nonetheless. Those things took time. He had just as important things on his plate—things he could control.

This morning was his hearing before Judge Georgia Smithson. By noon, all of AJAX's assets would be in his name. His accountant and lawyer were already hard at work drawing up the documents.

Georgia had called that morning and asked to see him in her chambers thirty minutes before the scheduled hearing. He knew what that meant and was willing to oblige. For the sake of the judge and the ruling he needed. He would enjoy it as well, but not as much as getting his hands on the two billion dollars, the yacht, the private jet, and whatever else might be out there that he didn't know about yet.

Fuller sat at his desk and let out a yawn. He'd had a restless night. A couple of things were bothering him. He was rethinking his plan to arrest Jamie and Alex and bring them back to the states for trial. Too many problems in that plan were rattling around in his mind. The duo were undercover CIA officers. It'd be easier to make them disappear. He already thought of a couple of ways to make that happen.

He was also rethinking his plan to have Jack August run AJAX.

So, first thing that morning, Fuller called the rehab center where his son was in treatment and told them to release him. They didn't advise it. His son wasn't ready. The chances of relapse were high.

That may be the case, but he needed his own man running AJAX. He didn't trust August. Actually, he shouldn't trust anyone other than his own flesh and blood to be running his company. Hopefully, his son could keep the blow out of his nose and his zipper up long enough to get things set up the way he wanted them.

His son, though an imbecile, should be able to do it with his direction. The boy had a degree from Wharton, which Fuller paid for, so he should know how to run a business. The kid passed by the skin of his teeth which still gave him concern. The generous donation to the college from some of Fuller's cronies had helped. Political capital he had to expend on his son's behalf. He hated calling in those favors, but he didn't have a choice if his son was going to graduate.

He looked at the notes for his to-do list that he'd scribbled in the middle of the night. As CIA Director, he was used to fighting battles on several fronts simultaneously. He knew how to multitask. So, he went from one phone call to the next with ease. He got most of the pressing matters off his desk so that he could focus on the Jamie and Alex problem. The clock on the wall said he had about an hour before he had to leave for the hearing.

He called Dietrich. The name at the top of the AJAX list.

"Any word on Austen?" Fuller asked.

"Yes, sir. We got a hit on one of her credit cards. It was used in Tajikistan. At a truck rental facility. Or she tried to use it. I made sure the card was declined."

"You idiot! Why would you put a hold on the credit card?" Fuller bellowed.

"I thought"

"I know what you thought, and you're as worthless as a tooth lying on the ground! I told you to put a travel alert on the passports and the credit cards. I never told you to put a hold on them."

"You told me to have her detained at the border so she couldn't use her passport. I also assumed you wanted me to make sure she couldn't use the credit cards as well."

He had given Dietrich all known CIA fake passports that had been issued to Austen along with credit card numbers. Now he was regretting it.

Fuller continued his tirade.

"How am I going to track Austen? I wanted the card to be good, so we would know where she used it."

More silence on the other end which was almost as infuriating as when Dietrich was talking.

Fuller contemplated his next move. The line was silent for nearly a minute.

"Director?" Dietrich asked. "Are you still there?"

"I'm thinking."

More silence.

"At least we have the name she's traveling under," Fuller finally said. "If she's in Tajikistan, she'll have to leave eventually. Her plane is in Turkey. She'll go there. I wonder why she was trying to rent a large truck?"

He asked the question aloud more for his own benefit. Dietrich wouldn't have a clue.

"I don't know, sir."

"Is there anything you do know? Call the facility and ask them! Use your brain, man!"

"I will. I do know that the primary way out of Tajikistan to Turkey is through Uzbekistan."

"That border is closed."

The two countries didn't get along. Most countries in that part of the region were sworn enemies unless they were fighting a common battle.

"No, sir. It was opened recently for limited travel. The border lets five hundred people a day through with the proper credentials. The only border facility that is open is in Panjakent. I'll check and see if that's how she entered."

"That's a good idea. I want you to go there now," Fuller said. "Get on the first flight to Panjakent. Take paperwork with you to have Jamie Austen detained if she tries to cross the border."

"What do I do with her if she shows up there?"

"Await my instructions."

Fuller abruptly hung up. He didn't know what to do with Austen. Bringing her back to the United States wasn't an option. He needed to figure out a way to have her disappear. Jamie Austen had made a lot of enemies over the years who would love to get their hands on her. The simplest thing would be to turn her over to one of them.

There were so many to choose from. Which one was closest to central Asia?

He'd figure it out later.

Fuller picked up his cell phone and called August. He was already in the AJAX office.

"I sent you the latest satellite photos from the island," August said. "They're in your email."

Fuller pulled them up on his computer and scrolled through dozens of unopened emails until he found it.

"What am I looking at?" Fuller asked.

"This is the island that matches the latitude and longitude sent to me in the anonymous email."

"Any idea who the email came from?"

"No. We traced it back through a number of servers and then lost the trail. Whoever sent it was an expert at covering his tracks."

"Not important. I see an airplane on a runway."

"Yes. We think that plane is the same one that left D.C. yesterday."

Fuller could feel the excitement building inside of him.

What if AJAX owned this island and airplane? That meant he could seize them as well and enjoy more fruits of Jamie and Alex's labor.

He scrolled through the photos and was amazed at what he saw. Swimming pools. Pristine beaches. An enormous mansion with tennis courts. Three other buildings. A place for his yacht.

August continued. Fuller couldn't quit looking at the photos.

"The island is not reported as an AJAX asset," August said. "If Halee owns it, then your suspicions about him were right. He has been skimming money out of AJAX for his personal gain."

This was why he needed to get August away from AJAX. He was too close to everything and already knew too much. Fuller didn't know if August could be silenced with money. Better to get him out altogether once he'd served his purpose. Which was immediate if Alex was really on the island.

"What do you want me to do now?" August said. "Do you want me to go down there?"

"No!" Fuller said with too much emphasis. He toned it down. "Your talents are better served here with me. In fact, I only need you for one or two more days at AJAX offices, then I want you back here. I have a new project for you to work on."

"I'm just getting started on this one. There's a lot to be done. AJAX is a much bigger operation than I realized."

Fuller was glad to hear that. He was anxious to find out how big.

That didn't change his mind about August. The man didn't know about the hearing with the judge or about Fuller's plans for AJAX and for Alex Halee. More than likely he wouldn't approve if he did. Best that he be kept in the dark. Fuller didn't need August looking over his shoulder. The entire operation needed to be outside the purview of the CIA. The way it was set up to operate which would work to his advantage.

"You've done a good job," Fuller said. "It will not go unrewarded. Finish up your work today at AJAX and report back here tomorrow."

"Yes, sir," August said with resignation.

Fuller hung up the phone and called Kyle Kelly. His go-to guy for complex military assignments. Kelly had executed the bombing in Syria that set the war in Syria in motion. Fuller called Kelly once he learned about the island and instructed him to assemble an assault team and fly to Panama. He wanted them ready if he confirmed that Alex Halee was on the island. While he didn't have proof positive, he had his suspicions. Enough evidence that he could act on it.

Kelly answered on a secure line.

"Are you ready?" Fuller asked.

"My team is on standby and ready to go," Kelly said.

"I'm going to send your instructions. There's a high-value target on an island north of Aruba. I'll send you the latitude and longitude and satellite photos."

"Who is the target?"

"Above your pay grade. All you need to know is that he's armed and dangerous. I'm sending you his picture now."

"What are the rules of engagement?"

"Whatever it takes. Secure the target and lock down the island. Take the target off the island and back to Panama. I have a team who will meet you for the handoff."

Fuller intended to hold Halee in Panama and turn him over to guerrillas in Colombia. He couldn't bring him back to the United States, where he'd have rights. The right to an attorney. Bail. The goodwill of a lot of people. Even the President of the United States was aware of Halee's distinguished service over the years.

Better that Fuller makes Halee disappear.

"You can count on us," Kelly said.

"I hope so. Once the island is secure, call me. I can be down there within a few hours. Just so we're clear, secure the island, take the target to Panama, and await my instructions. Detain anyone else on the island until I get there. Are we clear?"

"If we meet resistance, what am I authorized to do?"

"I said, whatever it takes! I don't care if Hal... if the target is dead or alive. I just want you to bring him in."

Fuller hung up. The last words were still ringing in his ears. If Halee did resist, that'd solve a lot of his problems.

17

Zakarov Compound
Kungrad, Uzbekistan

Jamie and her team took a longer route to get to Zakarov's compound in Uzbekistan from Clement's house in Khorog, Tajikistan. The straightest path would have taken them across the border at Panjakent. Jamie's credit card was compromised, so she assumed her passport was also. Fuller would likely have someone at the border ready to detain her if she tried to cross it.

Driving a large truck over the Tajik and Fann mountains was iffy at best. The narrow roads with the sheer drop-offs would mean certain death if a vehicle lost the slightest bit of control.

Ironically enough, Clement had been helpful in determining the route. He had smuggled his stolen art into and out of Tajikistan on numerous occasions and knew the best ways to go to avoid the authorities. Initially, Jamie had been skeptical of his suggestion, but after considering all other options, she ended up taking his recommendation. It worked out. They crossed the border into Turkmenistan, traversed the Karakum desert, and entered Uzbekistan at the sparsely populated northwest border. No one would be looking for her there.

The guys weren't as happy with the route since they had to drive the large truck filled with paintings across the desert. Colonel, in particular, didn't like the fact that between them, they only had four handguns and the two assault rifles they found in Clement's house that belonged to the two dead Russians.

His concern was probably warranted. If they had encountered hostile enemies along the way, their odds were not good if they had to go into a fight with so little firepower. It turned out to be a moot point since all they saw were villages and camels.

The issue of limited firepower had now reared its ugly head for a second time while they were surveilling Zakarov's compound.

"I have good news and bad news," Colonel said. He and Bond had just returned to Jamie's location after circling the compound on foot. "Which do you want to hear first?"

"Always start with the good news," Jamie said. Alex would've said start with the bad news first. The two of them were opposite when it came to most things.

"The good news is that Zakarov is probably here at the compound," Colonel said.

"Why do you say that?" Jamie had to ask, even though it was good news.

"The place is crawling with guards. We counted at least two dozen men armed with HK 417 assault rifles. They wouldn't have that much firepower guarding the house if he wasn't there."

"What's the bad news?" she asked.

Colonel smirked, then grimaced. "There are two dozen men armed with HK 417 assault rifles guarding the house."

Jamie wasn't surprised that an arms dealer would outfit his security with one of the best assault rifles available.

"That is a problem," Jamie said. "We can't match that. We don't have the firepower to take them on."

"We could if we still had the plane," Colonel said.

He was right. There had been plenty of firepower on their plane. A moot point since it was no longer on the ground in Turkey. Presumably, their plane was in Fuller's hands. Even if it were there, it wouldn't do them any good where they were now. Going back to

Turkey and then making their way back into Uzbekistan seemed like a risky proposition.

"The majority of the guards are clustered around the front gate," Colonel said. "That part's good. But they'd mow us down before we got within a hundred yards of them."

"What about a rear attack?" Jamie asked.

"The fence is electrified all the way around the compound. It's got motion detectors and alarms. They also have dogs roaming the back area inside fences spaced apart every twenty yards or so. If we could somehow get inside the fence, the dogs would bark, and we'd be discovered before we got to the house. Even if we somehow managed to breach security and infiltrate the house and capture Zakarov, how would we get the truck in to take out the paintings? The only way would be to kill everybody."

"I've got a plan, Jamie," A-Rad said.

"Shut up, A-Rad," Colonel said frustratedly. "Don't even start. We aren't going with your plan."

"Seriously, Jamie," A-Rad continued. "I know how to draw the guards away from the front gate."

"Ok, I'm listening. What's your idea, A-Rad?" Jamie said. She glared at Colonel so he'd let A-Rad talk. Although, if Colonel didn't like it, she was sure she wouldn't either. He was the expert when it came to strategy.

Nevertheless, she wanted everyone to feel like their ideas were being heard. Four heads were better than one was what Curly would have said in a similar situation. Sometimes the worst ideas turned into the best ones after they were hashed out and vetted.

A-Rad hesitated.

"Go ahead and tell me your plan, A-Rad," Jamie said to encourage him. He didn't often speak when it came to offering ideas. A-Rad was more of a follower than a leader..

His entire demeanor changed. A-Rad got all excited like a kid in a pizza place with a fistful of coins for arcade games. She'd seen him that way many times when they were about to go into a battle.

The team was positioned on a small berm just above the compound, looking down on it. A-Rad bent down and started drawing in the sand. Darkness had fallen, but Jamie had a small flashlight which she used to illuminate his drawing.

"Your plan is stupid," Colonel said condescendingly.

A-Rad ignored him and kept drawing. Bond was silent. He was lying down on the top of the berm, keeping watch on the guards who were a couple hundred yards away.

"Here's the gate," A-Rad said. He pointed to the opening on the east side of the rectangle on the ground.

"I'm with you, so far," Jamie said.

"This is where most of the guards are," A-Rad said.

On the way over, Jamie had formed a plan to breach the compound. She expected to find a gate with guards. Probably only two or three. Two dozen had been a surprise. Why would Zakarov need so many guards out in the middle of the desert? It made her think there were valuable paintings in the house that needed protection.

Two or three guards were manageable. Her team was skilled enough that they could take them out without a problem, even if the guards had assault rifles. They also had the element of surprise on their side. The sheer numbers left Jamie less optimistic.

A-Rad continued. "I'll circle around to the other side of the compound. Right here."

He pointed to the northeast side of the rectangle.

"Where are we going to be?" Jamie asked.

He drew two lines away from the rectangle. She presumed it was supposed to be the road leading in.

"You'll be back here. In the truck."

He drew a circle at the end of the road and tapped the ground in the middle of the ring.

"Ok. I've got it."

"I'll go running past the gate, yelling and screaming at the top of my lungs. I'll even get a shot or two off at the guards."

Jamie forced back a smile.

"Why don't you take your clothes off and streak in front of them?" Colonel said, sarcastically. "They might die laughing."

A-Rad's face formed a snarled expression. Jamie put her hand to cover her mouth so A-Rad wouldn't see her smiling. He was dead serious, and she didn't want to ruin it for him.

"Like I said. . . I'll run in front of the gate and distract the guards. They'll chase me. But I won't let them catch me. That will get most of the guards away from the gate."

"How are you going to get the truck inside the gate?" Colonel asked in a snarky voice.

"That's easy," A-Rad said. "We ram it with the truck."

"If all the guards are gone, why don't we just get out of the truck and open it at the guard gate?" Colonel asked with even more attitude.

"You could do that too."

Jamie studied the drawing, pretending to be considering it. There's no way she'd let him put himself in harm's way like that. Any plan they came up with that included a gunfight was out of the question. They'd lose a hundred out of a hundred times.

"It's a good idea, Jamie. It'll work."

"Make sure you're running away from the guards," Colonel said. "That way, when they start shooting at you, they'll hit your fat rear end. Then it won't hurt you."

"That's enough, Colonel," Jamie said. "We get your point."

She didn't mind the banter, to a point. She was used to it. The guys were like brothers. Always fighting but ready to die for the other when push came to shove.

Jamie took a deep breath and thought through her words. She had to let A-Rad down gently.

"It's a good idea, A-Rad," Jamie said. "But what if all the guards don't leave the guard shack? What if only a couple of them chase you? That'll still leave too many for us to take out."

"What if Clement drives the truck to the gate and he tells them he has a shipment for Zakarov?" A-Rad said. "We can all hide in the back of the truck."

"That's a halfway better idea," Colonel said. "It still sucks, but I give you a D on this one and a solid F on the other one."

"The guards will search it and we'll be sitting ducks in that confined space," Jamie said.

"I don't hear you coming up with any ideas," A-Rad said, to Colonel not acknowledging Jamie's objection.

The conversation was getting heated and they needed to keep their voices down. If the guards weren't on the other side of the berm and Jamie didn't do something, the guys would probably have come to blows.

"I don't have a good idea because there aren't any," Colonel said. "We can't get in a firefight with these guys. We don't have the weapons."

"That's what I thought," A-Rad said. "You don't have any ideas. You want to cut and run. At least I'm willing to get shot at if it'll get us in."

"We've heard enough of your ideas," Colonel said. "Why don't you stick to what you're good at? Oh, that's right. You aren't good at anything."

"I'll remember that the next time you need a plane ride."

"You're not the only one who knows how to fly. I was flying missions when you were in diapers," Colonel said.

"My point exactly. You're too old. You're past your prime. Your better days are behind you. That's why you're afraid of my plan. It might work."

"Guys!" Jamie said, trying not to say it too loud. "Will you two knock it off? We got better things to do than sit around fighting with each other. A-Rad is right about one thing. If you don't like his plan, Colonel, what do you propose we do?"

"I propose we parachute in."

"Oh, for heaven's sake," A-Rad said laughingly. "And you thought my plan was dumb."

"Hear me out," Colonel said in a severe tone. "We do a low altitude jump. Onto the roof of the building. That way, we have the high ground. From the roof, we can pick off the guards when they come running toward the commotion. That's when Jamie and Bond can drive the truck and open the gate. Take out whatever guards hang around. Most will come running to the house."

"That's the dumbest thing I've ever heard," A-Rad said.

"This will work," Colonel said.

"Do you see a helicopter anywhere?" A-Rad said. "Are you a magician who's going to produce one out of thin air?"

"A-Rad is right," Jamie said. "We don't have a helicopter. Or parachutes. Or assault rifles."

"We'll go back to Turkey and get them."

"We don't have any money," A-Rad said.

"I can get MI6 to supply them," Bond said. He was now standing next to them. "If I tell them what we're doing, they'll provide them in a heartbeat."

"Assuming we can get a helicopter, how many of us have ever done a low altitude jump?" Jamie asked.

"I have," Bond said.

"So have I," the Colonel said.

"Me too," A-Rad chimed in.

Jamie remembered hers like they were yesterday. "Curly made me do a few at the farm. But that was years ago."

She didn't want to tell them she almost broke her neck.

"You can drive the truck," Colonel said to Jamie.

"No. If you guys are going to jump, so will I," she said. "Maybe MI6 can supply a couple of men to drive the truck and even the odds in the gunfight."

"Does this mean we're going to do it?" Colonel said.

"I guess so. Although... I think I like A-Rad's plan better," Jamie said under her breath.

18

The hearing in front of Judge Georgia Smithson took all of five minutes. Fuller's lawyer did most of the talking, and Judge Smithson asked a few questions for the record. Her ruling was two sentences long.

"The Plaintiff's emergency motion and the relief requested is granted," Judge Smithson said in a regal voice. "All assets of AJAX corporation are hereby ordered transferred to the TITAN Corporation."

Fuller liked the name. The International Trade Art Network. TITAN. It represented who he was. A titan of industry. Arguably, the second most powerful man in Washington was now one of the most powerful men in commerce. He now owned a corporation with more than two billion dollars in cash and another billion in tangible assets.

"Anything else, Counselor?" Judge Smithson asked Fuller's lawyer.

"Yes, your honor. We ask that all records from this hearing be sealed."

"Reason?"

"National Security interests."

"Granted."

With the pounding of a gavel, it was done. It would take an act of congress for anyone ever to see what transpired in the courtroom that day. Now, Fuller had the green light to do whatever he wanted. The beauty of his well-orchestrated plan was that he was covered from every angle. His predecessor at the CIA was the one who set up the AJAX program. He was simply taking it over.

Running AJAX was within his power as the Director of the CIA. He'd have been negligent if he hadn't taken down AJAX considering the wrongdoing he'd uncovered from Jamie Austen and Alex Halee.

Judge Smithson had also now signed off on the seizing and transfer of assets. That gave him the additional cover he needed. A federal judge was all-powerful. The Fourth Circuit Court of Appeals was the only one who could overturn the transaction.

That was never going to happen.

Besides, who'd be around to challenge it? Alex Halee and Jamie Austen wouldn't be able to. They worked at the whim of the Director of the CIA. He was well within his rights to shut down AJAX if he chose to. The only person who could undo that was the President. And why would he? He had appointed Fuller. Why would he undermine him on a matter that didn't concern him?

Fuller knew it would never come to that.

Halee was powerless to do anything about it. And what would his argument be? That he should personally benefit from the assets? That the assets were his personally? He didn't pay taxes on them. That'd open him up to tax evasion charges. Fuller was satisfied that Halee and Austen were in a box.

Soon in a pine box, six feet under the ground. Or dumped in a South American jungle. He didn't care what was done with them as long as they disappeared.

The spirit of the AJAX program would live on. Just under a different corporate name. Because of the sensitivity of the program and the covert operations, Fuller would now oversee it. Not Brad. Not August. The only oversight of TITAN would be by him.

He'd see to it that no government money ever flowed into TITAN. That way, the operations would be entirely outside Congress' scrutiny. The cyber team could keep hacking into the financial accounts of criminals around the world and stealing their money. He would watch his growing empire with unbridled joy.

More importantly, he now has a corporation for influence peddling. Powerful men in other countries could purchase services from TITAN in exchange for access to him. His son could serve on boards of other companies and be duly compensated for filling that position. The positions would be figurehead only. His imbecile son didn't have the skills to contribute anything of value to multinational corporations. What his son did have was Fuller's good name. Which they'd use to build TITAN into a powerhouse corporation.

He'd also have a place to launder money. Foreign actors could donate money to his presidential campaign in a roundabout way without it having to be reported to election officials. Taking money from a non US citizen for a federal election was illegal. In this instance, TITAN could take in the donations under the guise of a business transaction. Then his corporation could set up the super pac to pay for his campaign ads.

The opportunities were endless.

Not that it'd be all business and no play. What's the point of having power and money if you can't enjoy it?

Fuller had a Gulfstream jet at his disposal. And an island. He could hardly believe it. He'd already made arrangements to have the yacht taken to the island immediately. It'd be docked there permanently outside the watchful eyes of authorities in the states.

He'd already had dreams about the wild orgies he could have on the island. They could even bring in younger girls from all over the world. Fly them in on his plane and pay them for their services.

He could wine and dine the richest men in the world who had the same propensity for young women. They would be out of the watchful eye of any legal authority. He had looked it up. No one had jurisdiction over that island.

The closest countries were Venezuela and Columbia. That was laughable. What would the dictators of those countries do about it? Nothing. The two countries that were the closest wouldn't give a hoot what he did on that island. Or the age of the girls he engaged. They were much more involved with their own money laundering and drug trades than a sketchy business on a tiny island. If push came to shove, he could offer to look the other way on their misdeeds. Or take the opposite approach and strong arm them. Threaten to put them out of business.

He had a lot of cards to play.

His cronies would be swooning at his feet to get an invitation to the luxurious, decadent paradise. He already had a woman in mind who could act as the madam and recruit the young girls.

Waves of desire swept over him just thinking about it. He could hardly wait to get to the island and fulfill some of his darkest, most illicit fantasies.

It'd be a lot better than the tryst he just had with the judge in chambers, who was enthusiastic but had a few miles on her tires. The sex was worth the favor, for sure. A small price to pay for such a monumental acquisition.

Judge Smithson smiled warmly as the business was concluded and she left the bench. He made a mental note to himself to send flowers to her home. Always a good idea to keep in her good graces. You couldn't put a price tag on having a federal judge who would rubber-stamp your activities.

After the hearing, Fuller went back to the attorney's offices and executed the documents.

The corporation and bank accounts were already established and only required his signatures.

His attorney, Lawrence Weigman explained things to him. "We will take the judge's order and these documents down to the bank and have the accounts unfrozen. The money will be transferred immediately."

"Excellent," Fuller said, rubbing his hands together.

"Here are the quit-claim deeds to Alex Halee and Jamie Austen's home in Virginia and the AJAX office building in Alexandria. Also to the yacht and plane."

Fuller signed them swiftly. He now wished he hadn't trashed the house with his search, but what was done was done, and he had more money than he knew what to do with, so repairs were a nonissue. The house needed renovations anyway.

He would immediately fire all the guards and hire new ones. He'd have the locks changed and a new security system in place by sundown. He probably wouldn't use the house much, but the house and acreage would be a good start to the portfolio of properties he intended to buy.

"I wonder why Halee and Austen didn't put their personal residence in their own names?" Weigman asked.

"I don't know," Fuller said. "It wasn't smart. I can't believe we didn't find any personal assets."

"Alex and Jamie didn't have anything in their names other than a couple of personal bank accounts," his accountant, Thomas Seppala, said. "From what I could gather, they lived on a modest salary from AJAX. Less than what the CIA was paying them."

"Did you find any wrongdoing?" Fuller asked.

"Nothing. The books are as clean as a newly groomed showpoodle."

"There has to be something they did that was out of line," Fuller said.

"I'm telling you there's nothing. We've been over the accounts and the books with a fine-toothed comb, and those two are as pure as a couple of choir boys."

"I was a choir boy, and I wasn't very pure," Fuller said with a hearty laugh.

"I don't doubt that one bit," Seppala said with a grin.

That was as close as he'd ever seen Seppala engage in humorous banter. Fuller's experience was that accountants were as dry and serious as a heart attack.

Fuller wasn't worried that the accountant didn't find anything. Now that he had access to the accounts and the records, he could doctor them to show dirty money flowing in and out. It only took one questionable transaction to prove wrongdoing on Alex and Jamie's part.

It didn't matter anyway. That was only for insurance. The two of them would never step foot in America again. If all went as planned, they'd be out of the picture altogether.

Fuller had finalized that part of the plan as well. He sat back in his chair with a wide grin on his face. He'd use Ladislao and Escobar Santos to make Alex and Jamie disappear. The Santos's were two brothers who ran one of the largest drug cartels in Central America.

Alex and Curly ran a mission in Costa Rica and wiped out Santos's operations in the area. They killed a lot of his men, destroyed millions of dollars worth of drugs, and siphoned millions of dollars more out of his bank accounts.

He sent word to them through back channels and arranged a call which he took after the hearing on his way to the lawyer's office.

"I know who stole the money from you," Fuller said to Escobar Santos. "I have the man in custody. Do you want him?"

He didn't have Alex but would shortly.

"How do I know I can trust you?" Santos asked.

"You have my word."

"The word of my enemy."

"Let's just say we have a mutual enemy. You'll be doing me a service. In return, I'll look the other way on your operations. Play a little misdirection. I'll notify you the next time one of your shipments is compromised."

"Who is this man?" Santos asked.

"I'd rather not say."

Better to keep Halee's name out of it. It was a federal crime to out a CIA officer's name.

"Where is this man?" asked Santos.

"In Panama. I'll be in touch. We'll arrange a handoff."

"How do I know you won't double-cross me?"

"You set the terms of the exchange. I'll see that they're followed. Just don't touch my men."

He didn't want an incident that would screw up the whole thing.

They finalized the plans. Fuller called Kyle Kelly as soon as he hung up the phone. "Are you all set?" he asked.

"My team is ready. We're moving on the target this afternoon."

"Not in the evening?"

"It's just one man. He'll be no match for my team," Kelly replied in a cocky tone.

"Don't underestimate the target. He has skills," Fuller said to drive home the point.

"So do I."

"He is the foremost assassin in the world."

The conventional wisdom was that Halee and Austen were one and two when it came to skilled operatives. Which was why he had to get rid of them. He'd have to sleep with one eye open every night if he didn't.

"I'd like to think that I'm the foremost assassin in the world," Kelly said.

"Then prove it, Kelly."

Fuller hung up the phone.

He hoped Kelly was right and they could capture or kill Halee on the island and the transaction with Santos would be unnecessary. As much as he'd like to see Alex Halee suffer in a South American jungle and die a slow and painful death, sooner rather than later was better.

He hung up the phone satisfied that Halee was no longer a problem. Now what was he going to do about Jamie Austen?

The last he heard, she was still on the loose, and from what he'd been told, even more dangerous than Halee.

19

Alex made his decision. He needed to get off the island.

Pok would give up his location. That's what he would do if he were in the same situation. Pok had to know that Alex wouldn't stop until he could get his hands on him and kill him. The only hope Pok had would be for Fuller to arrest Alex and put him away. The only way to do that would be to give Fuller his location.

At any time, Alex expected a swarm of FBI agents, or special forces personnel, to appear on the horizon, land on the island, and try to take him back to Washington. He sat on a lounge chair by the pool, staring off into that very horizon, wondering how long it'd take Fuller to make his move.

His gun was on the table next to his iced soda.

He almost wished Fuller would get on with it. If he didn't, Alex would get back on his plane and go back to Washington anyway. To defend himself. To protect his home, business, and assets. To be there for Jamie.

Alex almost preferred that he be captured on the island. In an ironic and strange twist of fate, Pok had actually done Alex a favor. All evidence of wrongdoing was gone, scrubbed from the computers and hard drives. Fuller would come to the island expecting to find bank accounts and proof of activity not reported to the CIA as required by the agreement with AJAX.

None would be found.

Alex would be cleared.

Not that he considered his activities wrong in any way. Everything they did made the world a safer place. It wasn't done for personal gain, and all the money stolen was taken from vicious fat cats, terrorists, pirates, drug runners, and sex traffickers. Admittedly, they ran the operations at the island outside the purview of the CIA so they could operate with more freedom and impunity.

What was wrong with that? The whole purpose of AJAX was so Alex and Jamie could run operations that the CIA couldn't. With a wink and a nod. Everyone knew what they were doing.

Was it illegal? Unfortunately, the answer to that question was yes.

So what. The CIA was involved in illegal activities every day of the year. Spying on other countries and wiretapping America's enemies was illegal. But that didn't stop them. The CIA even spied on its allies. Traveling to foreign countries on a fake passport was a crime. Recruiting double agents was against the law in those countries— considered treason. The crime was punishable by death in most countries.

If anyone knew Fuller pilfered CIA assets to put a ten million dollar hit out on Jamie, that information would land him in jail. But only if Alex could ever prove it. That didn't stop Fuller's despicable actions. He'd done so to make a name for himself and be named CIA director.

Alex had never done anything remotely close to Fuller's activities for personal gain.

The thought of Fuller's despicable endeavors made Alex's hair stand on end. The peaceful, idyllic blue water he was looking out at could not calm the stirring anger inside of him.

How did a man like Fuller get in a position of judging someone like Alex? What gave him the right to steal all of Alex's property that he'd worked so hard to attain? Fuller was no better than the crooks Alex and Jamie took out of circulation. Alex considered Fuller worse because he was operating under the well-respected government division of the CIA. His behavior was despicable.

Most importantly, America and her allies were less safe because of Fuller's actions.

Fuller got what he wanted. The damage was done. The lab on the island was closed indefinitely. AJAX was effectively shut down as well. Something that irked him to no end. Jamie was probably lurking in the shadows like a tiger about to pounce on a prey. She was no doubt livid at the sudden turn of events.

How many young girls would remain in sex trafficking because of Fuller's greed and lack of conscience? Alex could barely stand the thought and knew Jamie's hair would be on fire the moment she got wind of the situation. If Fuller and Jamie were in the same room when Jamie found out, he wasn't sure Fuller would make it out alive.

Alex wanted to get on his plane himself, fly back to Washington D.C., wrap his hands around Fuller's neck, and strangle the man. If he was going to go to jail, it should be for a crime he actually committed.

That's what Curly would do. Maybe not in that way. But Curly wouldn't hide. He'd face Fuller and take the threat head-on.

Alex downed the last of his soda and decided to go in the house, and packed his things. With a new resolve to go back to Washington and confront Fuller. Take the bull by the horns and throw him to the ground like a rodeo hand.

As he stood to his feet, he heard a sound in the distance. He recognized it immediately. A helicopter. He heard it before he saw it, mostly because he was looking in the wrong direction.

The helicopter was barely skimming above the water. Traveling at a high rate of speed.

Alex had designed a radar system to detect incoming threats by air or by sea. If he had been in the computer lab, he'd hear sirens going off.

The helicopter buzzed right past him, banked hard, and came in for a landing on the runway next to his plane.

Within seconds, half a dozen men armed with submachine guns emptied out of the helicopter with speed and precision. Their assault rifles were in the ready-to-fire position.

They ran toward him with guns raised.

Apparently, they didn't intend to kill him. At least not now. Not here. Fuller must have other plans for him.

Alex couldn't help but grin.

All this was for his benefit.

Fuller could have called him, and he would have turned himself in. He made no move for his gun. He certainly didn't intend to fire on American soldiers who were only following Fuller's orders. He held his hands out in front of him. They needed to see that he was not a threat to them.

He walked casually toward the men. They were sprinting toward him, shouting instructions.

"On the ground! Now! Spreadeagle," one of the soldiers yelled.

Alex stopped walking and held his ground. He wasn't about to lie on the ground like a dog. He'd at least make them work for it.

Two of them kept coming at him and tackled him to the ground.

"Hey," he protested. "What are you doing? This isn't necessary. I'm cooperating."

He didn't resist, although every ounce of his being wanted to.

One of the men sat on top of him with his knee on Alex's back. The other had a grip on one wrist and was bending his arm backward.

Alex could barely get a word out due to the pressure on his back.

When he caught his breath, he said, "I'm not resisting. You can let me up. I'll go with you peacefully."

No one said anything. A third guy grabbed Alex's other arm and twisted it backward. Alex had endured far more pain before, but it wasn't pleasant. The man on his back released his knee so Alex's two wrists could be restrained with zip ties. Once secured, they yanked Alex to his feet.

The soldiers turned Alex around, and he was face to face with a man about his height and weight. Military haircut. Armed to the hilt with a handgun, taser, baton, two knives on his belt, an assault rifle over his shoulder, and one gun pointed directly at Alex. A smug smile on his face as well.

"Very impressive takedown, soldier," Alex said.

He assumed the man he faced was the one in charge.

"I'm not impressed," the man said. "You're supposed to be some kind of elite assassin. It seems to me you've lost your touch."

"I can be lethal when I want to be."

"Doesn't look like you're very tough right now. I'm a little disappointed you didn't put up a fight. I was looking forward to some action."

"I didn't see you taking me down. Your men did all the dirty work. I've met a lot of guys like you over the years. You talk tough, but you let the other guys do the fighting for you. Take these zip ties off me, and let me have a go at you. You and me. If you win, I'll leave peacefully. If I win, you'll take your men back to whatever fox hole you crawled out of."

Alex was talking trash, but he really did respect the man. He was only doing his job and had probably taken great risks for his country on the battlefield. Under different circumstances, they could probably be friends and swap stories.

The man got right into Alex's face.

"I have orders to take you in."

Alex was defiant. "The Uniform Code of Military Justice Article 90 says that you are obligated to follow all lawful orders. It is a dereliction of duty to follow unlawful orders. Which this one is. I have not committed a crime."

"I don't care whether you have or have not committed a crime. That's above my paygrade. I swore an oath to protect the United States against all enemies, foreign and domestic. Apparently, you ticked off the wrong people back in the United States, and you are now a domestic enemy. My job is to bring you in dead or alive. Your choice."

"I prefer to be brought in alive. Thank you very much."Alex said.

The commander motioned to his men. Two of them grabbed Alex by the arm and led him back toward the helicopter.

"Do you mind if we go a little later?" Alex asked. "My favorite television show is coming on. Gilligan's Island. Have you ever seen it?"

"You're a funny guy," the man said.

"What's your name?" Alex asked.

The name on his fatigues was Kelly.

"Senior Officer Kyle Kelly."

"Pleased to make your acquaintance, Senior Officer Kelly. Sorry, it was under these circumstances. Where are you taking me? I don't think this helicopter has the range to make it back to the United States. Why don't we take my jet? It's stocked with food. I've got a pilot. We can travel in style."

"Why don't you just shut up and do what you're told?" Kelly replied angrily.

Alex had already loosened the restraints. They were about to fall off. He kept them on, so they wouldn't know he was about to break free. He contemplated resisting but decided against it. It would take all of his self-control not to kill a member of this special forces assault squad sent to take him in. No matter how obnoxious they were, he wouldn't take any of them out.

Alex glanced toward the compound that had served AJAX well until Pok threw a wrench in the works. He saw Radar and his pilot taken out of the computer building and put on the concrete with their hands secured behind their backs. He hoped neither would have to pay too high a price for their loyalty to AJAX and all the good they had accomplished.

As the helicopter took off, Alex wondered where they were taking him. Information was scant which was no surprise. He wasn't given a headset purposefully, so he couldn't hear the communications.

He could read lips.

They were taking him to Panama.

That's a good thing.

From Panama, they would take him back to the States. There he would wage his battle with Fuller and win.

20

"If any one of you wants to drop out of this mission, you can do so now," Jamie said. She had called the team together to discuss their options. There didn't seem to be many viable ones.

She could feel the emotions welling up inside of her. The seriousness of her situation was hitting her all at once. Fuller was systematically destroying everything she and Alex had worked so hard to build back home. She didn't know the full extent of the damage but her imagination was leading her to think the worst.

Here in the field, they'd reached a dead end, and it didn't look like they had a way to breach Zakarov's compound. Jamie was determined to do so, even if she had to do it alone. She couldn't ask the team to follow her over a cliff like a group of lemmings. The purpose of the meeting was to feel out the group's mood.

"You know that's not how it works," Colonel said emphatically. "I don't want to speak for anybody else, but I'm with you until you say we're done."

"Me, too," A-Rad said. "All for one and one for all. Or something like that. We're the three musketeers."

He raised his hand to high-five everybody, but Jamie was the only one who hit his hand.

Bond didn't say anything. He didn't have to. She knew he was just as committed as the others.

"I think we just want to understand the big picture," Colonel said. "Is capturing Zakarov worth the risk? Over some paintings?"

"When I start something, I want to finish it," Jamie said. "Besides, it's not just about paintings. Zakarov funds terrorists. He's a thorn in Israel's side. We need to bring him down."

"Then Israel should help," Bond said.

Jamie nodded in agreement.

"They should, but they can't. They'll give us operational support, but they can't supply us with men or with a military helicopter. They were adamant that this operation can't be traced back to them."

Jamie had called Saul Geller, a contact with Mossad. Saul was the head of the Duvdevan Unit, Israel's undercover strike unit. Mossad was the Israeli equivalent of the CIA. They specialized in intelligence and counter-terrorism. While Saul was highly interested in what they were doing, he needed time to coordinate and get approval to operate in a foreign country.

"How much time?" Jamie asked him.

"A couple of months."

She didn't have that long, she explained. Saul offered what support he could.

"Mossad is providing us with parachutes and weapons," Jamie said. "That's all they're willing to do at the moment. If we get Zakarov in custody, that changes things. They're all in and will move heaven and earth to extract him and us from Uzbekistan."

She stood to stretch her legs. They'd been sitting around a fire. They'd probably have to spend another night sleeping in the truck and SUV.

Jamie continued. "As soon as I give them the word, they'll organize a drop. They're also willing to take Clement off our hands and hold him until we decide what to do with him."

Clement was locked up in the back of the truck with the paintings.

"That's just great," Colonel said. "They'll let us get shot at, then take the credit for capturing him."

"We don't have a helicopter. What good will the parachutes do us?" Bond asked the obvious question.

Jamie knew why they'd be skeptical. This wasn't how missions ordinarily went down. Usually, they had time to plan. To organize. They also usually had the full weight of the CIA and AJAX corporations behind them.

At the moment, they had nothing but the four of them. And limited resources. Bond was right. The assault rifles would be helpful, but the parachutes were worthless without a helicopter or plane to jump from.

"At least that's more than your friends in London are willing to do," Colonel said to Bond. "I thought you still had some pull there."

Bond had received a similar response from MI6. They weren't willing to provide a military helicopter either. Otherwise, they'd do anything they could to help.

"They'll give us a couple of freelancers to drive the truck in for a price. We'll have to pay them. They won't come cheap.

That caused Jamie to let out another sigh. She wasn't sure she'd be able to pay them. All of her assets were tied up by Fuller.

"I do have an idea," Colonel said hesitantly. "But you're not going to like it."

He tilted his head to the side when he said it, staring right at Jamie.

"Is it better than my idea?" A-Rad said jokingly, poking Colonel on the shoulder. He was kidding, and there were no hard feelings from their previous verbal scuffle. Jamie liked that about her team. They were passionate and willing to speak their minds. Even go toe to toe when necessary. When the argument was over, it was over. Anger and resentment didn't linger around for very long. No use going into a firefight mad at the person you might need to save your life.

"Anything is better than your idea," Colonel said with a tone clearly meant to let A-Rad know that he didn't want him to be offended or get defensive.

"Lay it on us," A-Rad said. "Let's hear your Colonel of truth."

Uncharacteristically, A-Rad started laughing at his joke. "Do you get it? Colonel of truth."

"We got it A-Rad," Colonel said. "It wasn't funny."

"It was kind of funny," Jamie said, with a smile on her face.

"Do you know what happened when a soldier ran over a bag of popcorn?" Bond asked with his own smirk.

"No," Colonel said, "but I have a feeling you're going to tell us."

"He killed two kernels."

That got a hearty laugh. More than the joke warranted. The tension had been as thick as a bowl of lumpy gravy made with too much flour. Jamie was glad for the banter. The apprehension was lifting somewhat.

"That was a good one," she said.

"How long have you been waiting to tell that corny joke?" Colonel asked Bond.

"Just thought of it."

"Why am I not surprised?"

"What's your idea, Colonel?" Jamie said. "Give it to us since we're fresh out."

"As you know, I ran a lot of missions in Afghanistan. The Afghanistan border is not far from here."

The guys let out a groan. They'd heard enough Afghanistan mission stories to fill up the hard drive on a computer.

"You're right," Jamie said. "I don't think I'm going to like this."

"Hear me out," Colonel said. " It's about six hours as the crow flies."

He pointed toward the southeast.

"Where are you going with this?" Bond asked. "Please don't suggest that we go to Afghanistan!"

162

"The Afghans have a base just across the border in Herat. It's right at the border with Iran. As I said, it's pretty close."

"You've got to be kidding me!" A-Rad said. "You want us to drive to Afghanistan. Through hostile territory. Have you lost your mind?"

Jamie thought she knew where Colonel was going with this but kept her mouth shut.

He continued undeterred. "When the U.S. left Afghanistan, they left behind about seventy-five MD 530 helicopters."

"Are you suggesting we go to Afghanistan and steal a helicopter?" Bond asked.

"No. Let me finish. Right before the fall of the Afghan government, satellite images showed that a number of those helicopters were flown out of Afghanistan. Anybody want to venture a guess where they were taken?"

"Iran?" A-Rad answered.

The Colonel made a buzzer sound.

"Wrong! They were taken to a base in Uzbekistan. About ninety miles from here."

"Are you serious?" Jamie asked.

"Dead serious. Some of them might still be there. I've seen that base. I think we can get inside it."

"Are the birds still operational?" Bond asked. "I thought the U.S. sabotaged them so they wouldn't fly."

"That was propaganda to appease the folks back home. I don't know what shape they're in now. They were working when they left Afghanistan. Obviously, since they were flown from there to the base in Uzbekistan. I say we go check 'em out."

"This is crazy," A-Rad said, shaking his head.

"You don't like my idea?" Colonel asked. "When we get there, you can run in front of the guards and draw their fire if you want. Would you like that better?"

"I love the idea," A-Rad said with a massive grin on his face. "I paid for that helicopter with my taxpayer money. It belongs to me. I want it back."

"Can you fly an MD 530?" Colonel asked A-Rad.

"There ain't been a bird built that I can't fly."

"Don't you think we should go back home and regroup?" Bond asked. "We can get our own helicopter. Without having to fight for it."

"I don't know that I have anything to go home to," Jamie said.

Her voice cracked as she said it. The tears welled up in her eyes again. She pushed them off her cheeks roughly when a couple escaped.

"This may be our last mission together," Jamie said.

"Don't say that," A-Rad said, putting an arm on Jamie's shoulder to comfort her.

She let him.

"I have no idea what Fuller is up to," Jamie said. "I haven't heard from Alex. He could be in prison somewhere. Or dead... Who knows?"

"Don't say that. Alex is just lying low. Like us. Trying to figure out what to do," A-Rad said.

"All the more reason to go back," Bond said. "To find out what's going on."

"I can't go back," Jamie said. "Not yet. I know it's probably complete madness, but if we can capture Zakarov and secure the paintings, that'll put pressure on Fuller. If I can come home a hero, so to speak, then he might not be able to touch me."

"You're already a hero in our eyes," A-Rad said.

"And in the eyes of the CIA. Anybody who doesn't think so is a fool," Colonel said.

"Amen to that," Bond said. "You don't have to prove yourself to anyone."

The words warmed her heart but did nothing to make the angst go away.

"Maybe not. But what if this is my last mission? Ever. I don't want it to fail. I need to go out on top. Does that make sense to you guys?

Maybe it doesn't. It's stupid, I know. But it's how I feel. I have to leave knowing I did everything I could to make the world a better place."

"We're with you," Colonel said.

The three of them crowded around her in a group hug.

"So it's decided," Jamie said. "We're going to go steal a helicopter."

She wasn't sure how they were going to infiltrate an airbase and steal a helicopter, but they'd somehow figure it out.

21

The Uzbekistan airbase was in the middle of nowhere. It contained one hanger and a runway. The MD 530 U.S.-made helicopters were lined up in a row at the far end of the runway, fortuitously away from the tower, hangar, and barracks where the guards were probably sleeping.

Jamie counted seventeen helicopters. Colonel gave a further explanation of how they ended up in Uzbekistan.

"When the U.S. troops left Afghanistan, the Taliban moved in and filled the power vacuum. They didn't want the Afghan government to seize the choppers, so they flew them to Uzbekistan. The agreement was that they'd be returned once the Taliban gained control on the ground."

"I take it, the Uzi's double-crossed them," Jamie said, "which is why they're still here."

"You got it," Colonel said.

"Do you think they're operational?" A-Rad asked.

"We're going to find out," he said.

They were positioned by the last helicopter in line. The one furthest away from the tower. Colonel walked all the way around the copter, then he examined the engine and rotors.

He could do so because no one was watching from the tower. The only two soldiers they saw were at the main gate on the other side of the buildings and out of their view. The team had intended to cut through the fence on the far end of the base away from all the activity, but it was in such disrepair that they could climb through an opening and get to their position without being seen.

Security was lax, considering this was an air force base. The soldiers manning it clearly weren't worried about intruders.

"As soon as we fire one up," Jamie said, "we're going to have to get out of here in a hurry. We don't know how many soldiers are in the barracks, but they'll hear the noise. I figure it'll take them less than a minute to come running with guns ready to fire."

No one responded. Colonel continued his work. She was simply stating what everyone already knew.

Jamie could tell the men were on edge. As they should be. They were in a foreign country, had infiltrated an air base, and were less than a hundred yards from who knows how many soldiers sleeping next to assault rifles.

At least they were armed now as well. The Israelis had managed to get them assault rifles which were a godsend. And the parachutes, which they would need if they could get one of the helicopters working.

"This one looks good to me," Colonel said after ten minutes of inspecting it. It has fuel, and everything seems to be in working order."

"We don't have a key," Jamie said. "How are we going to start it up?"

"We'll hotwire it," A-Rad said with an all-knowing grin.

"He's kidding. You don't need one," Colonel explained. "Military helicopters don't have keys. Imagine being on a battlefield looking for lost keys. Not practical."

"Kind of crazy that anyone can steal a helicopter at any time," Bond said. "If you know how to get one of these babies off the ground, you can go for a joyride anytime you want. I'm surprised the Taliban haven't come for these and stolen them back."

Bond was an expert pilot as well. He once rescued Alex in London when a bomb was about to explode on a helicopter Alex was piloting. Something Bond reminded Alex of often.

Was it possible they were about to be brought down by one of their own? The Director of the CIA. After all the close calls over the years, it would be ironic, if their careers came to an end because of a corrupt politician.

"A-Rad and Bond, follow me," Colonel said, interrupting her thoughts. He walked to the next helicopter in line, and A-Rad followed, as did Jamie and Bond.

"What are you doing?" she asked.

"I'm going to show Bond and A-Rad how to sabotage the helicopters," Colonel said. "So the next time the Taliban fly one, they'll crash as soon as they reach an altitude above five hundred feet."

"Do we have time for this?" Bond asked nervously.

Jamie wondered the same thing. She kept a watchful eye on the barracks in case someone emerged.

"It won't take long," Colonel said. "I'm going to show you two what to do. That'll make it go three times as fast. I want to make sure they'll never be able to use these helicopters again."

Jamie lagged behind. She lifted her assault rifle and pointed it toward the barracks, even though they hadn't seen or heard anything. At least it made her feel like she was doing something.

After about thirty minutes, the guys came back to her position next to the one helicopter still operational. Or at least she hoped it was. They hadn't actually started it. She couldn't help but voice her concern.

"What if this one doesn't start?" Jamie asked. "Then we're stuck. We won't be able to use any of the others."

"Don't worry. This one will work," Colonel answered.

They'd soon know.

At Colonel's bidding, they all filed into the helicopter. A-Rad in the pilot's seat and Colonel in the copilot's seat. Jamie and Bond in the back. Both doors were off, making it easier for them to fire their weapons should the hostiles emerge from the barracks before they were out of the range of rifle fire.

"Let's pray this thing starts," Jamie said.

Colonel glanced back with a nod of the head and began to give A-Rad starting instructions.

"I'm going to walk you through it," he said. "One step at a time. It's like riding a bike. You might be on a different brand, but the concept is the same."

A-Rad laughed gleefully. He was in his element and loving every minute of it. Jamie didn't share his enthusiasm and wouldn't feel comfortable until they were out of there and back on the ground out in the middle of the desert.

Even then, she had the low altitude jump to worry about and the inevitable firefight upcoming at Zakarov's compound. If she allowed herself to think about all of it, the whole mission could seem overwhelming.

Colonel flicked on the cabin light. He must've anticipated what Jamie was thinking because he turned toward the back and said, "Can't be helped. We need to see the controls."

"Press Key On button," Colonel said, then waited.

"Check," A-Rad replied.

"Red Fuel button pressed in. Battery on."

From her vantage point, she could see A-Rad touching the controls.

"Check. Check."

Jamie was amazed at the skills of her team. She couldn't imagine having a better group of guys in the proverbial foxhole. If this was her last mission, she was glad it was with them. The only thing better would be if Alex were with them.

"Throttle should be in cut-off position," Colonel said like a coach calling plays.

"Check," A-Rad said.

Colonel took a deep and nervous-sounding breath.

"Don't do it yet, but the next thing you'll do is push the starter button and hold for five seconds. When N1 reaches twelve percent, open the throttle twist grip until the engine light goes off and watch the TOT. Pressure should immediately rise to about seven sixty celsius. Don't let the engine start temp go above nine twenty, or it'll kill the engine, and you won't be able to restart it, and Jamie won't be happy with you."

The instructions were over her head. She'd heard them before but didn't know what they meant.

"This isn't my first rodeo," A-Rad said.

He practiced moving the hand controls and she could hear the foot pedals moving as well.

"I know," Colonel said. "I'm just reminding you. When you're ready, increase the throttle until it reaches idle detent. You'll hear the throttle collar click."

"Like I said, I've flown a helicopter before," A-Rad said testily. "Not this one, but it can't be much different than the others."

"All right. I'm just trying to help," Colonel said.

A-Rad looked back at Jamie. "Are you ready?"

"I was ready thirty minutes ago," she said.

"Here goes everybody," A-Rad said like he was getting ready to take everyone on a sightseeing trip. "It's show time!"

A-Rad reached toward the controls and pushed the starter button, and held it. The engine roared to life, and the rotors began to turn. Since they'd been in almost dead silence for nearly an hour, the roar of the engine and rotors was deafening.

A-Rad let out a whoop and a holler. Jamie expelled a breath she didn't realize she'd been holding. She looked nervously at the barracks. Still no sign of trouble.

The helicopter began to lift off the ground. It shook and tilted slightly. The tail began to lift and the nose dived toward the ground.

Jamie choked back a scream. She began to voice a prayer, hoping it wasn't too late.

"Pull it forward!" Colonel shouted.

"Sorry," she heard A-Rad say.

The helicopter rocked back and forth. A-Rad was struggling to hold it in place. They were only ten to twelve feet off the ground. Jamie wondered if she could survive a jump or would be better off going down with the ship, so to speak.

"Hold her steady," Colonel said. "Give it more throttle."

The helicopter did steady and slowly lifted off. Jamie could hear the groans of the metal and wondered how long it'd been since it'd been flown.

It hovered above the ground and then stalled its ascent. She could see A-Rad strain to get it to rise.

"Come on, baby," she heard Colonel or A-Rad say. The noise in the cabin was so deafening she wasn't sure which one said it. Jamie had been on helicopters before, and this one wasn't responding like they usually did.

This might not have been such a good idea.

To make matters worse, the first soldiers emerged from the barracks. She didn't hear the gunfire but saw the sparks come out of the guns.

A bullet clanged off the metal and Jamie let out a scream.

"We're taking fire," she shouted above the din.

"We need to get going!" Bond said excitedly.

"I know!" A-Rad shouted. "I see them."

The soldiers on the ground were within range, but the helicopter was rocking from side to side so getting off a shot at the soldiers wasn't possible.

Fortunately, the men on the ground were still in a sleeping stupor and were firing wildly. Spraying bullets their direction, but none of the soldiers had taken time to aim before they fired. Jamie wanted to get a good shot off so they'd scatter back inside, but she couldn't aim and fire either. If she took her seat belt off and leaned out the helicopter, the odds were high that she'd plunge to the ground.

"Hit it!" she heard Colonel say to A-Rad.

The helicopter suddenly accelerated. Still low to the ground but steadier. Away from the soldiers and out of the range of fire.

"Good job, A-Rad," Colonel said.

"Let's see what this baby will do," A-Rad said.

Unexpectedly, he banked hard to the left, throwing Jamie back into her seat. He was heading in the opposite direction she had expected him to go. They were flying back toward the barracks.

"What are you doing?" Bond shouted angrily.

No response from the Colonel or A-Rad. They both gripped the controls and stared straight ahead.

They flew over the soldiers, and A-Rad banked hard to the right this time. He did a nifty twirl and then hovered over a field just off the runway. Jamie could see the soldiers on the ground sprinting toward the other helicopters.

One by one, the rotor blades of each bird began to spin.

A-Rad maintained their position about two hundred and fifty feet off the ground.

He suddenly accelerated again and flew at a high rate of speed directly at the helicopters still on the runway. He buzzed them.

Jamie thought she knew what he was doing but still wanted to wring his neck. He was trying to bait them into following them.

A-Rad circled the airfield.

The first helicopter on the ground lifted off and began flying toward them. A-Rad skillfully turned the bird and started to fly away. Jamie strained her neck to look behind to see if the helicopter was giving chase.

What she saw was petrifying. All sixteen were in the air now. Flying toward them.

A-Rad began to climb but maintained his speed. The helicopters were gaining on them. He appeared to be letting them.

A-Rad was laughing almost maniacally. Colonel kept looking in every direction. Like a wingman. Straight ahead. Then behind them. To the right and to the left. His jaw was clenched, and eyes set in steely resolve.

A-Rad abruptly banked again and began flying back toward the base. The other helicopters followed.

"You're at six hundred feet," Colonel said. They were now directly over the base.

One of the helicopters caught up and was beside them now. Jamie could almost reach out and touch the men in the back who had assault rifles. She pointed her weapon at them, and they banked sharply to get away from her.

When they did, the other helicopter suddenly began to spin violently. About twenty seconds later, it slammed to the ground. A-Rad shouted a roar of approval.

Another helicopter was spinning uncontrollably. It plunged to the ground as well.

A-Rad laughed hysterically while continuing to operate the control. He seemed to have a method to his madness.

Another helicopter fell to the ground and exploded in a fireball. One after the other did the same thing. Several landed on the barracks, and the hangar, destroying the buildings. Jamie now knew why A-Rad had led them over the base.

After the last one hit the ground, he turned south and accelerated away. The trip back to where their truck was hidden took about thirty minutes. They rode in silence.

Jamie was fuming. While it turned out okay, she felt like they'd taken an unnecessary risk.

In the darkness, they had to circle several times before they found the truck. When they did, A-Rad set the bird down, and they all exited the helicopter.

A-Rad was the last to exit the bird. Jamie pushed in the chest, knocking him backward.

"Was that necessary?" she growled. "You could've gotten us killed."

"It wasn't my idea," A-Rad said.

"Who's idea was it then?" she asked roughly.

"Colonel told me to do it. He wanted to see if our plan worked. And it did."

He looked over when A-Rad mentioned his name.

"Don't you think you should've run it by me first?" Jamie asked him.

He shrugged his shoulders and started examining the helicopter for damage.

Jamie wanted to protest further, but a black Mercedes SUV with darkened windows was headed straight for their position.

22

The dark Mercedes SUV approached slowly. The headlights flashed twice in quick succession. The vehicle came to a stop a short distance away. The passenger door opened, and a dark male figure emerged. He began walking toward them. The man appeared unarmed. Jamie had her weapon pointed at him, as did Bond, Colonel, and A-Rad.

They were all on edge and itching to use them if he made one wrong move. The headlights were blinding in their eyes. Jamie raised her hand to her eyes to shield it so she could get a better look at the person.

When he came out of the shadows, Jamie recognized him immediately. "That's a good way to get shot," Jamie said to Saul Geller, a director with Mossad.

She lowered her weapon while Colonel, Bond, and A-Rad kept theirs fixed on the man.

"We're here to give you some help," he said. "Do you mind?"

Geller was referring to the weapons still pointed at him. Jamie told the guys they could lower them.

He then motioned to the vehicle. Two men stepped out of the SUV.

Bond, A-Rad, and Colonel reacted by raising their weapons again.

"They're with me," Saul said.

"You should've called first," Jamie said somewhat roughly. "We might've fired and asked questions later."

She was already on edge from the incident with the helicopters at the airbase. A strange vehicle showing up in the middle of the night unannounced had to be considered a threat until proven otherwise.

Her first thought was that the SUV was someone from the CIA to arrest her. The last thing she wanted to do was let them. The next to last thing she wanted to do was kill them. She couldn't imagine firing her weapon at a fellow operative who was only following orders. Even if the orders did come from Fuller.

"I couldn't risk calling you," Saul stated matter of factly. "Communications are being monitored in this area. Apparently, Jamie, you're persona non grata with the CIA. They're looking everywhere for you. I have to assume that they're monitoring all cell phone communications. You should as well. You need to be careful. Even out here in the middle of nowhere."

He looked around as he said it. The desert terrain was quiet and peaceful. Jamie knew that could change at a moment's notice. Sixteen helicopters exploding had probably sent the Uzbekistan armed forces into high alert. Jamie now saw the wisdom of destroying those helicopters.

The men would've followed them. Probably all the way back to their location. As it was, the higher ups were probably busy trying to figure out what had happened.

"Can you tell your men to lower their weapons?" Saul added. "They're making me nervous."

Jamie nodded, and the guys stood down. Saul walked up to them with his hand outstretched.

"I'm Saul Geller. Mossad."

They all shook hands with a nod. They didn't identify themselves or who they were working for. Technically, it would be AJAX. However, Jamie wondered if that was still the case. AJAX may no longer exist for all she knew. In reality, they were working for her. Freelancing. In the middle of the desert.

When she framed it that way in her mind, she wondered why they were there. No one anywhere had given them authority to act in a foreign country against one of their citizens. Much less against the Uzbekistan Air Force in what could be considered an act of war.

She tamped those concerns out of her mind and introduced her men.

"That's A-Rad, Bond, and Colonel. They work for me."

"I know who they are," Saul said.

"How do you know who we are?" Colonel asked roughly. AJAX worked diligently to keep all of its operatives' identities top secret. Jamie wasn't even sure how much Fuller knew about her men.

"It's the Mossad's business to know," Geller said with a stone cold stare.

"Why should we trust you?" Bond asked. "Maybe you're here to turn Jamie in."

Saul shook his head no.

"Jamie's as good as gold in my eyes. If she's got a beef with Fuller, my money's on Jamie being the one who's right. Fuller is low-life scum with no conscience, as far as I'm concerned."

"You're a smart man," Colonel said. "Jamie's done nothing wrong."

She appreciated the support, but had some burning questions in her mind.

"Why are you here, Saul?" she asked. "I thought Mossad didn't want to be involved in this mission."

Was it still a mission if it wasn't authorized?

"Let's just say our interests have changed," Geller said. "Thank you for turning Clement over to us. He's been very talkative."

When Mossad brought them the parachutes and assault rifles, Jamie sent Clement back with them along with the truck and the paintings in it. Geller delivered an empty truck to them that they could use to load the paintings at Zakarov's compound. If there were any remaining.

The second truck was a godsend. Jamie was concerned that Fuller might be aware of the box truck they purchased in Khorog and had people out looking for it. The new one would have a different VIN number license plate and wouldn't have a GPS system that could be traced.

"What did you learn from Clement?" Jamie asked, although she suspected she already knew.

Jamie wasn't surprised that they'd been able to extract intelligence from Clement. Mossad were experts at interrogations. Clement was also easy to break. He seemed to have a low tolerance for pain and would melt at the sight of his own blood.

"You were right about the paintings in the truck," Geller said. "All of them were stolen by Clement. Mossad has little to no interest in most of them. We'll give them back to you when this is all over with, and you can decide what to do with them. There are a lot of valuable paintings in the collection from what I'm told."

Jamie wasn't sure she'd be able to do anything with the paintings. Her art business was no longer operational. Since she didn't know how much Saul knew about her plight, she decided not to say anything more. Maybe she could sell the paintings and have something to live off of. More than likely, she'd feel obligated to return the paintings to their original owners. It wouldn't be easy to try and find them, but something she'd have to do even if it was a pain in the neck.

"Two of the paintings are of great interest to us, though," Geller continued. "They were stolen from Jewish residents in Germany during World War II."

"How do you know?" Bond asked.

"About thirty years ago, we started creating a list of artwork and property stolen from our people. Not just in Germany, but Russia, France, Italy, Austria, everywhere. We interviewed people. We talked to holocaust survivors. Went back through old pictures. Newspaper articles and publications. We created a list."

"Sounds like a major undertaking," Jamie said.

"It's still ongoing, and we have no end date in sight," Geller said.

"Anyway, two of the paintings in the truck are on that list. Clement described more paintings he stole over the years. They fit the descriptions of a lot of the paintings we have proof were stolen from Jews during the war."

"Let me guess," Jamie said. "Clement sold some of those paintings to Zakarov. That's why you have a sudden interest in our mission."

His demeanor changed dramatically. From casual to dead serious in body language and in tone.

"Jamie, can I speak to you privately?" Saul asked.

"Anything you have to say to me, you can say in front of these guys. I don't have anything to hide from them."

Saul hesitated.

"Okay. Fair enough. Let's just say our interests include more than paintings."

"Zakarov!" Jamie said. "That makes sense."

"Not just Zakarov, although we'd like to get our hands on him as well. I'm here because of you."

"Me? I don't understand. Please explain."

"Your CIA director is intent on bringing you down. He's on a mission, and you're his target."

"I'm well aware of that," Jamie said. "That's not Mossad's fight. That's mine."

"Not exactly. We think the new CIA director has designs on the Presidency."

"I don't think there's any doubt about that."

"Director Fuller has made it clear that he's no friend of Israel. Neither is the current president, but at least he won't go as far as we believe Fuller will. If he had his way, Israel would be marginalized in the middle east."

"What does that have to do with me?" Jamie asked.

"Fuller is ambitious. You and Alex are the two people who can bring him down. For reasons you already know, he put out a hit on you."

She wondered how he knew about the hit, but asked a more pressing question. "Do you know where my husband is?" she asked.

"We're working on it."

"Does Fuller have him?"

"I suspect he does."

"Is he alive?"

"I don't know. We're trying to find him. I'm afraid that has been difficult to do."

Jamie could feel the ire reaching a fevered pitch inside of her. While she had been concentrating on the mission, and was able to compartmentalize, put Alex and Fuller out of her mind, at least to the extent possible, Saul was bringing it to the forefront.

As much as she cared about the paintings and Zakarov, she cared about bringing Fuller down more.

"I appreciate any help you can give me," Jamie said. "I'm surprised you'd go to these lengths now. The U.S. elections are a long way off. A lot can happen between now and then."

"I agree. We're not doing this for Fuller. We're doing this for you. We've been friends for a long time. You've helped me more times than I can count. I'm here to protect you and make sure Fuller doesn't succeed in bringing you down."

"I'm touched. I'm afraid it's my battle though. There's only so much you can do."

"We can do more than you think. If you need asylum, my government will grant it to you. I already have authorization from the Prime Minister to offer it to you."

"Do I need asylum?" Jamie asked in a questioning tone. Ignoring the ramifications of the gesture which were too many to calculate on the spot. She also hadn't thought that far ahead. What if she could never go back to the United States? She'd never be able to see her friends. Bae. Courtney. Brad. All her coworkers.

The thought seemed unimaginable two days ago. Now, hearing Saul's words, she wasn't so sure.

"I'm just saying it's available to you."

"Thank you, but surely it won't come to that. That would mean I could never go back to the United States again."

"If Fuller has his way, you never will."

"How do you know about all this?" Jamie asked.

"I'm not at liberty to share that information, but let me just say that we've been monitoring Fuller's activities for a while, and some of them are quite disturbing."

"Do you have any intel I can use against him?"

"I may have. Did you hear about a bombing in Northern Syria?"

"No I haven't," she answered. "We've been indisposed."

"I saw something about it on my phone," Bond said. "President Merali of Syria unleashed chemical weapons on his own people."

Saul shook his head no.

"We have it from good sources that the bombing was carried out by U.S. special forces. Fuller ordered the attack."

"What?" Colonel bellowed. "Are you telling us that the Director of the CIA ordered a mission to bomb innocent women and children with chemical weapons?"

"That's exactly what I'm saying."

"I don't believe it," Bond said. "I know a lot of Navy Seals, and I don't know any one of them who would carry out such an attack."

"They probably didn't know that's what they were doing," Jamie said. She wouldn't put it past Fuller to do something like that. Even as barbaric as it seemed.

"The men thought they were bombing a military position," Geller said. "The special forces operatives didn't know the bombs contained chemical weapons or that innocent women and children were in the village."

"How do you know this?" Colonel asked.

"We intercepted transmissions. That's all I can say."

"You have tapes?"

"Yes."

"Turn them over," Jamie said excitedly. "Fuller would be court-martialed and would have to resign in disgrace. That'd solve all our problems."

"The U.S. can't know we are monitoring their communications. It can't come from us."

Jamie rubbed her eyes roughly.

"Give them to me. I have contacts in the government who would be very interested in that information."

"They'd know it came from us. You need to get to the men who did the bombing and see if they'll talk."

"I don't even know who they are."

"You are extremely resourceful. I'm giving you this information, so you can find a way to use it."

"Thank you."

"Like I said, I want to help you. You're a good friend to Israel. We protect our friends. If it protects our interests as well, then all the better."

"So, that's why you're here and willing to help us with Zakarov?"

"That's a separate issue. We want the paintings and we want Zakarov. He supplies our enemies with weapons. My Prime Minister sees an opportunity to accomplish both without having our fingerprints on it."

"You're using Jamie to get your paintings back," Colonel stated in a serious tone.

"We're helping Jamie," Geller replied.

"How are you prepared to help?" Colonel asked.

"I brought these men along. I also see you found a helicopter. Israel was prepared to provide you one. I'm authorized to give you anything you need within reason."

"I wished we'd known that a few hours ago," Jamie said.

A wide grin suddenly appeared on Geller's face.

"I don't suppose you had anything to do with a dozen helicopters exploding at Tsoy airbase?" Geller asked. "It killed forty-five members of the Uzbekistan Air Force."

"Is that all?" Colonel asked. "Forty-five, huh? We were hoping to kill more than that."

"Impressive number, in my opinion," Geller replied. "For only four of you."

"Who are the men with you?" Colonel asked. "I like to know who I'm going to battle with."

Geller introduced the men. He went over their credentials in fine detail, which were impressive. Jamie had worked with the Duvdevan strike force before. They were highly trained and fearless. She was glad to have them.

Handshakes went all around.

"Tell us the plan," Geller said. "We're here and at your service. Just tell us what to do. Both my men know how to fly a helicopter."

"Nobody's touching my bird. I'm flying the helicopter," A-Rad said.

"The best pilot should fly it," one of Geller's men retorted.

Jamie had to force back a smile. Three testosterone-driven killing machines were one thing. Now she had five of them to deal with. Six including Geller who was a little more diplomatic, but she knew him to thrive on danger with the best of them.

The men would be annoying, but she liked her odds a lot better now.

She turned her mind elsewhere and decided to let the guys hash things out.

Geller had stirred something up in her. She couldn't shake the ominous feeling in her gut that Alex was in grave danger.

23

The conversation with Kyle Kelly wasn't going well. Fuller didn't like it when his subordinates questioned his orders. Kelly's job was to obey the Director of the CIA's instructions regardless of how he felt about them. That protocol was drilled into soldiers at boot camp.

Kelly was experienced enough to know better. The American Armed Forces were run by civilian leadership. The grunts on the ground had to accept that. Kelly might be a decorated soldier, but Fuller was his superior and didn't appreciate what he considered insubordination.

"Why do you want me to take him to Columbia?" Kelly asked in a disrespectful tone.

"You don't need to know why!" Fuller exclaimed. "Your job is to follow orders. I'm the Director of the friggin CIA, in case you've forgotten and need to be reminded."

That wasn't sufficient to get him to back down.

"My job is also to protect my men," Kelly retorted. "They're my responsibility. Colombia is an extremely dangerous territory. It's filled with drug lords and guerrillas who'd like nothing more than to get their hands on a few U.S. special forces members. I need to know why we have to put them in harm's way."

"You won't be in harm's way. I've taken steps to ensure your safety so you can take those concerns off your plate and do what I say."

"What about the man in custody? You just told me to hand him over to Colombian authorities. This is highly irregular and causes me great concern."

"Irregular, or not, that's the way the operation needs to be carried out. You'll meet the Colombians at the rendezvous point and transfer the suspect to their custody. Then you take your team and leave. My orders are pretty straightforward. It's what I'm ordering you to do."

Kelly wouldn't shut up.

"The man is a U.S. citizen. He has rights."

"He's been operating illegally within the Columbia borders," Fuller said roughly. "He's wanted in Columbia for any number of charges. Including murder, arms, and drug trafficking. Is that enough information for you, Kelly? Everything else is above your paygrade."

"With all due respect, sir, I find that hard to believe. He doesn't seem like the type of man who would traffic in arms and drugs. Or, the kind of operative who would betray the United States. I've heard about this man. He's practically a legend in CIA circles."

Fuller let out an exasperated sigh for effect. "Where do you think he got the money to buy that island? You saw it. The man is a gazillionaire. He didn't get it by twiddling his thumbs and whistling dixie. The man is a menace to the CIA. Hero or not, he's a criminal. He's not the first CIA officer to turn bad and won't be the last."

The other end of the line was silent. Fuller thought throwing the island argument into the mix was a good twist. That should win the day with someone like Kelly who didn't even make six figures.

"I still don't like it."

"You don't have to like it. You just have to carry out your orders."

"If he's who you say he is, he should be brought back to the U.S. and stand trial for treason. I'll put the noose around his neck myself if he's found guilty."

"He's already been found guilty. As I said, the house and island are proof enough. How many CIA officers do you know with that kind of money?" Fuller asked.

"None."

"That's exactly right!"

"How do I know the Colombians won't double-cross us?" Kelly asked. "They're not known for playing by the rules."

Fuller let out another huge sigh.

"How much money do you want, Kelly?" he blurted out.

"What are you talking about?" Kelly asked, in a confused tone.

"Name your price," Fuller said. "What's it worth to you to do the job I've instructed you to do and do it right?"

"Do you think I want money? I do what I do for God, family, and country."

"Yeah. Yeah. Yeah. I know all about your code. I've heard that line before. Every man has a price. How much is yours?"

"I can't believe you're offering me money. Isn't that what you are accusing the suspect of doing? Taking money illegally?"

"How much?" Fuller asked. "Is fifty thousand enough?"

Fuller had more than two billion dollars in the bank but wasn't about to be overly generous.

"It's not about the money."

"Fifty thousand for each of your men. Two hundred and fifty thousand dollars for you. It will be deposited into secure accounts for you and your team. Tax-free."

"I'm going to pretend we never had this conversation," Kelly said in a cross voice.

Fuller couldn't believe what he was hearing.

"Are you going to do the job, or do I need to get someone else to complete your mission? Going against my orders could be interpreted as treason."

"We'll finish the job. But I don't like it."

Before Fuller could throw out another 'you don't have to like it' answer, the line went dead. He sat at his desk for several minutes and thought about the conversation.

Something was unsettling about it. Not that he was worried about Kelly not following through with his orders because Fuller knew men like him. They followed orders. If a superior told them to run through a wall, they'd do it. These men had gone into harm's way, more times than they could probably count, and every time it was all based on someone's order.

Someone who wasn't going to get shot at and had never spent time under fire. That wasn't the problem.

Fuller recognized he had a different dilemma. As he thought about the entire conversation again, he concluded that Kelly was a ticking time bomb. Kelly was the one who carried out the bombing in Syria. He obviously hadn't put two and two together and realized that his men were the ones who planted the chemical bombs that killed the women and children in the village.

If he knew, no telling what he'd do. If Kelly would turn down two hundred and fifty thousand dollars based on principle, who's to say he wouldn't turn Fuller in for ordering him to plant those bombs.

That thought alone required him to rethink his plan. He needed to approach this whole impending disaster from a completely different direction.

It didn't take long for him to decide what to do.

Fuller opened his desk drawer and got one of his secure cell phones out of the desk. It was a burner. A phone that couldn't be traced. He dialed Escobar Santos' number. The drug lord in Columbia.

Santos answered on the second ring with a rude greeting followed by an expletive.

"The drop is all set," Fuller said to him, ignoring the rude comment. "I've given my men the rendezvous instructions."

"We're ready and prepared as well. How many men are you sending?"

"Five, along with the target."

"I want you to know that if you double-cross me, I'm prepared to kill all your men. I'm going to have a small army at the drop. If I get one whiff of a trap, all your men are dead. Mark my words."

Fuller was glad to hear the threatening tone.

"I have a proposition for you," Fuller said.

"What is it?"

"One million dollars. That's how much I'll pay you."

"For what?"

"To kill all of my men."

"You want me to kill all your men? Why?" Santos asked suspiciously.

"That's right. That's exactly what I want you to do. I want the bodies to disappear. Never to be recovered. And I'm willing to pay you a million dollars to do so."

"What about the suspect?"

"Do whatever you want with him? Just make sure he's dead as well when you're done with him."

"I want the money upfront."

"Send me instructions, and it'll be in your account by the end of the day."

"Done," Santos replied.

"Don't double-cross me either," Fuller said. "I'm not a man you want to come after you. I can make life extremely difficult for you."

"I will do as you say. Have your men meet us at the rendezvous point tomorrow at three o'clock in the afternoon. We'll be there waiting," Santos said.

"Excellent. We have an agreement. My word to you is rock solid. And remember to destroy the bodies after you've killed all of them."

Fuller hung up the phone.

He was pleased with the conversation with Santos. They had an understanding, and Fuller was confident Santos would carry out his end of the bargain. A million dollars was a small price to pay for eliminating any potential problems. He'd already saved the half a million by not having to pay Kelly and his men.

He logged into his computer and stared at the TITAN bank accounts. And all the zeros behind the numbers. In his wildest dreams, he never thought he'd have this much money under his personal control.

Then he wondered if he'd acted too hastily. Wiring the money could be problematic. It left a paper trail. He wasn't like Halee who could cover his tracks to the point that they couldn't be followed.

Fuller had to make sure the million dollars couldn't be traced back to him. Maybe he could backdate the transaction so it looked like Halee was the one who sent Santos the money. If discovered, he could blame it on the dead man.

It would take some finesse, but he was confident he could pull it off.

He was almost giddy and felt like giving himself a big pat on the back. His new concept was far superior to his original one and would be the best, most foolproof plan he had come up with to date.

Fuller sat up straight at his desk, picked up the phone, and called August into his office. He needed another paper trail within the CIA. One that could be seen by others.

When August came into his office, Fuller cut to the chase.

"I know where Alex Halee is," Fuller said to him.

"Where?" August asked in surprise.

"He's in Colombia."

"What's he doing there?" August asked. "We don't have any missions going on in Colombia that I'm aware of."

"According to my sources," Fuller said. "Halee has been working with Santos all along. He's been doing dirty deals for a while, selling him arms and drugs. That's how Halee made a lot of his money. He's also got some dirty Seals on his payroll. They've been working for him as well. Apparently, a half a dozen of them are in Columbia as we speak. It looks like this isn't anywhere near the first time they've worked together. I intend on taking them down."

"What are the names of the Seals on this rogue mission?" August asked.

"I only know the leader's name," Fuller said.

"What is it?" August asked.

"His name is Kyle Kelly. It's urgent you put him on our most-wanted list. He and Halee have to pay for what they've done."

"Yes, sir. I'll take care of that as soon as I leave your office," August said.

When August finally left his office, Fuller let out a sigh. He sat back in his wide leather office chair with a wide grin on his face. Things were going much better than he expected. He was satisfied that he'd set all the necessary wheels in motion.

He could already dictate the memo for the file. Kelly and Halee went to Colombia to work on a drug deal with Santos. His intel told him things went south, and Santos killed all of the Seals and Halee.

The bodies were never recovered.

24

Uzbekistan

The helicopter sped toward Zakarov's compound, flying low to the ground to avoid any possible detection by radar. A sense of déjà vu came over Jamie. A few years before, she had parachuted into the eye of a hurricane to rescue some teenage girls being held as sex slaves in Cuba. As far as anyone knew, jumping into a hurricane had never been done before and made her a legend in CIA circles.

Looking back, she felt more nervous today than she did then. Probably because fear feels more potent at the moment than it does in the memory. Also, in Cuba, she was parachuting from a normal altitude. She almost died but had two minutes to make whatever adjustments necessary on the fly, which helped her walk away from it unscathed.

Today, Jamie was doing a LALO, low altitude, low opening jump onto the roof of Zakarov's three-story house. The margin of error was so small it could hardly be calculated. From the moment she jumped from the helicopter to the time she landed on the roof would be roughly thirteen seconds.

Several factors had to be considered. Each element was highly critical, starting with avoiding the rotors when she exited. If she managed to do that safely, she had to have the presence of mind to deploy the chute in one motion. Any delay could be deadly. Assuming she got the chute opened in time, she had to remember to push her feet into the wind for maximum drag. Then she'd have to get her bearings and prepare for a roll landing, so she didn't break her legs on impact with the roof.

To make matters worse, a storm was brewing. The winds had picked up and were swirling. Instead of jumping from three hundred and fifty feet, the pilot said in the headset that he had to lower the bird to three hundred.

Two hundred and fifty feet was the lowest altitude they could safely jump from and the storm ceiling was getting dangerously close to that.

Colonel and Bond were jumping with her. One of the Israelis, Yossi, was flying the helicopter. Telling A-Rad he wasn't going to be the pilot had been a humorous conversation. Jamie liked to think of something funny when she was nervous. It took her mind off the impending danger.

"That's my bird," A-Rad argued. "I'm the pilot. I know how to fly that baby better than anyone else."

Colonel was explaining the plan to the team, and A-Rad wasn't happy.

"We need you with the truck," Colonel said stoically.

A-Rad grimaced. "Anyone can drive a truck. Not everyone can put a helicopter in position for a LALO. It's not as easy as you think."

"Actually," Jamie interjected. "Saul is going to drive the truck. You're going to do the heavy lifting and most of the fighting from the truck."

A-Rad started to protest further but Jamie cut him off. "Think about it. Would you rather fly the helicopter or be in a firefight?"

She knew he'd rather be in a gun battle than on a date with a supermodel.

"I want to do both," he said, twisting his lips to the side, clearly confused and thinking hard about the question. He was probably realizing for the first time that the pilot of the helicopter wouldn't see any real action.

"You can't do both," Colonel retorted.

"If I'm driving the truck, I'm not going to be in the action anyway. I might as well be flying."

Colonel violently shook his head no.

"Listen to the plan, A-Rad, before you draw any conclusions," Colonel said. "When the helicopter comes in, we need a distraction."

"Okay. What kind of distraction?"

Colonel looked at Jamie and grinned. The two of them knew the whole plan and how much satisfaction A-Rad would get from it.

"You and Saul are going to park the truck down the road from the house, just out of sight of the guards who are at the entrance. You'll take up a position near the guard shack. On my cue, I want you to run in front of the entrance to the compound and make a bunch of noise. Get off a shot or two at the guards."

Colonel could barely choke back a laugh.

"Hey!" A-Rad said. "That's my plan! Before, you said it was stupid."

"I changed my mind. It's a good idea."

"That's what I'm talking about!" A-Rad said smugly. He pointed at his chin. "This is not just a pretty face."

"No, it's not," Jamie said. "The most critical thing in this mission is timing. What we want you to do, A-Rad, is to distract the guards so they don't notice the helicopter until it's too late. Fire a couple of shots, then sprint back to the truck. Hopefully, a few of them will follow you. If they do, then take them out."

Colonel finished describing the plan.

"When the helicopter is in position, Bond will jump first, then Jamie, then me. We'll land on the roof, discard our parachutes, and get into position to open fire on the guards from the high ground. Once we are on the roof, Yossi will fly the bird toward the front gate, and Seth will open fire on the guards from the door of the helicopter."

Seth was the other Israeli.

"The guards are going to get hit from every direction," Jamie said. "They'll be pinned down from all sides. We have to keep them from getting to the house to protect Zakarov. Colonel and I will enter the house through the door on the roof and find Zakarov. Bond will try to keep the guards pinned down between the guard shack and the house. Once the building is secure, we'll search the house for the paintings."

"Saul will drive the truck to the gate and block the exit so no one can get out that way," Colonel added. "Just in case Zakarov tries to make a run for it in his car. A-Rad, you protect the truck and make sure Zakarov doesn't escape the compound."

"I like it," he said.

"You should like it," Jamie said. "It's basically your plan."

A-Rad beamed like a kid who'd gotten an A on his report card in his worst subject. For the next several hours after that, he was barking instructions like he was leading the plan.

The helicopter was being whipped around by the wind, but Yossi was holding it steady considering the turbulence. A-Rad radioed from the ground and said that he and Saul were in position and waiting for us to get in position.

They were getting close. Colonel had been relatively quiet on the ride over but was now barking out instructions into the headset.

"Thirty seconds to show time," Colonel said over the radio. "Willy, be prepared to go on my command."

Willy was A-Rad's mission handle.

"I'm ready to rock and roll," A-Rad confirmed.

Everyone had handles when they went into operation mode. A-Rad was named for Willy Shoemaker, the famous jockey was four foot ten inches tall and weighed ninety-one pounds. A-Rad was well over six feet and a mass of muscle. Hence the nickname. Handles were the team's attempt at humor and it did help ease the tension when you heard or said the funny names over the radio even in the heat of battle.

Colonel was called Private, as a slight since he'd earned his brass with more than twenty years of battlefield service. Bond was 007 for obvious reasons. A former MI6 operative with the last name Bond was never going to be able to avoid the comparisons. Although the guys had gotten to where they just called him seven. Or Mickey on occasion. The Yankee great Mickey Mantle's jersey number.

Jamie was Dolly. For Dolly Parton. Because her breasts were small. Jamie was tall and lanky without an ounce of body fat on her. Freakishly strong, but not sinewy. Muscular like a runner, rather than a bodybuilder.

She hated her nickname.

"Are you good, Dolly?" Colonel asked. She gave him the thumbs up even though her pounding heart was competing with Colonel's instructions in her ear. She'd rather have a root canal than make this jump.

"Now, Willy!" Colonel shouted, shocking her back into reality. It caused a jolt of adrenaline to pulse through Jamie's body like a fire hose had been unleashed and set on full blast.

She took several deep breaths to settle her insides. Her mind settled into her pre-fight routine. Jamie had been through this with her body hundreds of times before in dangerous situations. She always got a huge adrenaline rush right before it came time to act. Then she always felt a sudden calm. A peace. Maybe it came from God. She wasn't sure, but it happened every time.

Time actually slowed down. Her senses heightened. Every part of her being shifted to optimization. She no longer felt fear. Just determination and deep resolve. A survival instinct, maybe. A winner's mentality. Alex talked about it in football. When the game was on the line, the cream rose to the top, and the players with the strongest minds and training excelled.

The difference between the ones who succeeded and the ones who choked was razor thin. The best of the best knew how to channel that rush of adrenaline into excellence.

Jamie had never choked in a dangerous situation. Not once. For whatever reason, she always came out on top. Her bullets seemed to find the mark, while her enemies' bullets whizzed by without finding their target.

She said a prayer, which was another part of her routine. Maybe one of the reasons bullets missed her. Angels were watching out for her. Something she never took for granted. She wasn't invincible. Not the Superwoman of the movies. Bullets wouldn't bounce off her. She needed to be great. Especially today, when she was out of her element.

Bond got into position to jump first, practically leaning out of the helicopter which was now hovering. It couldn't be moving when they jumped or they risked being splattered on the side. They had to wait until the pilot settled the craft.

Because of the danger and the fact they had a new pilot on board, Colonel had insisted they take several practice jumps. Rather than doing it over land, they'd jumped into the Caspian Sea from three hundred meters.

The practice had given her confidence she could do the jump, although hitting the target was still a concern. In the sea, there was no real target. Just a spot in the water to hit. Who knew if they actually hit it since the water gave no point of reference?

Jamie looked out the open door to assess the situation and visualized doing it. The guards at the gate were scrambling. A-Rad must be doing his thing. Firing random shots into the darkness towards the guards. They were returning fire at the phantom. She could imagine their confusion.

No guards were on the roof. Several were at the gate, though, and had noticed the helicopter and were running toward the house. The driveway was long so it'd take them more than a minute to get there.

A-Rad's distraction would hopefully be enough time for them to get into position. From the roof, they should be able to pick them off like a lake full of ducks floating on the water.

Assuming the jumps went well. And they didn't break their legs in the process. The worst possible scenario was missing the roof completely and landing on the ground. Then they'd be the sitting ducks.

Colonel pushed Bond from behind, and he plummeted out of the helicopter. Jamie moved into position. She saw the parachute open, but didn't wait to see if Bond's jump was successful and that he landed on the roof.

She needed to go before his jump was finished.

Colonel asked if she was ready.

She nodded her head. He pushed her, so she cleared the rotors.

The rush of air was violent from the impending storm and took her breath away.

Suddenly, the wind shifted.

Instead of blowing in her face, it was behind her.

Jamie instinctively pulled the ripcord with no time to consider the consequences of the weather change.

The chute opened.

The roof was rapidly approaching her.

She was coming in too fast.

The landing target was the center of the building. The wind had pushed her toward the edge of the roof.

Dangerously close.

She was in danger of missing the building altogether.

Jamie forced her legs out and up to keep from smashing them on the landing. Rolling was no longer an option. She might roll off the edge of the roof and fall three stories.

She had to make a split-second decision. If she lifted her legs high enough, she could clear the building and land on the ground. But she'd be out in the open. She wouldn't have the high ground to her advantage. The soldiers on the ground outnumbered her more than twenty to one.

One of them would almost certainly get in a kill shot.

Landing on the roof was still the best option.

Jamie lowered her legs and braced for impact in an attempt to land on her feet.

She tightened her thigh muscles to dig in when she made contact.

She landed on her feet but lost her balance. She had overcorrected. Like a gymnast trying to stick a landing but took two steps forward.

The force of the speed caused her to bounce forward unexpectedly. She was propelled headfirst over the building.

25

Jamie braced for the impact that came, but not in the way she was expecting. She relaxed her legs but tightened her abs and back, prepared to crash into the ground, hoping she was at the right angle to roll and that her core would sustain the jolt.

Instead, about halfway down the side of the three-story house, she was suddenly jerked upward in a whiplash motion, like a crash dummy who'd just smashed into a brick wall. Her back slammed into the side of the house with such force that it took her breath away.

So hard, it took several seconds of dangling in the air and swinging back into the wall a couple more times to get her wits about her.

What happened?

All she could figure was that her parachute lines were caught up in the satellite antenna she tried to grab on the way over the side of the roof. She looked down at her hand, which had blood on it from a laceration. Out of all her injuries in the throes of battle, it never ceased to amaze her how the adrenaline masked the pain at the moment. Or at least until she allowed herself to think about it.

The cut suddenly throbbed.

"Dolly, are you okay?" Colonel shouted. She could hear his voice on the headset and from the roof.

She looked up and saw Colonel leaning over, holding on to the parachute lines.

Were they about to give way? What did he know that she didn't?

Before Jamie could know what to say or do, she quickly assessed the damage to her body. She didn't want to make things worse if she had an injury that the adrenaline was covering up.

The concentration of pain was in her neck and back and right under her shoulders where the parachute harness had stopped her momentum. She probably had bruises on her chest and under her armpits.

Her breath still escaped her, but she knew how to get that back. With a weak voice, she said to Colonel, "I think I'm okay. I won't be for long if the guards come around the corner anytime soon."

That was her most significant concern. Even the worst shot could kill her if the guard could hit the broad side of a barn. Or the broad side of a multi-million dollar mansion as it were.

"Hang on," Colonel said. "I'm going to get you out of this difficulty."

An interesting choice of words. Difficulty.

A math problem was difficult. This was one of the most precarious situations she'd ever been in. She could think of a few more colorful terms Curly would use in this situation.

Thinking of Curly caused the fog of war to lift, and her heightened senses returned. The gunfight was still raging at the gate. The helicopter was now at the back of the house and not the front. She wondered why. Probably because it started taking fire from the ground and retreated.

Heavy gunfire was coming from the roof—likely Bond unloading his weapon on the guards on the ground to keep them away from her.

Thank you, Bond.

But hurry up, Colonel.

He was probably trying to think of a plan. What could he do? Pulling her up by the parachute lines would take more strength than he possessed. Even with Bond, the two of them couldn't do it. Maybe they could, but Bond was preoccupied.

She should be helping them.

Don't wait for someone else to save you, she remembered Curly saying.

Jamie pressed her feet against the side of the house and pushed out. Then she turned her body, so she was facing the house. The momentum slammed her back against the wall, sending another jolt through her spine, but at least she was facing the right way.

She grabbed the lines with her hands and put her feet out against the wall like a rock climber scaling a mountain. She cried out in pain when her lacerated hand gripped the ropes.

Didn't matter. Not a good plan anyway. Apparently, when she felt the parachute lines giving way and heard Colonel yelling for her to stop.

"The antennae won't hold you!" he shouted at the top of his lungs.

Jamie pressed her chest against the side of the house to try and lessen the weight on the lines.

She looked down.

The fall wouldn't kill her but might break her legs or her already traumatized back.

Avoid falling, she heard Curly say.

Duh. I can figure that out on my own, she said to him in the conversation that was raging in her mind.

Those arguments with Curly in the heat of the battle were a lifeline. She hoped they never went away. It helped her think through her options.

Before she could think any further, a soldier rounded the corner leaving her only one option. Kill or be killed. He looked up and spotted her. Their eyes met. He raised his weapon. It became a race of time and skill. He had a head start and got the first shot off. The bullets bounced off the brick and stone of the house sending shards into her face.

Jamie let out a shout.

Where was Colonel?

Probably looking for a rope or something to help her with.

She didn't let the man get off another volley of rounds. She raised her weapon and fired. Two shots to the chest. The most significant area of mass with the best likelihood of success. He dropped to the ground in a heap.

In the movies, the spy would spray a dozen shots. Curly taught Jamie to be efficient with her ammo rounds and keep count.

More guards could come around the corner at any time.

She reached for the knife in her belt, then thought better of it. Cutting the lines and falling to the ground was not the best option. Not yet.

She reached out for the windowsill to a second-story room. It was too far below her. Climbing up to the third-story windows wasn't an option either. She might be able to release her parachute and fall to the second-floor but didn't trust her lacerated hand to hang on to the sill.

Another soldier rounded the corner.

This time she was prepared and got the first shots off. Mainly because he hesitated when he saw his comrade lying on the ground. Curly warned her not to get distracted. Ever. Focus on the necessary, not the peripheral—human nature. The guard had to look. Because of that, and because Curly hadn't trained him, the man was on the ground next to his fellow soldier seconds later.

Where was Colonel?

"It's getting hot down here, Private," Jamie shouted into the com.

"I'm on it. I'm trying to find a rope."

An idea came to her when he mentioned the rope.

"Forget that! Go after Zakarov. I'll figure out something."

"Are you sure?"

"Go. We can't let him get away."

By her calculations, he'd already had a couple of minutes to prepare for them to breach the house. If he had an escape tunnel, he might already be out of their reach.

"Yossi! Do you copy?" Jamie said with urgency.

"Roger!"

Yossi was piloting the helicopter.

"Swing around to the northeast side of the house," Jamie shouted. "Drop me a rope."

It didn't take long for the bird to come around the corner of the house. It sent a torrent of wind rushing toward her. Jamie turned her head away to keep the dust and dirt from blowing in her face.

Yossi lowered the helicopter to about a hundred feet above her.

"Toss me a rope," she said.

"You aren't wearing gloves," Seth replied. He was the other Israeli in the back of the helicopter. She could see him looking out the open door and could practically read his lips. "The rope will rip the flesh right off your hands."

Seth was also right. The rope would burn her hands like touching a hot iron. Especially with the laceration which he didn't even know about.

"I'll wrap a sleeve around my hands," Jamie said.

"You might slip," Seth argued. "I'll send down Jacob's Ladder. That'll be safer."

The ladder wasn't as long as the rope, but Jamie could wrap her arms around one rung of the ladder and hold on for dear life.

The ladder appeared and flopped down toward her. Seth barked instructions to Yossi to lower the bird by thirty-five feet.

The helicopter would have to get dangerously close to the side of the house for Jamie to reach the ladder.

"Can you clear the house?" Jamie asked Yossi.

"It'll be close."

"Don't put yourself at risk," Jamie said.

"Are you going up or down?" Yossi asked.

"Up. To the roof."

It'd be easier for her if they lowered her to the ground but more manageable for them to elevate and drop her on the roof and get back out of harm's way.

The ladder was within reach.

A new problem arose.

Jamie had to get out of the parachute while holding on to the ladder. She wrapped one arm through the lower rung, so she was being held up by one elbow.

Jamie pulled the breakaway handle to her chute and then held on for dear life as the ropes of the chute no longer held her up against gravity. She swung out away from the house with her legs dangling off the ladder.

Jamie's heart pounded in her chest and reverberated in her ears.

"Go!" she said to Yossi.

"We've got a rabbit!" Colonel suddenly shouted in her ear. "Out the back door."

Yossi had lifted Jamie up to the roof, and he was about to set her down.

"Yossi! Take me to the ground. Now!" Jamie shouted.

Thankfully, she didn't have to ask him twice. The helicopter suddenly jerked her into the air again.

The figure of a man was running away from the house into the shadows. Presumed to be Zakarov, or Colonel wouldn't have even mentioned him.

A gust of wind jerked the helicopter forward, causing Jamie to swing violently underneath it. Back and forth like a pendulum. It was all she could do to hold on.

"Take me down, now!" Jamie shouted.

Zakarov was getting away. Tracking him in the darkness would be next to impossible given that he knew the terrain and they didn't.

Jacob's Ladder swung back and forth like a carnival ride. Yossi struggled to gain control of the bird.

"Any time now, Yossi," Jamie said. "I don't know how much longer I can hold on."

Finally, he gained control and set her down slowly. When she was within ten feet of the ground, she let go and fell the rest of the way, rolling on her side. She felt the impact, but it saved time.

Jamie was on her feet and sprinting within seconds, ignoring her body which was protesting all the abuse. She could no longer see Zakarov but ran in the direction she'd last seen him.

He had to be heading for the back fence. The dogs in the fences were barking violently. She could hear gunfire starting to dissipate back at the house which meant someone was getting the upper hand—hopefully, her team.

Jamie had sprinted this hard many times, but her lungs were still burning. Her legs, neck, and back were aching from the trauma of the fall off the rooftop. She put that out of her mind and quickened her pace.

She got off a shot in the air ahead of her. It might make Zakarov fall to the ground or try to take cover.

It had the desired result.

Just ahead, she saw him hesitate, fall to the ground, then stand and scale the fence and drop to the other side.

For a second, their eyes met.

When she got to the fence, she scaled it quickly as well. Ignoring that it was an electric fence. Zakarov must've had the presence of mind to disable it before he ran out of the house.

"House secure," she heard Colonel say.

"We'll bring the truck in now," A-Rad shouted through the headset.

"I'll keep watch from the roof," Bond said.

The good guys did win.

Not yet. There was one loose end, a big one, and it fell on her. The main reason they'd taken this much risk.

Zakarov was headed for the treeline. Jamie assumed he had a weapon on him. But it was much easier to shoot running toward a target than away from one, so she threw caution to the wind and went into a dead sprint.

She had to get to him before he made it to the thick forest.

He looked back. She was gaining on him.

209

His arm raised, and he pointed a gun behind him. Jamie ser-pentined and slowed slightly but then resumed her speed when the bullet bounced harmlessly away from her. Not even close enough to hear the whizzing sound.

She could fire on him and bring him down, but she wanted him alive. Mossad wanted him alive. To question him. Gain intelligence beyond just what they'd find in the house.

She was on him now.

Zakarov looked back and raised his arm again. This time she was close enough for him to fire a bullet and hit her. She didn't give him a chance.

Jamie launched herself like a cougar pouncing on its prey. She adjusted her trajectory, so she was to the opposite side of his body to the gun.

He never got a shot off.

She landed on his back, and her momentum pushed him to the ground and broke her fall. She felt the air leave his lungs. Pressing her knee into his back made sure he couldn't replace it with another breath. Not until she was ready.

The gun fell to the side. Somewhere on the ground. She didn't bother securing it.

Zakarov tried to struggle, so Jamie elbowed him in the back of the head. He let out a windless yelp of pain. It worked, because he quit resisting.

"How does it feel to be taken down by a girl?" Jamie asked with as much vitriol as she could muster.

She usually never played that card or mocked a defeated sus-pect. She usually just saw herself as a skilled operative doing her job. It didn't matter that she was a woman or that she had bested a man.

But she was ticked off. Why? Because she almost broke her neck on the LALO. Because Zakarov trafficked in arms and drugs. Because he was a basic low-life scum of the earth, who should be taken off the face of the planet so he could meet God and receive his eternal judgment.

Also, because Russian oligarchs were pigs. Women were like hood ornaments. They needed to look pretty but not say anything.

Then she realized the real source of her angst.

Fuller.

That's why the pent-up aggression was coming out at once.

Why did her mind keep going back there?

Because capturing Zakarov didn't bring her the satisfaction she thought it would.

She'd never have it until she dealt with Fuller once and for all.

26

Washington, D.C.
One week later

Fuller needed answers, and he needed them now. Dietrich was on the other line and was being extremely evasive.

"I don't know where Jamie Austen is," he said. "I tracked her to Uzbekistan. Then the trail went cold."

"Did she have anything to do with the attack on the Tsoy airbase?"

"I don't know."

Fuller had gotten word that sixteen American-made helicopters were destroyed in a coordinated attack on the Uzbekistan airbase. The details were sketchy, but eyewitnesses on the ground said a blonde-haired woman and several men were behind the attack. They escaped in one of the helicopters.

"The Uzbekistan government seems to think Americans were behind the attack," Fuller said. "They've lodged an official protest with the United Nations claiming the attack was carried out by the U.S. government. The President has called me to the White House. I'm on the way there now. I suspect that's what he wants to talk about. I need to provide him with answers. I'd like to have proof that Austen was behind the attacks."

Fuller was in his black SUV and would arrive at the White House within minutes. As Director of the CIA, his job was intelligence. 'I don't know' would not be a sufficient answer for the leader of the free world.

"What about the missing helicopter?" Fuller asked. "Where is it?"

"I don't know."

"You are as worthless as a strap of leather in the garbage dump!"

"I only know what I know. I agree that Austen is probably behind it. She's been in this area. Too big a coincidence not to be her."

"What's she doing operating in that part of the world? What could she possibly be up to?"

"I don't know."

If the man said 'I don't know' one more time, Fuller was going to fire him on the spot. Actually, he made a mental note to reassign Dietrich. Somewhere humiliating. Like Iceland or Finland. Maybe Libya.

Fuller was nearing the White House and needed to get off the phone. If the President asked, he could always make things up. It wouldn't be the first time and certainly not the last. If it served him to move up the ranks, he rationalized his unethical actions. He would say Austen was behind the unauthorized attacks. Who could refute it?

His caravan pulled through the White House gates after a security check, and a White House staffer met him. She was perky and friendly. She looked him in the eye and greeted him warmly. She must be new. He'd given specific instructions to the White House staffers never to look him in the eye.

"This way, sir," she said.

A secret service agent was also with her, and Fuller was led through the West Wing to the Oval Office. He couldn't help but think it'd be his office someday. When he entered, he was reminded how small it was. Hardly fitting for a U.S. President. There was nothing he could do about it. Even when he became President.

President Rutledge sat in a wingback chair. On one of the two couches facing him were the Prime Minister of Israel, Sheldon Jaffe, and the Prime Minister of Great Britain, Graham Stuart.

He was surprised to see them, but tried not to show it on his face or demeanor.

Two other people had their backs to him on the other couch. He kept his focus on the dignitaries.

"Mr. Prime Ministers," Fuller said. "I didn't know you'd be joining us today."

He did know that they had arrived at Andrews Air Force Base earlier that morning for a meeting with the President. Very few things he didn't know as Director of the CIA. What he didn't know was why. Why wasn't he notified as to the nature of the meeting?

He walked straight toward the two men and extended his hand. After some awkward pleasantries, Fuller turned to acknowledge the other two people in the room.

His mouth gaped open and would've hit the floor if it wasn't attached to his neck.

Jamie Austen was one of the two people sitting on the couch. She remained seated.

What the hell?

Brad was the other person. Why was he in the room? Without Fuller knowing about it. What possible business could Brad and Jamie have with the President of the United States and the two Prime Ministers.

This was highly irregular and unnerving.

Fuller's mind was spinning. He was completely caught off guard. Still, he had to maintain a poker hand face.

He gathered himself and greeted them. Even extended his hand. Neither Jamie nor Brad accepted the gesture.

"Hello Jamie," Fuller said cordially.

If looks could kill, he'd be dead a thousand times over. She glared at him like a woman who'd been scorned ten times over. Fuller didn't know why the shrew was at this meeting, but perhaps it was fortuitous.

This was his opportunity to crush her in front of the President.

President Rutledge motioned for Fuller to sit in the wingback chair next to him. He was not his usual warm self.

Something was up.

What had Jamie told him? How did she get into the United States without him knowing it? Was a disaster brewing?

He racked his brain, trying to think of what she might have on him.

Nothing.

Fuller decided to go on the offensive.

"There's a warrant out for your arrest, Ms. Austen," Fuller said coldly. "I'm surprised you'd show your face in the United States again."

She glared at him but didn't respond.

"That warrant is going away, right now." President Rutledge said.

"Perhaps you won't be so flippant when you hear what she's done," Fuller retorted in his cocky tone usually reserved for people that reported to him, not the President.

"Ms. Austen has done my country a great service," Prime Minister Jaffe of Israel interjected. "She has recovered more than six hundred paintings that were stolen from my people during the Second World War by Hitler's regime in Germany."

What did that have to do with anything? Fuller was perplexed.

"The Queen is also in her debt," the Prime Minister of England said. "Jamie, uh, Ms. Austen has recovered the paintings stolen from the Royal Museum of Art. It's the largest art heist in history to date, and she single-handedly, and at great risk of bodily harm, brought those paintings back to their proper place in the museum. We are forever in her debt."

The Prime Minister smiled at Jamie when he said it. She smiled back.

The woman was good. Fuller would give her that. This was obviously some kind of sinister plot to get her in the good graces with the President.

"I never authorized a mission to recover stolen paintings," Fuller argued. "Where did she find them, and why was she operating outside my purview?"

"One Mister Clement of Tajikistan was the culprit. He's an art thief," Prime Minister Stuart said.

"I'm aware of Clement but wasn't aware of his location," Fuller said.

"Apparently, Ms. Austen was able to track him down," Prime Minister Jaffe added, the jab at Fuller crystal clear.

"Clement sold the paintings to a Russian oligarch in Uzbekistan," Stuart continued. "Zakarov is his name. I'm sure you're familiar with him."

"Of course I am. He's an arms dealer. We've been trying to get our hands on him for years."

"You can quit looking. He's now in the custody of the Israeli government. He will never see the light of day again."

"All this is well and good, but it doesn't change the fact that Jamie Austen and her husband Alex Halee have been siphoning money from their illegal activities for their own personal gain. I have the proof. That's why a warrant was issued."

"That's not true," Brad said. "If anything, you're the one who has acted illegally."

Anger rose up inside Fuller like a volcano getting ready to explode. Brad worked for him. Who was he to challenge the Director of the CIA? As soon as the meeting was over, Brad would be out the door faster than a pile of trash on garbage day.

"You shouldn't be throwing around accusations that you can't prove," Fuller said roughly. "I'm the Director of the CIA."

Brad had a recorder in his hand. He held it up and pushed play. Fuller's voice suddenly filled the room.

He recognized it immediately. It was a crude recording of his conversation with Kyle Kelly when he directed him to bomb the village in Syria.

Fuller felt the blood rush from his face.

Where did Brad get that recording? He was clearly being betrayed by one of his own staffers. His mind could barely process all the ramifications of the revelations.

"This tape is proof positive that you ordered a chemical attack on a village in Syria that killed many women and children," Brad said. "That act propelled us into a war with Syria."

"I didn't know there were civilians in that village," Fuller argued. "I thought they were soldiers."

"And yet you authorized a chemical attack?" the President said. "Against soldiers? What you did was a war crime!"

"You wanted war with Syria. I made it happen."

"Be that as it may, you can no longer continue as Director of CIA. I'm relieving you of your duties immediately."

He paused to let that sink in.

Fuller was speechless. He couldn't believe his ears. The President had just fired him.

"Now we have to contain the fallout. The information on that recording can never leave this room," the President said. "No one can ever know that the United States unleashed chemical weapons on civilians in a foreign country to start a war with Syria."

"You can't fire me," Fuller said. "You need me in this position. I did your dirty work. You knew about the bombing. Now you're throwing me under the bus."

"I did not know about the bombing."

He did, but Fuller couldn't prove it.

"Here's what you're going to do," President Rutledge said. "You're going to resign your position as CIA director. Make up an excuse. State that it's because of some health reason. The press will have a field day, but no one will be able to say otherwise. I'll make a statement thanking you for your years of service. You'll go off into the sunset and be able to keep your pension."

"And if I refuse?" Fuller asked.

"I will destroy you!" Rutledge bellowed.

"What about her?" Fuller asked. "She went into Uzbekistan and blew up sixteen helicopters. Without authorization."

"The woman sitting here with us is a hero," Rutledge said.

"Yes, she is," Prime Minister Jaffe added.

"Here, here," the English Prime Minister agreed enthusiastically.

Fuller didn't know what to say or do. He just stared at Jamie Austen. She was the one behind all this. He didn't know how, but somehow, someday, he'd get her back. He already had all her money and assets. That wasn't enough. He needed revenge.

"Where's my husband?" Jamie asked, sitting forward in her chair.

"He's dead," Fuller replied smugly.

That was all the revenge he needed.

27

"Do you really think Alex is dead?" Jamie asked Brad nervously.

"I don't know," he said soberly.

"Fuller seemed pretty emphatic," she said.

"You can't believe a word he says."

President Rutledge had dismissed Fuller from the White House meeting with orders to have a letter of resignation on his desk by the end of the day. He was also instructed to clear out his desk by the end of the month. As long as he cooperated, he'd keep his security clearance and pension, and the whole mess with the Syrian chemical weapons bombing would never see the light of day.

Jamie and Brad were given a similar warning. The President gave the bombing the highest security classification level, and the unauthorized disclosure of classified state secrets was tantamount to treason.

Other than that harsh admonition from the President, Jamie was dismissed from the meeting with the profound thanks of all three of the world leaders.

Prime Minister Jaffee of Israel said, "If Rutledge doesn't take care of you, young lady, you can always come to work for Mossad. We can use someone like you."

"Same with MI6," Prime Minister Stuart said.

They all laughed, but Jamie wondered in the back of her mind if it might come to that. She had no idea what the future held.

Brad left with Jamie, and the two came back to his office at CIA headquarters in hopes of finding some clues as to what might've happened to Alex. They wanted to rummage through Fuller's office but he had already beaten them back to headquarters.

What they did find was troubling. Fuller locked down Brad's computer and access to any of Fuller's files. Brad wasn't even able to log into areas his security clearance entitled him to.

Fuller was clearly stonewalling and covering his tracks. The end of the month was more than enough time for Fuller to make all of his wrongdoings go away. That's probably why the President gave Fuller until the end of the month rather than forcing him to leave his post right away.

Fuller was part of his administration. Any malfeasance reflected negatively on the President as well.

Jamie hated to think of her President in those terms. She used to think politicians really were public servants. Many of them were. Far too many were in it for personal gain. Power, fame, and money or some combination of the three.

The reality of it made her blood boil when she saw it first hand in men like Fuller.

Politicians as corrupt as the criminals they prosecuted.

"What are you going to do now?" Brad asked after they'd exhausted several attempts to get around Fuller's actions.

"I guess I'll try to find Alex on my own," Jamie said. "The problem is that I don't even know where to look."

Neither of them said anything for a good thirty seconds.

"Do you have a place to stay?" Brad asked.

Jamie hadn't even thought about that. Fuller had her house. Her bank accounts were empty. Her credit cards were frozen. She couldn't afford to stay at a dive hotel or even buy a decent meal at the moment. She was, in essence, homeless.

Dozens of friends would take her in, but surely it wouldn't come to that. Or could it?

The reality was hitting her all at once.

How could she go from being a billionaire to destitute in a few short days?

The only thing she had to her name was literally the clothes on her back. No telling what Fuller did with all the clothes in her closet. It made her sick to her stomach to think of Fuller taking possession of all of their property.

What about her photo albums? Her wedding album? Her Alex box where she kept all their keepsakes? What happened to them? The things her mother gave her before she died? Tears welled up in her eyes just thinking about it.

They had a million dollars in the storage unit, but she assumed Alex took that out when he executed the Cardinal Red. Or at least he was supposed to.

What would she do with no money and no credit cards?

She could always go to a seedy part of town and steal some money off a couple of drug dealers. That thought brought a faint smile to her face. She'd been in a lot of foreign countries with no money and had used that tactic to get resources in a hurry.

In retrospect, she should've taken the nineteen million dollars out of Clement's bank account when she had the chance.

Curly was immediately in her head chastising her for even thinking about it. Hindsight would never help her current situation.

She actually had no idea what she was going to do. What would Curly do? What would Alex want her to do?

Never give up.

"You can stay with me," Brad said, tamping down the raging emotions boiling up inside of her.

"I appreciate that. But, I'll figure something out."

"I'm sorry this has happened to you," Brad said. "I wish I could've done more to stop it."

"It's not your fault. You did everything you could. When did you last see Alex?"

"When I sent him the Cardinal Red. We followed protocol, and I met him at Lady Bird Johnson Park. He showed up, and after we talked briefly, he was on his way."

"Did he say where he was going?"

"I presumed he was going to the island. It's my best guess."

"Something happened when he got there," Jamie said. "I think Pok double-crossed Alex and took all the money out of those accounts. They all show zero."

"We all should've seen that coming."

"I can't disagree with that. Alex put safeguards in place. But Pok is almost as good as Alex. He probably found a way around them. Obviously."

Jamie felt bad. It'd been her idea to hire Pok. She hoped she also hadn't gotten Alex killed.

"No use speculating at this point," Brad said. "We need to hope for the best."

A thought came to Jamie. "Now that Fuller has been forced to resign as CIA Director, won't he have to give us our property and money back?"

Brad shook his head no.

"Why not?" Jamie asked, forlorn.

"He transferred that property to a new corporation. Best I can tell, it's called TITAN, and he's the sole stockholder."

"How can he just take our property like that?"

"He probably went to a judge and had him sign off on it."

"Can he do that? Don't we have to be given notice of a hearing?"

"He probably told the judge that he tried to serve you but that you were out of the country. I'm sure he lied to the judge. Fuller is a powerful enemy. Our system is supposed to be set up with checks and balances, but it doesn't always work that way. Absolute power is a heady aphrodisiac. Men like Fuller know how to play the game and work the system to get what they want. I doubt you'll ever be able to get those things back. In fact, I'm sure of it. Fuller has the rest of the month to tie down his resources and see to it that you never see a dime of it."

"I'm pretty resourceful myself," Jamie said, angrily. "I don't have the computer skills Alex has, so I might not be able to get the money back, but I can extract a pound of flesh. Maybe two."

Her fists were in a ball.

"Jamie, promise me you'll stay away from Fuller!" Brad said in a nearly commanding voice. "He's still the Director of the CIA. At least until the end of the month. He can still cause you a lot of trouble. You've already seen what he can do to you with his power. He intended to arrest you today. If you hadn't shown up with the Prime Minister of Israel and Great Britain, and we hadn't had that damning tape, he would've succeeded. He still might. If you hurt him, you could end up in jail for the rest of your life. It's not worth it."

"What about all my things?" Jamie asked. "The things in my house. My wedding albums. My jewelry. The keepsakes from my mom. What happened to all of my stuff?"

"Let me ask Fuller," Brad said. "I'll try to get them back for you. In the meantime, I'd suggest you lay low. I'll help you find Alex."

"I appreciate your help."

"It's the least I can do."

"I'm going to go," Jamie said. "I've got things to do. Places to go. People to see."

She stood to leave.

"I'm serious," Brad said. "Stay away from Fuller. He'll get what's coming to him."

She nodded.

"Promise me!" Brad said.

"I promise," Jamie said in a defeated tone.

She lied.

Brad walked Jamie out of the building. He wanted to make sure she didn't run into Fuller. At least a dozen people stopped her. Jamie was like a rock star in that building. She took time with each one of them and put on her best smile. They'd never know the pain she was feeling on the inside.

Jamie gave Brad a warm hug, then summoned a cab. She instructed the driver to take her to the storage units. He actually dropped her off half a mile away so she could determine if she was being followed. Satisfied she wasn't, she found the unit and entered the combination into the lock.

Once inside, she found a package from Alex addressed to her.

Inside was a cell phone and ten thousand dollars in cash, along with a passport and credit card in the name of Grace Gallup. That made her smile. Jamie had said, on several occasions, that if they had a daughter, she'd like to name her Grace.

The passport had her picture on it and would pass any TSA security check and get her into any foreign country. At the moment, she wasn't sure where she'd go.

Also inside the package was a folded note. From Alex.

Hi love. Sorry about all this. Call the number on the cell phone. Leave me a message. I'll call you back when I can. The credit card has a hundred-thousand-dollar limit on it. Use it to get somewhere safe. Don't come to the island until you talk to me. If something bad happens to me, use the money in AJAX to start over. Don't worry. God causes all things to work together for the greater good. We'll get through this. I love you more than you know. Always. Alex.

The note brought more tears to her eyes. It warmed her heart and it gave her hope. A connection to him. Like he was still alive.

He had to be. That's the only way she could picture him.

The note was also a good reminder to trust God.

She powered up the cell phone and found one saved number in the contacts. She dialed it immediately. It went to a voicemail with no greeting.

"It's me," she said. "Call me back. I hope you're okay."

There were so many more things to say, but caution overrode her emotional desire to say them. She had no idea who might be hearing the message. Hopefully Alex. If he was alive, he'd call her back. If she never heard from him, then she'd have her answer and would have to start over again.

That thought sent a sharp pain through her heart. She couldn't imagine a life without Alex.

For the first time since this whole thing started, she allowed herself to really get in touch with her emotions.

She felt so alone.

Probably because she was in that storage unit.

The sense of loss was overwhelming. The unknown. Had she lost everything?

The material possessions could be replaced. Alex couldn't be.

She tried to fight off the tears. Jamie always considered herself stronger than most of her colleagues. Solid as a rock. She wasn't the one to buckle under pressure.

This was different.

She couldn't think of a good reason to suppress her feelings any longer.

Jamie sat down on the floor and leaned back against the wall of the storage unit. She looked at the phone still in her hand and set it down on the storage unit floor.

For the first time in years, she buried her head in her hands and began to sob.

28

Neal Fuller had always been a glass-half-full kind of guy.

In this instance, his glass was more than half full with two billion dollars of Alex Halee and Jamie Austen's money. Along with a yacht, a plane, and an island. Not to mention a half-billion dollars worth of paintings he still didn't know what to do with. Probably put them up for auction with a major auction house, or hold them as an investment if he was advised that they would increase in value.

The newfound riches didn't lessen the blow of the day's events. He'd been humiliated in the President's office. Made the scapegoat. Forced to resign so Rutledge could keep his reputation intact. If he allowed his emotions to run unchecked, he'd be so furious he wouldn't be able to think straight.

Staying level-headed was job number one. His experience in the CIA had taught him to keep emotions in check so he could think clearly. There were a lot of things to do. Mainly, cover his tracks and then figure out how to enjoy his money and make the best of the situation.

Would he trade all the riches for the Presidency? In a heartbeat. Power was always the first aim in politics. If you had power, the money would follow. Fuller was already a rich man. The years in politics had been good to him. But now he was a billionaire. He had more riches than he could ever spend.

Although, making the effort would be the thrill of a lifetime.

Actually, if he played his cards right, he could have both. The Presidency and the riches. His resignation could be crafted so that he could maintain his political viability. The door could be left open for a triumphant return, especially if he was able to work behind the scenes to discredit Rutledge. The man was a buffoon who'd eventually make a mistake that would cost him reelection.

At the right time, Fuller could swoop in from the sidelines to save the day for the party. The knight in shining armor, so to speak. Being outside the fray was a good thing in a weird sort of ironic way. It meant he couldn't be blamed for anything.

He sat at his desk and finished crafting his resignation letter. It took several tries to get it right. Actually, it was more of a statement. He wouldn't give the President the satisfaction of an actual resignation letter.

He read through it one last time.

This morning, I went to the White House and asked the President to accept my resignation from my position as Director of the CIA for personal health reasons effective at the end of this month. The President graciously accepted my resignation with regret.

I have served my country in the CIA for more than thirty years. Working with the men and women in the finest intelligence agency in the world has been the highlight of my life. Thank you for your extraordinary service to our country, and I wish you ongoing success as you face the many challenges that lie ahead for our country and our Agency.

With utmost admiration and appreciation.

Neal L. Fuller, Director

He reread it several times. Satisfied, he sent a copy to the President and another copy to the P.R office with instructions to release his statement to the press and circulate it among his staff.

Then he turned his focus back to covering his tracks.

He'd already made progress on that front. Before starting the goodbye letter, he issued a directive to lower Brad's security clearance to the lowest level and officially blocked him from accessing files and records above that level. That'd handcuff the traitor for a short time and allow Fuller to get his act together.

Brad's credentials would eventually be reinstated, but it'd take him a few days to lodge a protest and get his case heard. He'd like to do the same thing to Alex and Jamie, but they no longer worked for the CIA. They were freelancers. He didn't see any way to get it done.

Alex was dead anyway, so it didn't matter. But, Jamie was alive and well, and an ongoing threat. He needed to figure out how to cut off her access.

Someone messaged him and said Jamie was in Brad's office at that very moment. He'd like to go down and confront her but thought better of it.

Instead, he spent the next three hours going through everything in his office and on his computer to make sure that there was nothing that could incriminate him. Satisfied, his tracks were covered, he moved on to equally pressing matters.

He reassigned Dietrich to Assistant Station Chief in Rome. Rather than demoting him, he gave him a promotion and a raise. He already had enough enemies. The gesture would be appreciated by Dietrich and buy his silence. He called him to make sure.

After he was confident Dietrich was handled, Fuller called August into his office. He gave him a promotion as well, and a raise. He moved him to Assistant Station Chief in London. Having eyes and ears on the ground in Great Britain would be beneficial after the way Prime Minister Stuart had blindsided him in the meeting.

Fuller asked August for all the files pertaining to Halee and the Colombia mission. He'd keep those in his possession until he decided what to do with them. August was then instructed to pack up his office and leave for London immediately.

The kid was ecstatic. He was single and unattached to any material possessions in the states. The boy had risen through the ranks of the CIA faster than any other person in history, Fuller reminded him. Hopefully, he understood why and would repay the debt when called upon in the future.

Fuller turned his attention to the newly acquired assets. His son would still run the TITAN offices, but with a different purpose. All employees would be let go, and new ones hired. He didn't want anyone working for him with ties to Jamie or Alex.

He jotted down more things that needed to be done, then he gave himself a break. He couldn't do everything at once.

His secretary's voice interrupted his work. He'd given her instructions that he was not to be bothered, but she called him on the intercom anyway.

"Director, Brad is here to see you," she said.

Fuller bristled, and the hair on the back of his neck stood at attention.

The nerve of Brad showing his face in his office. He almost sent him away, but curiosity got the better of him.

"Show him in," Fuller said.

He didn't bother standing when the Benedict Arnold entered.

"What do you want?" Fuller asked with as much frost in his voice as he could muster.

"I want to know what you did with Jamie Austen's personal effects. The ones from her house."

Fuller was surprised that the visit was personal in nature. Of all the things he expected Brad to confront him on, that would've been the lowest on the list. If it even made the list.

"They're gone," Fuller said with no emotion. "I gave them to charity."

That wasn't actually true. The clothes and personal items were taken to the dump. The jewelry and items of value were put in the safe at the house. A few were sold to a pawn shop.

"If I were you, I'd figure out how to get them back," Brad said coldly.

"You're not me."

"Just a word of advice. Jamie Austen is not someone to be taken lightly."

"Are you threatening me?"

"I'm stating more of a fact than a threat."

"Noted. Jamie Austen threatened the life of the acting Director of the CIA."

He wished he'd had the presence of mind to turn on the recorder in his desk.

"I'd watch my back if I were you," Brad said. He abruptly turned and walked out of the office.

Fuller didn't need Brad to remind him that Jamie Austen was the most dangerous female operative in the world. He wouldn't sleep well until he knew she was out of the picture. Right now, things were too hot to act against her. He figured it was that way for both of them. She wouldn't dare act against him. If something happened to him, she'd be the first suspect.

She'd also be looking for information on her husband. If Fuller were dead, then the secret would die with him, and she'd never know what happened to her beloved Alex. That's why he had to destroy the Colombian paper trail. No use giving her a road map she could piece together. Once she knew the truth, she had no reason to keep him alive.

With Kyle Kelly dead, too, no one would ever know what happened.

After Brad left the office, Fuller breathed a sigh of relief. The confrontation with Brad was more docile than he had expected. It barely raised his blood pressure.

With that out of the way, it allowed him to turn his attention to more important things.

Fuller took a burner phone out of his desk and dialed a number he knew by heart.

Meme answered on the first ring as she usually did.

"Abelard," she said. "How is my favorite *grand amant*?" He knew that meant great lover in French. It wasn't the first time she'd called him that.

Peter Abelard was a famous Frenchman of medieval times. Meme was French and gave all her famous clients French names from a famous figure of the past, to maintain their anonymity. According to Meme, Abelard seduced Heloise. They had an affair, and he was known to be a skillful lover.

Fuller looked it up once and wasn't sure why she made the connection. Abelard's affair ended tragically. Perhaps she was foretelling the events of that day.

"My handsome Abelard," she said. "So wonderful to hear from you."

With her sultry voice and thick lips, she could call him Peter Cottontail if she wanted. Meme never disappointed. Her girls were the best. Professional and discreet. Knockdown gorgeous. Adventurous and accommodating.

"I have a request," Fuller said.

"The usual?" she asked.

Once a month or so, Meme sent a girl to an apartment he maintained in Virginia for an afternoon liaison. Two thousand dollars. Pricey, but it was always worth it.

"No," Fuller said. "I need ten girls. For two weeks. I'm going to fly them to an island in the Caribbean. Money is no object."

Whatever it cost would be well worth it. Eventually, he'd get his own girls. For now, he wanted professionals. Meme would know exactly what he wanted. The only downside was that Meme didn't provide underage girls. He'd have to get them from his other source.

Not on this trip. People might be watching him.

Jamie Austen in particular.

"Twenty-thousand each," Meme said.

"I was thinking ten," Fuller replied.

"I thought money was no object, *mon amour*."

"I'll go up to fifteen. The girls will love it. They'll have the whole house and island to themselves. The beaches and swimming pools are pristine. Unlimited liquor will be flowing. They'll have everything they need. It'll be a paid vacation for them. They just need to be at my beck and call."

"Of course. And, fifteen it is," Meme said. "When do you want them?"

"They'll leave with me on my private jet on the first day of the month."

"Shall I use the normal payment method?" she asked.

"Let me give you a different one."

He read her the numbers on a debit card from one of his new TITAN bank accounts.

"*Plaisir à faire affaire avec vous*," she said.

"A pleasure doing business with you as well. As always."

Fuller hung up the phone. The conversation left him burning with desire. While he'd never had sex with Meme, her voice was mesmerizing and always left him wanting one of her girls.

He couldn't help but smile broadly. In a way, the sudden turn of events would work to his advantage. Much easier to carry out his plans for the island if he wasn't the CIA Director. Now that he had no one to answer to. Not the President. Not the press. Not Congress. No legal authority. As far as he knew, the island wasn't under any jurisdiction.

No one was going to arrest him for bringing hookers to the island. Even underage girls. He just had to make sure he brought them from foreign countries that would easily look the other way with a little money greasing their filthy hands.

Fuller was surprised when the burner phone rang a few minutes later.

"Hello," he answered hesitantly.

Meme was on the other line.

"I'm sorry, but the card you gave me was declined," she said.

"I must've given you the wrong numbers."

Fuller pulled out the card and read the numbers to her again.

"Those are the right numbers," she said. "Let me rerun them."

A few seconds later, she came back on the line and said, "It's still declined, dear."

Strange.

Did his attorney forget to activate the card?

"Let me call you back," Fuller said and hung up the phone.

His heart was beating faster. He logged into his computer and pulled up the bank account for that card.

He couldn't believe what he was seeing! The balance in the account showed zero.

How was that possible?

Panic coursed through him like he had a taser pointed at him.

He pulled up one account after another. It took him nearly two hours to go through all of them.

Every single one showed a zero balance. All the money in the accounts had been transferred out earlier in the day.

This couldn't be happening. What was going on?

When he was finished, the reality hit him like a tsunami wave.

His two billion dollars was gone! All of it!

29

The call from Alex came after Jamie finally put her cell phone away.

Not because she'd given up hope, but because she'd given up on the anticipation. For several hours after she found the note from Alex in the storage unit and left him the voicemail message, the phone was always in her hand. Every few seconds, she'd look at it as if she could will him to call her.

When he didn't, she went through a range of emotions, from hope to hopelessness, to anger, to resignation, then back to hope.

Since she had nowhere to go, Jamie went to *Lady Bird Johnson Park*. Alex's last known location. That's where he had met Brad, and they discussed him getting out of the country. She sat on the same bench Alex sat on, hoping to make a connection.

It only made her sadder.

Her imagination ran wild like a wild stallion let out of a corral for the first time. She conjured up all kinds of ridiculous scenarios in her mind. Based on their line of work, none of the plots spinning through her head were that far off base. Anything was possible when they faced danger as often as they did.

There was one question that she couldn't shake. She knew that it wasn't absurd, and it was burning a hole in her mind. If Alex was alive, wouldn't he call her back as soon as she left him a voicemail message?

Not necessarily. An argument raged in her head as she tried to come up with logical explanations as to why he couldn't call.

He could be on a mission or in an area that didn't have cell phone service. He might be waiting for a better time. When he was sure the call couldn't be traced. He might be chasing Pok. Or on his computer trying to get their money back. The list of possibilities was endless.

None of those things were more important than calling her back, though. Wouldn't she be the first priority?

Her thoughts had become an obsession.

For sanity's sake, Jamie finally put the phone away in her backpack. Less than ten minutes later, it rang. She almost didn't answer it in time.

"Alex!" she practically shouted into the phone.

"Hi, honey."

Hearing his voice made her heart melt in her chest. She slumped back on the park bench but immediately bolted back to her feet. The relief was overwhelmed by the exhilaration.

"You're alive!" she said, practically dancing a jig on the sidewalk in front of the bench. Oblivious to the dozen or so people in the park. She couldn't care less what they thought. Her husband was alive, against odds stacked like Jenga blocks that could have come down on him at any moment. She was overcome with elation.

"I am very much alive!" he said, the words bringing an elation unlike any she'd ever felt before.

"Fuller said you were dead! I didn't believe him. I knew it couldn't be true. Where have you been? What's been happening to you that you couldn't call me right back or answer the phone?"

The words came out of her mouth a mile a minute. She needed to take a breath.

"Where are you now?" she asked.

"Sigao," Alex answered.

"Our island. I thought Fuller stole it from us."

"He tried. But it's one thing he can't touch. It's not in AJAX's name."

Jamie was standing now. She headed for the walking trail that ran along the Potomac River. Away from any possibility that someone might overhear their conversation. She had so many questions, and she had already made a bit of a scene. Not that anyone appeared to have noticed.

"What happened to you?" Jamie asked.

"Fuller sent some Navy Seals to the island to arrest me."

"How did you get away from them?" Jamie asked.

"It's a long story."

"I got all day."

She had a lifetime now. A few short minutes ago, she didn't know if she'd ever have time with Alex again.

"The short version is that they took me to Panama."

Alex explained that a man named Kyle Kelly led the mission to arrest him at Fuller's direction. Kelly didn't trust Fuller. He became suspicious when Fuller instructed him to take Alex to Colombia and turn him over to Colombian authorities.

"I told him it was a trap," Alex said. "That Fuller intended to kill him as well. Kelly didn't believe me until he saw a news report of a chemical bombing in Syria."

"Fuller ordered that bombing!" Jamie said emphatically. "We have the tapes to prove it. Mossad intercepted the conversation between Fuller and Kelly."

It was all starting to come together in Jamie's mind.

"Kelly never told me he carried out the bombing," Alex said, "but I could see it in his face. He was devastated. Kelly's a good man. Anyway, he refused to take me to Colombia and brought me back to the island. We kind of hit it off. I kept getting out of my restraints. He'd put zip ties on me, and I'd break them. Then he tried handcuffs. I got out of those as well. It became a game for us. Eventually, he wanted me to show him how to do it, so I did. After multiple attempts at removing the various restraints, he got pretty good at it."

"How do you think Fuller knew about our island?"

"I suspect Pok tipped him off. All he would have had to do is give Fuller the latitude and longitude."

"So, Pok double-crossed us?" Jamie asked bitterly. "I was afraid of that."

"He took all our money," Alex said. "All three billion dollars. As soon as I sent you the Cardinal Red, I met with Brad and then got on our plane to the island. When I got here, Pok was gone. I figured he'd sell us out to Fuller and give away our location, so I just waited."

"You wanted to be caught?"

"I was hoping Fuller would personally come to arrest me. Then I could kill him and dump his body in the bottom of the ocean. Instead, he sent the Seals. I wasn't going to hurt them. They were there under orders and clueless about Fuller's illegal activities. I figured if I went back to the States, I could help you and also bring Fuller down. It turns out you didn't need my help. Good job."

"So you know Fuller is no longer Director of the CIA?" Jamie asked.

"Yes, I do."

"Where did you hear that?"

"From Brad."

"You talked to Brad?"

She was suddenly angry.

"Are you telling me that you called Brad before you called me? Why on earth would you call Brad before calling your own wife?"

She asked it in a cold tone.

"I needed to make sure it was safe to talk to you. Your safety is the most important thing to me."

He was surprisingly calm.

Jamie had to admit to herself that it sounded like a reasonable explanation. Alex was in a desperate situation. He didn't know who he could trust or who might be listening in on our conversations. The CIA's reach was far and wide. Alex usually erred on the side of caution. He was speaking freely now. He must be confident the call was secure. It occurred to her that she hadn't even thought to ask.

Since Alex was using Fuller's name, she did as well.

"Fuller took all our money!" Jamie said although she was sure Alex already knew that fact. "It's all gone. So is our house. Our business. All of the paintings are gone too. Even our plane and the yacht have been taken. All my stuff. My clothes. Jewelry. My Alex box."

Jamie's voice trailed off. Verbally listing all the assets made the loss seem so staggering that it made her head spin. Hearing Alex's voice made her temporarily forget about all of the things that were stolen from them. Truthfully, she'd give them all up in a second to have her husband in her arms again.

She reminded herself to thank God for saving her husband from harm.

"Fuller doesn't have our money," Alex exclaimed.

The words made her head spin again. This whole saga had more twists and turns than the Snake River. She couldn't wrap her head around the enormous, insanely complicated situation.

"Brad said he took our two billion dollars and started some company called TITAN," Jamie said. "Where is the money now?"

"I stole it back," Alex said cheerfully.

The conversation went into an extended pause as Jamie contemplated the ramifications of that statement.

Of course, Alex managed to get their money back. That didn't surprise her.

Alex was as resourceful as a busy beaver building a dam. If anyone could have gotten that money back, it was Alex. She would've loved to have seen the look on Fuller's face when he found out all the money was gone.

"Won't Fuller know you took it?" Jamie asked the obvious question.

"He will, but what's he going to do about it? He can't prove it."

She didn't have a comeback for that. The financial scenarios were over her head. She'd just have to take Alex's word for the great news he just shared with her.

"Anyway, Alex continued. "The money trail wasn't hard to follow. Fuller put up some firewalls to keep me from getting to it, but... well... you know a few firewalls weren't going to stop me."

"So you got all of it?" Jamie asked.

"Most of it. He'd already spent some. A few thousand dollars."

"That's a drop in the bucket," Jamie chuckled.

"What should I do?" Jamie asked. "Do you want me to pay Fuller a visit? I could easily make him disappear."

"No. You need to get on the first plane to Sigao. Then we can figure out what to do from here. Now that we have our money back, we need to regroup and find Pok."

"What about the plane, the yacht, and the paintings? Fuller still has those."

"I don't think there's any hope that we can get those back."

She couldn't believe what she was hearing. It wasn't like Alex to accept defeat like that.

"Are you saying he can just steal them from us?"

"He already has."

"The yacht and plane are ours. The CIA gave those to us to use for missions. Everybody knows they belong to us."

"Honey, I've got bad news."

Jamie stopped walking.

What could be worse than the news they'd already gotten?

"I'm almost afraid to ask," Jamie said.

"There are no more missions," Alex said soberly.

"What are you talking about?"

"According to Brad, the President has cut us loose. The CIA is no longer allowed to work with us anymore."

"That's not fair! What did we do?"

"Nothing. But we know too much."

"What happens to AJAX?"

"AJAX is no more."

"I love our company. I love collecting art. I was looking forward to setting up the art gallery."

"I'm sorry, honey, but there's nothing we can do about that. Our careers are over."

The blows just kept coming.

30

"I can't believe you found Pok so fast," Jamie said to Alex. "I mean. . . I can believe it. You're amazing. You told me it would take a long time, is what I meant to say."

Jamie had learned early on in their relationship to be careful when discussing Alex's cyber hacking skills. To never say anything that could be considered questioning of them. He wasn't as sensitive about it as he used to be, but she still chose her words carefully.

"I've been in Pok's head for a while," Alex said.

If he was bothered, he didn't let on.

He added, "I've learned to think like he thinks."

They'd just cleared customs at *Jeju International Airport* and walked into the parking garage where they found an all-terrain SUV vehicle left for them in one of the parking spaces by a CIA field agent in South Korea. Weapons and supplies were presumably stored in the space meant for the spare tire.

Alex and Jamie no longer worked with the CIA, but they both had contacts everywhere. People willing to assist them off the record and outside the watchful eyes of the acting Director of the CIA, Martin Parnas. A sympathetic friend, but not one to defy the wishes of the

President who specifically ordered that no more assistance be given to Alex or Jamie to conduct missions.

Alex and Jamie hadn't gone on any missions since everything went down with Fuller. The AJAX team was dismantled. Bond, A-Rad, and Colonel were all released from their contracts. Tearfully. There wasn't money to pay them.

Alex and Jamie had decided to give away the two billion dollars they stole back from Fuller. Hanging on to it was too risky.

Alex felt reasonably confident he could keep it hidden by managing it out of the island but not on the mainland. But Sigao was now on the CIA's radar. They knew he had a cyber lab on the property. He had to assume they were watching his every move. Intricate firewalls would only confirm to the watchful eyes that Alex was operating again. With no governmental authority.

Complicating it further, if the CIA knew about it, then their enemies did as well. There weren't many secrets in the world anymore, and Alex and Jamie had made a lot of enemies over the years. They never felt more vulnerable, so they stayed on the island where Alex felt like he could protect them. Venturing out occasionally for supplies and a break from the monotony.

Turns out, stealing the two billion dollars had been problematic for former CIA Director Neal Fuller, who was arrested and now awaiting trial. Mainly because he wasn't smart enough to figure out why it was a problem.

Alex knew why.

Every banking transaction over ten thousand dollars was reported to the IRS. When Fuller deposited two billion dollars into his TITAN accounts, it raised all kinds of alarm bells in Washington.

When he didn't report the income on his corporate or personal tax returns, he was arrested for tax evasion.

The money was gone, but Fuller had no logical explanation as to where it was. He'd have to make the case in a trial that it was stolen, even though he had no proof of that fact. The prosecutors in the indictment claimed that Fuller transferred the money and hid it from authorities.

The whole sordid affair left Fuller a shell of a man. All his assets were seized. Actually, Alex and Jamie's assets. The plane. The yacht. The paintings. Their former residence. Fuller would argue in court that a Judge awarded him those assets. But just because a judge signed off on the transaction didn't mean Fuller didn't have a financial gain when he acquired them.

The two billion was income that had to be reported to the IRS.

When Alex and Jamie learned of Fuller's arrest, rather than throwing a party, they had a frank discussion around the swimming pool on the island.

"That's why we can't touch the two billion dollars," Alex said. "We can never spend it. If we buy anything with it, it'll raise all kinds of red flags, and the IRS will be all in our business as well."

"I don't want it anyway," Jamie said.

"It came in handy when we were running sex trafficking missions," Alex said.

"Not really. Every year we brought in more money than we spent. The balance in our AJAX accounts kept growing. We were never touching the principal. It was just sitting there gathering dust."

"All that money was reported to the CIA. The three billion dollars Pok stole technically should've been reported to the IRS. If they knew about it, we'd be sharing a cell with Fuller."

"That's why I think we should get rid of the money. Now. While we still can."

"What if we need it later?"

"I think money should always be moving. Like a river. Or like the wind."

A gentle breeze constantly blew off the Caribbean Sea. Alex and Jamie spent most afternoons by the pool. When they became too hot, they took a dip in the pool or the ocean to cool off.

"What do you mean?" Alex asked after taking a long sip of his beverage.

"Think about the money like it's a pond," Jamie said. "If it doesn't have water flowing in and out of it, the pond becomes stagnant. Everything in it dies. Water needs to be flowing. Constantly fed by a water source. That's what keeps it alive. What good does two billion dollars do for anybody hidden in bank accounts?"

"What do you propose we do about it?" Alex asked.

"I think we should give that money away."

And that's what they did.

Over six weeks, they gave away two billion dollars. *Save The Girls* got nearly five hundred million dollars. They gave to orphanages, planted churches, supported missionaries, set up endowments, and funded an art school. All anonymously.

It felt good.

Once that task was accomplished, Alex set out to find Pok. It didn't take him long. He tracked him to Jeju-Do Island in South Korea, just off the southern tip of the mainland in the East China Sea.

Alex even knew where Pok was hiding the three billion dollars. He hadn't taken it yet. They'd just gotten rid of a two-billion-dollar problem. Why add another three billion-dollar one?

They flew to Jeju to confront Pok. Not confront him, really. They were there to kill him. Justified because Pok was one of the foremost cyber hackers in the world. Second only to Alex. It was only a matter of time before Pok resumed his nefarious activities. This time outside the watchful eye of Alex, who made sure Pok only stole from the bad guys.

Pok had to be stopped before he set up operations again. So far, he hadn't, to Alex's knowledge, but the world would be a safer place if Pok weren't in it.

Pok's house was on a secluded road at the base of Hallasan Volcano just outside the town of Seogwipo.

The location was ingenuous. Pok would fit into the general population. The island was secluded but densely populated. Easy for him to be another face in the crowd. It even had an international airport for Pok to fly in and out of.

Asia also had a vast and intricate banking system. China, Japan, Singapore, the Philippines, and even India moved trillions of dollars of financial transactions every day. Pok's three billion dollars was substantial but still a minor player in the grand scheme of things.

Alex and Jamie parked a distance away and hiked in with their rifles and supplies. They had to assume Pok was monitoring the only road into his house, so they took the long way around, above the house, on the volcano side. The terrain was rough, and Pok wouldn't suspect Alex and Jamie to launch an attack from that angle.

When they reached their ideal vantage point, they were within two hundred feet of the house. The structure was modest and had a steeple and a cross above the front door. A lame attempt on Pok's part to make it look like a church and not a personal residence. Alex became suspicious when satellite photos showed that the building never had cars in front of it, even though a website showed service times.

When he spotted Pok in one of the photos, he knew he'd found him.

They prepared for the kill. Alex and Jamie had not said two words since they began the hike. Partly because of the steepness of the climb and partially to protect their cover. Pok could have listening devices and motion detectors on the volcano. They hadn't seen any, but microphones could have a range of up to a mile.

Alex decided they were being paranoid. It didn't seem like Pok had taken that many precautions. He must be confident he wasn't going to get caught or certain Fuller had made Alex and Jamie disappear.

They'd been off the radar for three months now so Pok wouldn't know what had happened to them.

They sat down on the ground, drank some water, and caught their breath from the strenuous climb.

"Maybe we should take time off from missions," Jamie whispered. "I miss sitting by the pool."

Alex let out a muted chuckle.

"Weren't you getting a little bored? And a little out of shape? I can feel this hike in my legs."

They hadn't done anything over the last three months other than stay in shape the best they could on the island. By running, swimming, and exercising in their island gym.

"It's kind of been nice not being shot at," Jamie said.

"You miss it. Tell me you don't."

"I'm not sure I do. Maybe it's time we retired and let the younger generation take over."

That caused Alex to laugh a little louder.

"You sound like you're over the hill. Most of the younger kids I know couldn't do the hike you just did."

"I know. We're still at the top of our games. But how long will that be? Eventually, those skills will fade. When are we going to start thinking about having a baby? I'm not getting any younger."

"A baby? You want to talk about that now?"

Jamie hadn't brought up the topic of a baby in a long time. When they were married, they agreed they would quit the CIA when she got pregnant. Neither of them wanted the baby to grow up without a father or mother. They were no longer with the CIA. Not their choice, but a reality nonetheless.

"Don't you think a little Alex running around would be kind of cool?" Jamie asked.

"I want a little girl," Alex said. "A little Grace."

"A daughter would be fine as well. Then you'd have two girls around to torment you on a daily basis."

"We don't have any prospects for missions anyway," Alex said.

"Saul Geller said we could always work for Mossad."

"I've always wanted to live in Jerusalem. You know. Walk where Jesus walked. That'd be awesome."

"MI6 would hire us in a heartbeat."

"I thought you said you were ready to retire from missions. Besides, I kind of like our freedom. We set our own schedule."

The door to the house opened, and Alex and Jamie both reacted simultaneously and were flat on the ground. A man came down the steps and walked into the yard. He looked their way, but they were well hidden as long as they weren't standing.

He turned his back to them. Alex took out his binoculars and looked through them. Then handed them to Jamie.

"That's definitely Pok," she said after the man turned to the side so she could see him better.

Alex's sniper rifle was propped up on a log next to where they were sitting. He reached for it, careful not to make a sound alerting Pok to their position.

He was already in the prone sniper position, facing Pok. It didn't take long to have the rifle in the firing position.

"Showtime," Alex whispered.

Alex wasn't the best sniper but could easily make this shot with the scope and range of the rifle.

"Spot me," Alex said. "We might as well get this over with."

Jamie looked through the binoculars. Pok was milling around, clearly at ease. Not concerned at all.

With no idea that his life was about to end.

"No wind," Jamie said. "It's not a factor."

Alex would have to adjust the shot for the downward trajectory, but he knew how to make those calculations. He didn't need her help with that.

"He won't know what hit him," Alex said. "Count me down."

"On my cue," Jamie said.

"Three, two, wait!" she suddenly shouted.

A movement had caught her eye. Coming from the house.

"What's wrong?" Alex asked, raising his eye from the scope.

Jamie pointed. A little girl had come out of the house. She ran up to Pok and threw her arms around his leg. She appeared to be no older than four or five.

Jamie peered at the girl through the binoculars. She had beautiful jet black hair. Freckles. She had Pok's features.

Jamie handed Alex the binoculars. He stared through them, then let out a groan.

About that time, a woman came out of the house and walked over to Pok, and put her arms around him. The three of them formed a group hug right in the yard.

They heard Pok say something but were far enough away that they couldn't tell what it was.

The girl responded to his words and ran back into the house and came out with a ball.

Pok and the girl began kicking the soccer ball back and forth. The woman sat down on a chair and watched them with a pleasant smile on her face.

"Did you know Pok had a daughter?" Jamie asked.

"I did. He mentioned her. Back in North Korea."

"Do you think that's them?"

"I don't know. Pok assumed that they were both killed when he disappeared. Or maybe sent to prison."

"The girl looks just like him. It has to be his daughter. I bet that's why Pok left the island and took the money. So he could find his wife and daughter."

"It looks like he succeeded."

"I don't blame him. I'd want to find that little girl as well. She's precious."

Alex looked back through the lens of the rifle. Jamie put her hand on his shoulder.

"I know," Alex said. "We can't kill him in front of his wife and daughter."

"We can't kill him at all," Jamie said. "We can't leave that little girl without a father."

Alex let out a sigh of resignation. Then stood to his feet and began to pack up his rifle. They no longer tried to hide their position. Pok must've seen the movement because he stopped playing with the girl and looked right at them.

He didn't move. Didn't panic. Didn't run.

Just stood there. Staring at them.

Jamie stepped forward so Pok would see her too. She took Alex's hand and held it.

The mother noticed Pok looking into the forest. She stood and stared at them. A panicked look crossed her face.

Alex nodded toward Pok.

Jamie thought she saw a pained look cross his face. Like he was sorry. At least that's how she interpreted it.

"Let's go," Alex said.

They hiked back down the volcano in silence. Holding hands.

Satisfied they'd done the right thing.

The only thing they could've done under the circumstances.

31

"What are you doing?" Alex shouted angrily at Jamie.

"Did that hurt you?" she said mockingly.

Jamie was in the pool on Sigao Island and had just playfully splashed water on Alex who was sitting on a lounge chair drinking a virgin Rum punch.

"I don't want to get wet," Alex said.

"You're wearing a bathing suit."

"I'm resting."

"You slept 'til almost ten o'clock."

"I need my beauty rest."

She splashed him again.

"Get off your duff and play volleyball with me," Jamie said. "I've beaten you the last three times we played."

That usually was enough to get him out of the chair. If Alex was anything, he was competitive. Or at least he used to be. They'd spent the last seven months on their island, relaxing and sunning. The respite had done them both good in terms of their mental health. Neither of them had realized the mental and physical toll month after month of dangerous missions had had on them.

"Don't make me come over there and drag you out of the chair," Jamie said.

"That I'd like to see," Alex said.

Jamie got out of the pool and approached him cautiously.

"Don't start something you can't finish," Alex said.

She poked him in the stomach. He was wearing a tee-shirt along with his swim trunks.

He tried to grab her hand but missed. She was too fast.

"Slowing down in your old age, aren't you?" Jamie said mockingly.

She circled behind the chair and slapped his hat off his head.

"Hey! That's my hat!"

He scrambled to get it off the floor.

"It's wet now."

The hat had landed in a puddle next to his chair.

She circled back around and poked him again. This time Alex was able to get a grip on her hand. They began to wrestle. He maintained his hold and was able to stand. With her free hand she poked him in the side of his ribs.

He grabbed her around the waist.

Jamie screamed.

He was twice her size, but she didn't go quietly. Jamie was kicking her legs. Alex had his back to the pool and was trying to throw her in, but she was resisting.

They were breathing heavily now.

Alex lifted her high in the air and attempted to sling her into the pool. Jamie managed to grab his shirt and pull him in with her. Ripping it in the process.

For more than two minutes, they wrestled in the water. With an intensity that went beyond playfulness. Each trying to get the other under the water.

When it looked like one was going to succeed, the other pulled something out of their hat and negated the advantage. Jamie finally let Alex get her back and he locked his massive forearms around her neck and squeezed. Pulled her under the water and held her.

When he let her back up, she faced him and wrapped her legs around his waist and they kissed passionately, although it didn't last long since they both were struggling to catch their breath.

"That was fun," Jamie said.

"If you think having a heart attack is fun," Alex said.

Alex got out of the pool and went back to his chair. Jamie propped her elbows up on the side.

"We're pathetic," Jamie said.

She got out of the pool and stood in front of him.

"Look at this," Jamie said. She grabbed the side of her stomach and squeezed. "I'm fat."

"You're not fat."

She held up her arms.

"Look at my sagging triceps. I used to be pretty and in good shape."

Alex laughed. "You're still pretty."

"Exactly!"

"What?"

"You said I was pretty, but you didn't say I'm in good shape."

"You still look good."

"I doubt I could even do our triathlon."

When they first secured the island, Alex and Jamie would run around the island five times. The equivalent of five miles. Then they'd swim around the island twice. Then get on the exercise bike and go fifty miles. Their version of a triathlon.

Over the last few months, since they came back from the mission to find Pok in South Korea, they'd settled into a lifestyle of leisure. Sitting by the pool. Eating too much. Sleeping too late. Watching television together. Something they'd never done.

"I'm losing my edge," Jamie said.

"That's a good thing. We could both use a little less edge."

"I don't like it."

"Do something about it."

Jamie sat down next to him.

"Don't you miss it," she asked. "The missions. Getting to shoot people."

"Not really," he said. "This has been nice. I'm enjoying being with you."

"How come you don't take your shirt off at the pool anymore?" Jamie asked.

"I take my shirt off."

"No, you don't," Jamie said. "Whenever you go in the pool, you always wear your shirt. Why?"

"Let's just say that I haven't been able to see my abs for a few weeks."

"That's what I'm talking about. We're getting soft."

"I do have love handles for the first time."

"And they're cute, but you and I both know that once you lose the edge, you're never getting it back."

"I don't know if I want it back. I thought you wanted to have a baby."

They weren't trying to have a baby. They just weren't trying to prevent it.

"I hate to tell you this, but once you have a kid, you'll lose your figure."

"Lela Hope won three gold medals in the Olympics after having her first kid. It can be done."

"It takes a great sacrifice."

"I just think we're coming to the point of no return. If we keep sitting around the pool drinking rum runners and eating bon bons, we're going to get fat and lazy."

"I'll have you know, I haven't had a bon bon since we got here."

Jamie glared at him.

"I hear you. I know what you mean. Tomorrow, we'll start working out again. But let's start out slow. Maybe we don't want to get back to where we were. I don't have to remind you that we were a little insane."

Jamie sat down on the chair with Alex and they snuggled. She kissed him passionately. He moved over to give her more room.

The chair collapsed throwing them to the ground.

They lay there laughing hysterically.

"See what I mean," Jamie said.

"Tomorrow," Alex said. "We'll start working out."

Jamie stood to her feet and grabbed Alex's arm and jerked him to his feet.

"Right now. Not tomorrow. Let's go for a run."

He groaned but agreed.

Later that night, they were eating on the patio. The sun was setting in the distance.

Alex got up from his seat to refill his drink. "I'm sore," he said, walking gingerly.

"Me too," Jamie said. "I'm feeling it all over my body."

A cell phone rang, causing them both to jump.

"Who could that be?" Alex asked.

Jamie answered it.

"Jamie, this is Saul Geller."

"Hello Saul. It's nice to hear from you."

Jamie put it on speaker so Alex could hear the conversation.

Saul was with Mossad. She hadn't heard from him since the mission in Uzbekistan to capture Zakarov.

"Are you two on a mission?" Saul asked.

Jamie smiled at Alex.

"We're between missions right now," Jamie said.

"Excellent. Mossad would like to engage your services."

Jamie could feel the excitement rising inside of her. Like it used to when Brad would call with a new mission.

"We're listening."

"It's an unusual request."

"What is it Saul?" Alex said.

"As you probably know, the Olympics is coming up this winter. In four months."

Jamie hadn't realized that, but took his word for it.

"Yes."

"Our intelligence says that the Iranians are planning an attack on our athletes at the Olympic Games."

"I'm not sure how we could be of help," Jamie said.

"I'm getting to that," Saul said. "There is a sex trafficking angle. For the last several years, girls have been hired to work private flights to and from the Olympics. They think they are signing up to be flight attendants but end up being expected to have sex with the customers. Some get caught up and can't get out."

A flame ignited in Jamie. Something she hadn't felt for several months.

"I'm interested," she said.

Saul hesitated. He clearly was trying to carefully choose his words so he could convince them to do whatever it was he wanted them to do.

"We'd like for the two of you to be on our Olympic team."

"Pardon me," Alex said.

"Hear me out. If you are part of the team, you'll be able to stay in the Olympic Village and get close to the athletes. You can protect our team members, but also find out if the plot is real and then stop it."

"What would that entail?" Alex asked. "If we're part of the team, doesn't that mean we'll have to compete in the events."

"Yes. But the two of you are in better shape than most of our athletes as it is."

Jamie rolled her eyes.

"What events did you have in mind?"

"I thought Jamie could be in the biathlon and Alex on the bob-sled team. The biathlon combines cross country skiing and shooting. Jamie will be a natural. Alex is bigger than most bobsledders but you're an athlete. You'll do finc."

"You want me to plunge down a mountain at eighty miles an hour?" Alex asked. "I don't know what I'm doing. The team will never win."

"We never win at bobsledding anyway. The goal is not to win. The idea is to stop the terrorist attack."

"Can we think about it?" Alex asked.

"Yes, but let me know soon."

For two hours they discussed it.

They called Saul back.

"We're in," Jamie said.

"I'm so glad to hear," Saul said.

"What do we do now?" Alex asked.

"I need you in Israel as soon as possible. You'll go to the Olympic training facility where you'll start preparing for the Olympics and will be briefed on the mission."

"The Olympics training facility? Sounds intense."

"I'm sure you're already in great shape, but you need to be in Olympic shape. Not so you win, but so you can avoid injury and at least make a respectable showing."

Jamie hung up the phone.

"What in the world have we gotten ourselves into?" she said.

NOT THE END

Thank you for purchasing this novel from best-selling author Terry Toler. As an additional thank you, Terry wants to give you a free gift.

Sign up for:

Updates
New Releases
Announcements

At terrytoler.com

We'll send you an eBook, *The Book Club*, a Cliff Hangers novella, free of charge.

READ MORE BOOKS FROM TERRY TOLER

Jamie Austen Thrillers

Read all the Jamie Austen Thrillers. They must be good.
They've been number one on Amazon in ten different countries.
Click on the link below.

THE JAMIE AUSTEN THRILLERS (12 book series)
Kindle Edition (amazon.com)

https://amzn.to/3vmPUy7

Cliff Hangers Mystery Series

Who wants to read a good mystery? We've got you covered! Read the Cliff Hangers where homicide detective, Cliff Ford, solves crimes in Chicago, with help from his wife Julia. These books have everything Terry Toler is known for. Page turning suspense, a hint of romance, and an ending you won't see coming.

The Cliff Hangers Mystery Series (4 book series)
Kindle Edition (amazon.com)

https://amzn.to/36WX3go

About Terry

Terry Toler is an Amazon international # 1 best-selling and award-winning author. He writes clean fiction with a message and life-changing nonfiction. He's a public speaker, entrepreneur, and has authored more than forty books.

Sign up for his newsletter where you'll get free stuff, exclusive content, and news of releases and promotions. He can be followed at terrytoler.com.

If you like his books, please take a few minutes to leave a review on Amazon. We really appreciate it. It helps draw more readers to his books. Thanks!